THE HOUSE
OF IZIEU

We gratefully acknowledge the support of the Canada Council for the Arts and the Ontario Arts Council for our publishing program. We also acknowledge the financial support of the Government of Canada.

Cover design: Val Fullard

Library and Archives Canada Cataloguing in Publication

Title: The house of Izieu : a novel / Jan Rehner.
Names: Rehner, Jan, author.
Series: Inanna poetry & fiction series.
Description: Series statement: Inanna poetry & fiction series
Identifiers: Canadiana (print) 20200208217 | Canadiana (ebook) 20200208225 | ISBN 9781771337250 (softcover) | ISBN 9781771337267 (epub) | ISBN 9781771337274 (Kindle) | ISBN 9781771337281 (pdf)
Classification: LCC PS8585.E4473 H68 2020 | DDC C813/.6—dc23

Printed and bound in Canada

Inanna Publications and Education Inc.
210 Founders College, York University
4700 Keele Street, Toronto, Ontario, Canada M3J 1P3
Telephone: (416) 736-5356 Fax: (416) 736-5765
Email: inanna.publications@inanna.ca   Website: www.inanna.ca

THE HOUSE OF IZIEU

A NOVEL

JAN REHNER

Inanna poetry & fiction series

INANNA PUBLICATIONS AND EDUCATION INC.
TORONTO, CANADA

For Jake and Kyle

ALSO BY JAN REHNER

Almost True
Missing Matisse
On Pain of Death
Just Murder

THE CHILDREN

Sami Adelsheimer
Hans Ament
Nina Aronowitz
Jean-Paul Balsam
Max-Marcel Balsam
Elie Benassayag
Esther Benassayag
Jacob Benassayag
Jacques Benguigui
Jean-Claude Benguigui
Richard Benguigui
Barouk-Raoul Bentitou
Albert (Coco) Bulka
Majer Bulka
Lucienne Friedler
Egon-Heinrich Gamiel
Liliane Gerenstein
Maurice Gerenstein
Henri-Chaïm Goldberg
Joseph Goldberg
Claudine Halaunbrenner
Mina Halaunbrenner
Georges Halpern
Arnold Hirsch
Isidore Kargeman
Liane Krochmal

Rénate Krochmal
Max Leiner
Claude Levan-Reifman
Fritz Löbmann
Alice Jacqueline Luzgart
Marcel Mermelstein
Paula Mermelstein
Theodor Reis
Gilles Sadowski
Martha Spiegel
Senta Spiegel
Sigmund Springer
Sarah (Suzanne) Szulklaper
Herman Tetelbaum
Max Tetelbaum
Charles Weltner
Otto Wertheimer
Emile Zuckerberg

PRESENCE AND ABSENCE

THE HOUSE STILL STANDS, a large white house on a long, sloping hill, nestled against the blue-shadowed foothills of the Jura mountains in a tiny corner of France. To the right of the house, sprays of arching, red-berried shrubs border a path that leads to the barn; to the left, a decorative terrace with white balustrades stretches toward lush fields of wild grass that ripple in the wind. A wide circular fountain filled with clear water dominates the front courtyard, while brown cows graze in the lower meadow, just below the old granary.

The view from the house is stunning, uninterrupted, bordered by pine-covered mountains, and centered by wide-open sky and the shine of water, a sweeping slice of the Rhône River. A flock of birds catches the eye, a mass of silver wings swinging in upward drifts across the sun.

All this beauty, and yet no one stumbles upon this place accidentally. The village of Izieu, a mere scattering of houses, is miles away and the narrow road twisting up the mountain is a wilderness of ivy and brambles. Encroaching tree branches meet overhead, turning the road into a green tunnel.

Step into this space and the air is electric, charged with all that once happened here. Time slides in some unfathomable way and suddenly you are there at the moment it began. The clock ticks. The hour strikes.

You want to shout out to the children, "Run! Hide! It's not too late!"

But the children are playing, drawn back to the place where they were happy, their spirits woven into the woods, sparking off the surface of the river. Their bodies are sketched in shadow, their movements slightly out of rhythm, jumpy, as if you were watching an old black-and-white newsreel.

Three young boys swing from the limbs of a craggy apple tree. Two sisters, hand-in-hand, shyly watch from the mossy edge of the woods, lingering in patches of shade. Another group of children has turned the fountain into a wading pool. You hear the lilt of their voices above the splashing. A toddler bounces up and down as if there is too much energy in him to be contained in one small body. In one corner of the terrace, two teenagers steal a kiss.

The rush of a child's breath whispering into your ear is like the flutter of a butterfly wing, a soft puff of displaced air that you wish you could capture in a jar and keep forever.

You lay the palm of your hand on the bark of a tree just to check on reality and you imagine that a child once lay their hand on that very spot, or maybe that spot is now further up the tree, further than you can reach, up in the tangle of branches above your head.

But time buckles again and you are back in the present, abandoned amid an aching vacancy.

You squint your eyes and blink and blink again, but the children are gone and it does no good to shout into the wind that they should have been safe. They should have been.

You wander inside now, hoping to find their sharp presence again, touching, naming, and identifying, acknowledging the significance of a child's crayon drawing, row upon row of empty desks in a makeshift classroom. Upstairs, there is a dormitory, yawning space where once there were beds, pillow fights, faces reflecting the light of candles, warm hands reaching out to comfort.

There are photos of the children, some blurry, some clearly in focus. You feel an urgency to learn every name, memorize each set of eyes, each nose, each smile, every freckle and twist of hair. But you are quickly defeated. Each face is a universe.

The stillness of the photographs is inherently elegiac. Sometimes, the paper evidence of a crime is more reliable than memory or testimony.

Outside again, you stand in the front yard and stare up at the House of Izieu, solid enough to have survived for over a hundred years and yet, in retrospect, as ethereal as a dream. The dream lasted for only a moment, but that moment was brilliant.

Then the light goes out. Nothing prepares you for it. The loss. The darkness. Nothing moves, not a leaf, not a bird, not you. The river stops flowing. The moment has come.

The story is too terrible to speak of in the present tense. You must slide into it from the past, the details trapped in the tangled nets of history.

THE GATHERING

NANCY, 1927

SHE STUDIED HIM BETWEEN SIPS of espresso in the café in Place Stanislas. He sat two tables away, reading a book, and would occasionally glance up over the rim of his glasses to catch her looking at him.

She turned a page in her sketchbook and began again, tracing the contours of the longish face, the high brow, the strong line of the jaw. He had thick, dark hair combed straight back from his forehead. He had fine grey eyes and smile lines around his mouth. She thought he must be a student at the University of Nancy, and that if he had any curiosity at all, he would introduce himself.

She deliberately caught his eye again and then stared out at the square as if it were the most fascinating place on earth. It was impressive, with its grand baroque buildings, gilded wrought iron gates, and a rococo fountain where mythical figures speared oversized bronze fish. As an architect's daughter, she could not help but admire the beauty of the place, but she considered it a cold beauty, lacking gaiety and the warmth of a more human scale.

A tall shadow fell across her table. Finally.

"Bonjour, Mademoiselle. I couldn't help but notice your sketching. I'm Miron. Miron Zlatin."

He spoke to her in French, but she could hear that it wasn't his first language because it wasn't hers either.

"Sabine Chwast. Please, sit. Are you a student here?" She noticed that he looked younger when he removed his glasses, and that, up-close, his shirt and pants were clearly expensive and finely tailored.

"I am. I'm studying agronomics at the university."

"You want to be a farmer?" Sabine tried to keep the surprise from her voice. She had no wish to offend, but this man, with his fine clothes and refined manner, did not look like a farmer. A lawyer, perhaps, or an estate manager, or even a banker. She was relieved when he smiled, ignoring the bluntness of her question.

"I want to be an agronomist. You might think that's just a fancy word for farmer, but I see it differently. I was born on a large estate in Russia, the heir to fields and farms, badly run and lost now. I want to modernize the business of farming with new efficiencies and even new inventions."

"You are an inventor? Of what?"

"Nothing but dreams right now. But what of you, Sabine? Are you an artist?" he asked, nodding at her sketchbook.

"I'd like to be. My father worked as an architect in Russia sometimes, even though we lived in Poland. My love of sketching comes from him. Did you leave Russia because your estate was lost?"

"Partly. And partly because it's not easy to be a Jew in Russia. And you? What brings you to Nancy?"

"It's not easy to be a Jew in Poland." Sabine shrugged, but the truth was she couldn't get away fast enough from holy Polish earth and the rise of nationalism there. She felt too deeply the lack of tolerance in the new national character so widely praised in her homeland. The worry was that as she travelled and worked in Dantzig, Köenigsberg, and Berlin, she'd recognized signs of the same fervour again and again.

"Well, then," Miron said. "You've landed in the most appropriate place. This grand square is named for Stanislas

Lesczcynski, deposed king of Poland in the eighteenth century."

"Perhaps that's why I prefer the old town," Sabine laughed. "I don't like the geometry of kings or their grandiose visions. I prefer crowded and winding streets. I've never been comfortable inside straight lines. I'm here to study Art Nouveau, the flowing, organic line."

"You're a most interesting young woman, Sabine. Tell me, do you like concerts?"

"I prefer dancing."

"Ah, perhaps I'll see you again someday when you come here to sketch. I'm afraid I don't dance."

She watched him walk away and felt a little sad. Once again she'd talked too much and been too opinionated. Her mother had always told her it was better to be pretty and shy than plain and intelligent. She was too tall and her dark hair too unruly. She was too disobedient, she was told, and she ought to find her proper place in the world as a modest Jewish woman and abandon her mad dreams of being a painter.

But Sabine, the youngest of twelve children, did not like her proper place and she turned away from her family who did not understand her, all but her father who never liked the name Sabine and called her Yanka instead. Because of him, Sabine was given far more freedom to travel than other girls her age. He understood her restlessness and her thirst for a life different from the old ways of her mother.

"Yanka," he would say. "The world is big and somewhere there is a place for you and your bright talent. Find that place and the world will smile back at you."

Was this the right place, she wondered? She was happy enough in France, but she would have been happier if Miron had smiled back at her. She supposed she would never see him again, or at best might catch sight of him in the square, or browsing in a market, or reading in the café. But she was wrong.

A month or so later she was in the home of a fellow student, Collette, who'd invited her to see her small collection of Gallé glass. Sabine was excited. Emile Gallé was her favourite, born near Nancy and a leader of the Art Nouveau movement. His glass vases and boxes were exquisite, every shape and size, with smooth contours and whimsical designs, decorated with dragonflies or lilies or fish or birds or even landscapes. Some of his glass was called *clair-de-lune*, because it appeared to capture moonlight.

The two young women were in the living room admiring the glass when they heard music coming from down the hall. Jazz music with its strident, driving rhythm. "That'll be my brother," Colette said. "Come, let's peek."

They slipped along a corridor to a doorway, slightly ajar. Underneath the music, they could hear male voices and laughter. Sabine put her eye to the open space and looked into the room.

For the rest of her life she would never forget that precious moment when she spied Miron Zlatin, elbows cocked and knees splayed, trying to learn how to dance the Charleston with Collette's brother. Perhaps the only thing that surprised her more was that three months later, she agreed to become a farmer's wife.

It was a decision Sabine would never regret, even though her mother disapproved of Russians and insisted she was too busy with a brood of grandchildren to attend the wedding. Her father and Colette acted as witnesses to the simple civil ceremony at the *mairie*, and Miron's parents, too old and uncertain of the world to travel so far from Paris, sent a fat cheque and an antique ruby necklace that Sabine would never wear, a family heirloom intended for Miron's wife. Sabine wore her best blue dress since she didn't own a white one, and Miron was elegant in a grey suit. He held her hand tightly and whispered that she was beautiful, and Sabine smiled back because she knew, for the first time in her life, that she was beautiful in his eyes.

After the ceremony, her father pulled her aside. "Yanka, you have found a good and loyal man who will not break your heart. Be a wise wife, kind and solicitous, but do not forget who you are. This is my gift to you and I only wish it could be more."

He placed a box in her arms, a polished box of cherry wood with her old and her new initials carved on the top, YZ. Inside was a set of sketching pencils and paintbrushes and little pots of oil paint in every shade, but especially tones of pink and ruby, which he knew were her favourites. Sabine ran her hand over the smooth wood, her fingertips tracing the initials.

"Y and Z," she said. "The last two letters of the alphabet. That must be lucky. Thank you, Papa. I promise I'll remember."

He pulled her close and kissed her cheek. "That big box that I gave to your husband? It's from your mother. I can't be sure, but I think it's an iron."

Amidst a flurry of good wishes and goodbyes, names called out and kisses blown into the wind, Sabine and Miron ran down the steps of the *mairie* into their new life together and somehow the heavy box was left behind, unopened and unmissed.

The first years of their marriage were pure happiness, pure exuberance. Except for their studies, which they both continued diligently, they were carefree vagabonds. On weekends, they rode bicycles into the countryside and shared picnics beneath leafy trees and the lazy buzz of bees. They talked about everything from the best kind of tractors, to the worst kind of government. They read aloud to each other in the evenings and made love in the mornings when dawn was blooming and the world belonged only to them.

Sabine felt intensely alive, curious about everything, able to be fully herself. She drew so many portraits of Miron she could have used them to paper the walls of their small kitchen in their apartment on Rue Sainte-Anne. He was a man who never doubted that he was born to be happy with a simple life that balanced physical labour with the refinement of the mind. When he was deep in thought, there was a soulful cast to his features that seemed to reveal his innermost self. Sabine learned to read his moods by looking deep into his eyes, which she claimed changed colour depending on his frame of mind: bluish when he was content, grey when his brow was furrowed with a problem, green when he reached out his arms for her in the pale light of dawn.

Within two years, they both had graduated from their respective colleges, and the future was filled with possibilities and forking paths like a book they'd just begun to read together. But sometimes Sabine felt guilty about being so happy when so much of the world was going wrong. She'd told Miron about the terrible poverty she'd seen in Berlin where hundreds of homeless people lived under the bridges and searched in garbage bins for food. Once, she saw a woman trade a sable coat for a loaf of bread. People slept on the ground with nothing to protect them from the damp, unhealthy air, and the sound of children crying from hunger echoed eerily in the underpasses of the highways.

Miron tried to reassure her. This was not the time to tell his compassionate wife about Russian unrest and the misery that had caused his own family to flee their homeland. "We must try to help when we can," he said, "but we can't save the world."

"Surely we're meant to try," was her reply.

In the meantime, their marriage was a fortress against the world, and the well of all comfort. They finished each other's sentences, and anticipated each other's needs. They shared pillows, blankets, and dreams. They lit candles on Friday night and said the prayers of their faith, but they didn't really believe anymore. It was their culture and their people they honoured those nights. Memory. Ancestry. History.

LANDAS, 1929

THE SNOW SEEMED ETERNAL, infinite. Sabine stood at the window and watched as it swept across the garden, across the roof of the barn, and down to the smooth round pond at the bottom of the field. There was not a single footprint, not a single mark to show a human presence in the silvered landscape.

But this snow-blanketed farm in Landas in the north of France was their first real home where they would raise children and chickens when the spring came. Miron had bought the farm in an estate sale with the last of their savings. Though he knew his father was rich, it was not until the family was forced to leave Russia that he understood the breadth and depth of that wealth, how far it stretched and how many lives were held in its grip. He had no desire to be one of those lives. Sabine, who had left home when she was only sixteen, had no quarrel with Miron's decision. The farm was small and surprisingly cheap. They would work hard and be glad of their independence.

That was the plan, Sabine thought.

But when the last lick of snow finally melted, and they stood on the land they'd been so proud to own, their optimism melted too, because the land was entirely contaminated by chicken shit. Miron had a laboratory in Lille confirm what their noses already knew. It would take more than a year before they could grow so much as a single bean or raise one single chicken. They worked from dawn to dusk and fell into bed exhausted. All summer, they shovelled out the contaminated soil and raked in the new. In the autumn, they built a large and sturdy chicken coop and burned the wood of the old one on what was surely a sad day for the foxes in the neighbourhood.

Slowly, the land began to mend its way back to health. Sabine grew radishes and tomatoes, feathery stalks of asparagus, and purple skinned garlic. She came to love the pale pink and white blossoms of the fruit trees in the spring when petals floated on the currents of the air like a thousand butterflies. Sometimes, she walked several miles to a neighbour's farm with a basket of eggs just so she could see the blaze of scarlet that was his wheat field covered in poppies.

Despite the long days and the exhausting work, Sabine realized she loved Miron even more than in their halcyon student days—his loping stride, his openhearted smile, his innate goodness. They had forged a life together and she wanted to make it even fuller. She wanted a child.

A year passed and she felt a flutter of worry that there was no pregnancy, but there was so much to do and the farm seemed knee-deep in yellow chicks that needed to be fed. She was convinced that she could alter fate with the sheer power of her desire, so she kept on trying to conceive a child.

A second year and the flutter became a permanent crease in her brow. Month by month, slowly and insidiously, her sadness deepened. Why couldn't she do what every other ordinary woman could do with ridiculous ease? How was it possible to feel such grief over a child that never was? She refused to let Miron see her cry, but her tears were falling nonetheless, salty tears, tinted green for bitterness, falling drop by drop deep inside her, like the slow dripping of a faulty tap, eroding her confidence and turning her dreams to rust.

Many nights, she would touch Miron's face in the darkness. She would open his pyjama top and feel his chest with her eyes closed, his muscles and ribs, feel his words as he spoke them, trying to comfort her. She would lie in his arms and try to be grateful for what she already had.

But the pain grew worse. By the end of the third year, she felt there must be a block of ice inside her womb that not even the fire of her longing could melt. Or perhaps her longing was so great that her womb had become an inferno, a whirl of hot white sparks. She began to turn away from Miron. She was unlovable. She was flawed in some fundamental, profound way. She hated the body that betrayed her. She did not want to abandon herself to him, to float in a sea of sex, only to crash into the jagged rocks that lurked just below the surface of pleasure, reminding her that her body had failed, again and again.

Slowly, the Sabine that Miron loved began to disappear. She became thinner and she laughed less. She seldom touched him. She often complained of headaches and an indefinable ache in her chest. She left plates and dishes on the table with crusts of bread and bits of fruit, flies gathering on the rims. The chicks she used to love to scoop up in both hands wandered about, unnoticed. Her wavy brown hair grew dull. The wide, intelligent eyes that used to light up when Miron walked into a room seemed to dim. She did not sleep, but wandered the farmhouse at night in a white nightgown that made her seem as insubstantial as a ghost.

Neither did she seem to notice or care that the world was changing around them. There was nasty trouble brewing in Germany, a lawlessness that portended evil. Synagogues and books were burning, and every Jew in Europe could smell danger in that smoke. Miron read the newspaper aloud to her over a breakfast she didn't eat. Her expression was unreadable. She didn't even seem to blink.

One night as she drifted aimlessly from one room to another in the farmhouse, she caught a glimpse of her reflection in a mirror and almost cried aloud at the stranger she saw there, for surely that haggard, haunted face couldn't be hers? She was shocked by the physical changes her grief had wrought, and slowly raised her hand to the glass to trace the hollows under her eyes and the paleness of her skin.

She heard Miron approach her but couldn't look away from her reflection. She saw his face appear beside hers in the mirror and saw, too, the sadness she'd painted upon it by her refusal to love him. He had a dark blue shadow over his jaw and a way of narrowing his eyes that made his gaze intense. He circled his arms around her and in the dark he whispered. "You broke your promise to your father and to me. Come back to me Sabine. I love you, but if I can't make you happy, just me, I'll go."

He stared at her dark, beautiful mouth. He was going to kiss her. She knew it, and she wanted him to, so much. A truth had been glimpsed, if only for a moment, like a door opening and closing.

After that night, Sabine let go of her dream. She just let go and felt a lightness she hadn't experienced in years. It sounded simple and incredible, and probably would not even have been possible without suffering the years rimmed with hurt, but letting go allowed her to breathe deeper, without the stranglehold of an unfulfilled desire. She knew she was letting go of something dear, but Miron had forced her to realize she had risked something even dearer. With Miron by her side, she knew she was strong enough to carry her sorrow with dignity and step back into life.

The world came back to her in bits and pieces, not in a rush. One pale morning filled with birdsong, she found herself smiling. On another day, her skirt brushed against a clump of lavender, releasing an aroma that filled her with delight. She ate two apples, one after the other, letting the juice run down her chin, thinking she had never tasted anything so good. She baked a cake for Miron, which he declared was delicious, but when she caught him throwing bits of it behind him to the rooster, she laughed out loud.

Sabine knew she was changed and still changing. Her depression had driven her back into herself, forcing her to examine what was important to her and what was not. She had a will to create, if not a child, then the will to create meaning and purpose in her life. Her tools were her education, her mind and her heart. From these she built her own ethical code, as if she were building a new house to inhabit, viewing the world through its windows. Her faith was in people, and if she could not bear the cruel, the careless, and the powerful, then she would seek out the good and the vulnerable. The important thing was to seize the bright moments and let them guide her through the darkness.

And there could be no doubt that the darkness was gathering. One night, Sabine and Miron went to the movies and saw a newsreel from Berlin that left them shaken: lines of men marching to triumphant music, arms extended in salutes to madness.

Taking her hand, Miron swore to keep her safe, and for a very long time he kept his word.

LANDAS TO MONTPELLIER, 1939

ALL THAT EXHAUSTING WORK to restore the ruined land, slogging shovel after shovel full of fresh soil with blistered hands, all the doubt suffered, wondering whether they would ever succeed, and then, slowly, month by month, watching the green tip of a plant burst through the earth, or hearing the clucking of the first healthy brood of chickens, had all come down to this one unalterable fact: the farm was six kilometres from the Belgian border, behind a Maginot line that was about as effective against a German advance as a strand of chicken wire.

In July, Sabine and Miron were granted French nationality. Under a murky sky on an overcast September day, war was declared. They would have to leave. It made no difference that the farm had become the leading producer of eggs and poultry in the district, or that Miron had won prizes for his Blue Hollands, White Leghorns, and Red Rhode Islands at the agricultural exposition of 1939. For thousands of years, their Jewish ancestors had known when it was time to uproot, move on, and start again, and so Sabine and Miron stood hand in hand in their garden to say goodbye to their home of ten years.

The farmhouse was so rooted in Sabine's heart that even the things that used to annoy her, like the slope of the kitchen floor, or the tap in the bathroom that always leaked a little, or the crack in the upper pane of the bedroom window that Miron was always too busy to fix, now seemed endearing, as familiar to her as her own hands or the curve of her brow. Had she actually complained when the winter wind had rattled the windows? Had she really been so bleary-eyed from lack of sleep one morning that she had stood in the yard and cursed every feather of every chicken she had ever seen?

"It does no good to cry over things you can't control,"

Miron said stoically, but the last night in Landas, Sabine did just that. She wept for all the birds that had sung to her in the mornings, for the purple spears of lavender whose scent had helped bring her back to life, and for the ghost of the unborn child that had followed in her footsteps as she had wandered the house night after night.

Then she packed her bags and went to train as a nurse for the Red Cross in a military hospital in Lille, while Miron put the farm up for sale.

The smell of the hospital, a mix of antiseptic, blood, and burned flesh became for Sabine the smell of war. It clung to her clothes and her hair, and no matter how much she scrubbed she could not eradicate it. Miron had rented a small apartment for them in Lille, and at night she opened all the windows, welcoming in the winter air because she preferred shivering in the cold to feeling the nausea triggered by that pervasive odour of pain and beckoning death. When it inevitably snowed and the water in their taps turned to ice, Miron finally closed all the windows and gave her a bottle of lavender perfume.

"Here," he said. "Dab a bit of this under your nose and let me thaw out."

Sabine smiled and thanked him and did not tell him that no perfume, even if she bathed in it, could block out the smell of those rows upon rows of broken men who cried out to her day after day.

She had been at the hospital for several months, when a critically wounded man cried out to her. "Madame," he pleaded. "I'm dying. I must have the blessing of a priest."

Sabine ran for the director, a nun from Saint-Vincent-de-Paul.

"This man will die before the priest can get here," the nun said. "We must do the best we can. Are you a good Catholic?"

"No, Sister. I'm a Jew."

Surprise flashed in her eyes, but only for a moment. She traced the sign of the cross on the man's forehead, and then reached for Sabine's hand. "Pray with me," she said. "You say your prayers and I'll say mine and together we'll get this poor man into somebody's heaven."

The nun never spoke of Sabine's heritage again until May of 1940 when the Germans began pushing into France, the Maginot line leaking like a sieve. "My dear, Sabine," she whispered. "People in Paris are beginning to panic and soon the roads and trains to the South will be overflowing. I hate to lose you, but I fear a dark time for your people. Go. My prayers go with you."

The two women embraced and Sabine did not tell her friend that Miron had already bought a small farm in Montpellier and was waiting for her there. They did not need to be told what was coming. But to go with the blessings of a Catholic nun? That much surprised her.

MONTPELLIER, 1940

THE FARM IN THE SUBURBS of the city had a pigsty, but no pigs, and a chicken coop with two scrawny and lonely looking chickens that seemed better fit for stewing than for laying eggs.

"Leave all of this to me," Miron said, already busy setting up his incubators. "In a few weeks, you won't recognize the place."

There was a great deal that Sabine didn't recognize. In Montpellier, the air was hot and murky, as if a storm were brewing, and the hot wind carried bits of sand and the smell of the tide. The light was bright yellow and its glare often left her feeling dizzy. At night she dreamed of rain and the drenched fields that had surrounded Landas.

Thousands had fled to the South hoping to escape the German advance, and there was a sense of unease and tension in the city. Most accommodations were overcrowded and the trains were packed. People of all classes and nationalities were on the move, adrift, bereft, and desperate. When France was inevitably defeated, and the state divided into Occupied and Unoccupied Zones, there was a great sigh of relief that Montpellier would not be ruled or patrolled by Germans. But that relief evaporated as quickly as the summer rain of Sabine's dreams. The rule of Vichy, headed by the old war hero, Pétain, propped up by leaders of the conservative right wing, smacked of the kind of blind nationalism that Sabine had smelled in Poland and Berlin. Work, Family, Fatherland were code words for collaboration and conservatism. Women were expected to stay home and make babies to replace the fallen soldiers. Foreigners of all backgrounds, Jews especially, were suspect, potential betrayers of the holy state. It was a grand hypocrisy, that morality, but it had to be borne.

Sabine reported for duty with the Red Cross at Montpellier and was placed at the military hospital of Lauwe. There, with one other nurse, she was responsible for the care of forty men, some French, some Algerians, and some Senegalese, packed into two rooms of twenty beds each. She did her best to keep the men comfortable and keep up their spirits. She was especially fond of the Senegalese, who had lilting, lyrical voices and sometimes kissed her hand when she left for the day.

Still, the work was discouraging. For several months, she watched the life in these skeletal figures ebb and flow. The lack of medicine meant that many died needlessly. Their weakened state offered little resistance to any infection. Sabine often spoke to Miron about how tragic it was for these men to have escaped the strafing of machine guns, only to be wiped out by gangrene or typhoid in their hospital beds.

It was almost with relief that she received her letter of dismissal from the hospital's director, Dr. Meunier. The word *Jew* did not appear in the letter. Meunier simply said he was obliged to let her go, with regret, but since the only other Jew on staff received the same letter on the same day, the implicit message was clear.

"What will you do now?" Miron asked.

"I don't know. It's clear no hospital will hire me."

"But the Red Cross hasn't dismissed you. Surely they need you."

So Sabine went back to the Red Cross and was directed to the office of the magistrate, or *préfecture*, of the *département* of Hérault. A social worker in that office led her into a small meeting room, gestured her to a chair, and shuffled some papers on his desk, studying her intently all the while.

Sabine was suspicious of any form of officialdom, but this fidgeting young man lacked the usual haughty manner of Vichy rule. He couldn't be more than twenty, she thought, and the steel-rimmed glasses balancing on the end of his pug nose, made him look even younger. He did not seem to be trying to intimidate her; rather, he seemed to be trying to read her character from her face, her clothes, and her demeanour. She stared back at him and decided that if he was going to refuse her employment just because she was Jewish, this time she would force the true reason to be spoken aloud.

Finally, the young man cleared his throat and leaned toward her. "I am Jean Fridrici. Tell me, Madame Zlatin, have you ever heard of the camp at Agde?"

"Of course."

Everyone who was honest had heard of the camp at Agde. Formerly a camp for Spanish refugees from the Civil War, it now housed refugees from all over Europe, Jews for the most part. But Sabine was a naturalized French Jew, so far untouched by Vichy. Surely this man was not threatening to send her there?

"And have you also heard of a French Jewish humanitarian organization for the care of children, *Oeuvre de Secours aux Enfants*?"

Now Sabine was truly surprised and could not hide that surprise from her voice. "The OSE? Yes. Oh, please, if I could help the children, I'd be truly grateful."

The young man sat up straight and smiled at her. "I'd hoped you'd say that. But you might not thank me. The camp is some fifty kilometres from Montpellier, next to the sea, and a tiresome journey. Conditions at the camp are not pleasant. If you are willing to make the journey, this office has the authority to allow the release of four or five children under the age of ten on each visit. You will have to work with OSE to find placements for them. There are a number of children's homes, some private families, and some orphanages that will help."

"When can I start?" Sabine answered.

"Tomorrow. As you know, time is of the essence."

Agde. Sabine would never forget her first sight of it. Bumping along in a truck that had long lost its shock absorbers, with her driver, Marius, she saw pastel stucco houses with red-tiled roofs, agave cactus, and a curving, hilly shoreline. Flocks of seagulls were a shock of white against a deep blue sky and the gentle waves of the azure Mediterranean.

But there was nothing gentle about the camp itself and Sabine found it difficult to stomach either the contrast or the smell. The barracks, each about one hundred feet long, were made of heavy cardboard, coated with a layer of tar and separated from the outside world by a fifteen-foot fence topped with barbed wire. The floors were slabs of concrete, the beds were straw mattresses resting upon hard wooden benches, and the windows were square holes covered in plastic.

Men and boys fourteen years of age and older were separated from the women and children, thus tearing families apart. Privacy was a series of thin blankets hung from low ceilings. Inside, the heat was stifling.

Outside the barracks, a few taps provided water for drinking and washing, but there were no containers for transporting water inside. The latrines, almost hidden amid clouds of flies and crawling with vermin, were concrete structures with spaces for standing or squatting over large petrol drums sunk into the ground. Sabine saw more than one rat in the camp kitchen that served two meals a day, usually a thin potato soup and a small slice of brown bread.

The medical tent was predictably overcrowded and disease was rife. As in the hospitals, medicine was scarce and despair abundant.

The guards of Camp Agde were all French. There were no beatings, no overt incidents of violence. No prisoners were shot. They simply grew hungrier and thirstier, weaker and more vulnerable, and finally more susceptible to tuberculosis or pneumonia.

Sabine was rooted to the ground, unable to move, as still as she'd ever been. In the pocket of her Red Cross cape was a list with five names. Five. From where she stood, she could see dozens of children, more than she could count, maybe hundreds. Some of them played soccer, kicking at an old lop-sided ball. Some of them drew pictures in the dirt with sticks. Some of them clung to their mothers' skirts and looked at her through eyes older than their years. All of them were too thin, too ragged, and too young to be prisoners.

Sabine trembled with fury and indignation and marched up to the nearest guard.

"How can you be a party to this?" she demanded. "Look at these children!"

The guard, grimly silent, looked right through her as though she did not exist.

Sabine wanted to scream. She wanted to shake him until his brains rattled and arouse whatever scrap of conscience he might once have had.

She opened her mouth to speak and felt a hand on her back. Whirling around, she found herself face to face with a young woman with curly black hair and a look of pure compassion in her eyes. Her features had an indefinable quality of grace. "It does no good to be fierce with the guards," she said softly. "Try another way."

"But how?" Sabine wailed. She clutched the official papers

in her fist and waved them at the woman. "Look at this list. Five names and there are so many children."

"One day at a time, Madame. Five today, and in a few days, five more, and a few days after that another five."

Sabine took a deep breath. "I'm sorry. It's just—"

"Yes. The first visit is a shock. I'm Léa, by the way. Léa Feldblum. I work as a teacher and counsellor at the children's home in Palavas-les-Flots."

Sabine introduced herself and then asked again: "How do you deal with the guards?"

Léa smiled. "Learn from the children. The guards they speak to have a heart. The guards they ignore pretend to be blind and so are susceptible to distractions and bribes. The children have been known to come up with some ingenious distractions—everything from fist fights, to hysterical fits of crying and even, just once, racing from the kitchen screaming *Fire!* I see by your ring that you're married?"

"Yes. Miron and I live on a farm on the edge of Montpellier."

"Does he smoke?"

"No."

"Use his ration cards for cigarettes. That's a good place to start."

And so the journeys back and forth between Montpellier and Agde began and continued two or three times a week for several months. Sabine grew braver and smarter and learned when to bring out the cigarettes, when to bargain with a chicken or two donated by Miron, and when to use her tall stature and her voluminous Red Cross cape. More than once, she strapped an infant to her chest, covered the baby with her cape and strode past the guards.

Marius and Léa had many contacts in OSE who helped her find placements or homes, and she grew especially fond of the Paillarès family whose two teenaged daughters, Renée and Paulette, volunteered at the camp and at Palavas-les-Flots. She also found a well of kindness in the person of Berthe Mering, who lived frugally in order to give generously to the OSE.

But Sabine never got used to the mothers crying out *take my children*. She wanted desperately to guarantee these mothers that their children would be safe, but as the women looked into each other's eyes, they knew no spell, or promise, or prayer could make it so.

PAULA MERMELSTEIN, TEN YEARS OLD

I WAS SENT TO THE DUMAIS FAMILY in the south of France. That was after the German soldiers marched into Paris. My parents paid money to Monsieur Dumais to hide me.

"You'll be safe here," my father said.

But I didn't like Monsieur Dumais. He was fat and sweated a lot in the heat, and he laughed at me.

There was a girl my age, Jeanne. I don't think she liked Dumais either, even though he was her father. When he lit up a smelly cigar, she said I should watch and he would blow smoke through his nostrils like a dragon. But that wasn't why I didn't like him.

He watched me. I could feel his eyes on my back.

Sometimes he would imitate my voice. We'd be at the table and I'd ask Jeanne to pass the salt, please, and he'd say, *Pass the salt, please*, in a high squeaky voice. He thought that was funny and I should learn to take a joke, but it made me feel small and itchy.

Madame Dumais noticed, but she didn't like to cross him. Sometimes I'd glimpse bruises on her arm and she'd pull down her sweater to hide them. Jeanne said Dumais hit her when he was drunk.

I wanted desperately to go home. I wanted to sit at my own kitchen table and swing my legs and eat Challah with strawberry jam. I even missed my little brother, Marcel. I didn't think that would ever happen.

One night, after about two weeks, Madame Dumais came

down to my room in the basement. "Tomorrow," she said, "when my husband's at work, you have to leave. He's threatening to turn you in. I'm sorry."

I just sat on the bed, scared to death. So, my father didn't know everything, after all. I wasn't safe.

"Jeanne will take you to a good family."

She pushed some money into my hands, a fraction of what my father had paid Dumais.

"But how will my parents find me?" I asked.

She shrugged. "They'll never find you if you stay."

So Jeanne and I set out the next morning. I wanted to know where she was taking me and I pestered her with questions but she wouldn't answer. I could tell she was angry.

"You're nothing but trouble," she finally said. "Maman will get a good beating for this."

I started to cry because I didn't want to be trouble. My parents always told me I was a good girl. All I could see with my head down were my shoes on the pavement and the bruises on Madame Dumais's arms.

Finally we stopped walking in front of a blue house with red tiles on the roof. Jeanne gave me a little shove. "Go on. Go in."

She ran off without another word.

I opened the gate of the little fence, but I couldn't go any further. I didn't know where I was or who the people in the house might be. I just sat down on a corner of the lawn.

It seemed a long time before the door opened. A girl came out and crouched down in front of me. She handed me a handkerchief because my face was all snotty from crying so much.

"What's your name?" she asked.

"P-Pa-Paula. Mermelstein."

"I'm Paulette Paillarès. I don't blame you for being scared, but it's very nice inside. Would you like to come in?"

I nodded and she took my hand. I noticed how pretty she was. She had clear smooth skin and long black eyelashes. "I don't want to be trouble," I said.

"You? You're no trouble at all."

That's when I fell in love with Paulette and I love her still.

MAX TETELBAUM, TWELVE YEARS OLD

I REMEMBER WHEN I HEARD the word "refugees" for the first time. It was spoken harshly by a man in the doorway of a hotel who took one look at us and shut the door in my mother's face. "What does it mean, refugees?" I asked.

"It means us," my mother explained with a sigh. "People who have lost their homes and are in search of shelter."

We didn't seem to be searching in any of the right places. All the hotels and restaurants were full. People sat down right on the sidewalk or even right on the road. One night, a bar maid on her way home caught sight of my little brother, Herman, asleep on the ground with his head on my mother's lap. "Come with me," she said. "I haven't much, but it's more than this."

She fed us a thick vegetable stew and hunks of bread and she slept on the floor of her living room with Herman and me so that my mother could have a proper bed for once. The bar maid's name was Francine and she was kind, but there were other nights when I saw money change hands and all we got were straw mattresses with fleas on the floor of an outhouse.

When we weren't searching for shelter, we were waiting. Waiting in long lines for transport, waiting for stamps on visas, for the next train, the next meal, the next chance.

Only the present counted. That, and where you stood in line, or how much money you could raise for papers.

I looked around and saw that refugees were sad people caught between a past that was ruined and a future that lay just over the border, or in the next town, or on the other side of the ocean, which might just as well be the other side of the moon.

Father said we should meet him in Montpellier, but when we finally got there in mid-summer, the sky was hot and the earth was dry. Dust swirled in the air and the fronds of the palm trees rattled in the wind.

We were able to rent a room in a small pension, and every day mother would leave us for a few hours while she searched for my father in the appointed meeting-place, the market in the Place Jean Jaurès.

On the fifth day, she didn't come back.

We still had some food, a bit of sausage and bread, and I tried to persuade Herman to eat a little, though I could see by the way he bit his lower lip that he was trying not to cry.

Suddenly there was a knock on the door and I told Herman to hide under the bed. When I opened the door, there was a lady in a nurse's uniform. That was the first time I saw Madame Zlatin. She was very calm and respectful and asked if she might come in.

"Your parents have been taken to an internment camp in Agde, not far from here," she said. "I've spoken to them and their only thought is for you."

My heart sank, but I was grateful that she didn't pretend that this was anything other than bad news. It made it easier to accept my responsibility to look after Herman. He was sitting on top of the bed now and I went to his side and put my arm around him. I looked Madame Zlatin in the eye. "We won't be separated," I said.

"I promise," she replied.

And I could tell by the kindness in her face that she would keep her word.

MAJER (MARCEL) BULKA, THIRTEEN YEARS OLD

I WAS SCOLDED BY MY MOTHER a lot. She said I was a naughty kid, without manners or common sense. "Majer," she would say, wagging her finger. "Wild boys come to wild ends."

It's true I was bad. There was something in my legs that made them want to kick out at rules. I figured that just because something was a rule didn't necessarily mean it was fair. And I sure didn't trust people that made up the rules, seeming to spin them out of thin air. These were the same people who spat on the sidewalk after a Jew passed by.

So I broke the rules. I pinched apples from the fruit seller around the corner. Once I stole a bottle of Shabat wine and drank until I fell on my face. I teased girls and chased dogs and threw stones at squirrels. I took every kind of dare. I climbed unto rooftops, crossed streets in traffic, broke into any empty house that might be haunted. I threw a few punches, too.

But in the end, my rule breaking was nothing compared to the way Vichy twisted the law. My whole family was rounded up and sent to a wretched camp. "You see," I told my mother. "The bad boys are penned up now with the good boys, so what's the point of being good? What good did it do you to follow the rules?"

In the camp, I learned that my bad behaviour gave me certain skills. The guards would sometimes give me a bit of sausage or cheese if I could recite every French swear word I knew, and I knew lots. On nights so black that even the trees and shrubs were black, too, I'd sneak into the guardhouse and raid their supplies, never enough to raise the alarm, but enough to ease the hunger of my younger brother, Albert. His pet name was Coco, and he was only three.

My mother smiled at me then. "If you get the chance, my son, run away and don't look back."

But now that I had her permission, I wanted to stay.

She begged me to go.

Several weeks later a nurse came with a list of children to be released from the camp. Our names were not on the list. My mother approached the nurse and held up Coco.

"Please," she said quietly. "He's such a good boy. He never complains when he's sick, just puts his head on my shoulder and waits to get better. My eldest son, Majer, will look after him."

I watched as the nurse held my mother's gaze for what seemed a long time, but was surely only seconds. I thought she was going to say *no*, but instead she told me she was going to smuggle Coco out under her Red Cross cape and I should try to follow and slip by the guards.

"Carry one of the younger children to the truck and, while I distract the guards with paperwork, jump into the back."

"He can do it," my mother said. "He's clever."

So I did what the nurse said and when the truck started to move, I looked back, even though my mother had told me not to. I could see her waving behind the fence, and I can see her there still, a tall woman growing smaller as the distance between us grew.

I never got to say how much I loved her.

EGON-HEINRICH GAMIEL, NINE YEARS OLD

I WAS AT PALAVAS-LES-FLOTS with my cousin, Arnold Hirsch. I remember the sea best of all. The fishing boats and even the fish were bright red, green, blue, and yellow. We made a game of learning those crazy fish names, shouting them out loud as we ran along the shoreline.

"Gulper shark!" Arnold shouted

"Lizardfish!" I shouted back.

"Starry sturgeon!"

"Butterfly blenny!"

"Velvet belly!"

"Tonguesole!"

Every day, there were sardine barbeques on the beach. We took off our shoes and went barefoot in the sand dunes. We waded into the sea where the water was pale green. We wandered along the alleys beside the wharves. They stank of drying fish. Some days, the sea was smooth and glassy. Arnold said it almost seemed we could walk across it, hopping onto the backs of turtles and fish, all the way to neutral Spain. I loved the way the tide left the beach washed and clean. Every morning seemed like a new beginning.

The end of days on the beach was the only part of being at Palavas that made me sad. That was when the town's mothers and grandmothers would stroll along the sand, as predictably as the incoming tide, and gather in all the other children. Arnold and I would just sit and watch. Both of our mothers had been arrested and deported. We never talked about where they might be, or how much we missed them. If Arnold ever hoped, as I did, that we would see our mothers again, he never spoke of it. I understood. It was a hope too huge to risk speaking aloud.

We walked along the edge of the water toward the sanatorium that housed the Children's Shelter. When I looked back, I saw that the wet sand had already swallowed our footprints, leaving no trace of us.

MONTPELLIER, 1941-1942

SABINE AND MIRON WERE ARGUING. Notice had been given that all Jews, under the authority of René Bousquet, the despised Vichy official in charge of French police, must register at the local *gendarmerie*. Miron thought they should obey the order. Sabine did not.

"How can you even think that this is a good idea? I see the results of this tactic over and over again at the camp," Sabine argued.

"If we don't register, we'll be fugitives. Nothing will protect us."

"And you believe that if we do register, we won't still be fugitives?"

Sabine stood up from the kitchen table and retreated into the bedroom, slamming the door behind her. She just didn't want to fight anymore. They'd been going back and forth for hours and she was beginning to see that no words would change Miron's mind.

Hunger drove her back to the kitchen several hours later. Miron was standing by the window, hands clasped behind his back and his head bent. The sunlight caught his profile and for one moment, gone so quickly she might have imagined it, she saw something different in him: not his usual certainty, not defiance, but something pale and unvoiced. It was vulnerability and fear. She knew because she felt it too, as though a car on a slippery road was skidding straight towards them. Who should they trust—the law, their French neighbours, themselves? She didn't know, and neither did her husband. She walked toward him and held him in her arms.

The next morning, Miron registered their names and their identity cards were stamped with the word *Juif*.

Sabine knew she wouldn't be able to travel with such a stamp. She asked a number of discreet questions of her friends at OSE, and was directed to a shady character in an even shadier boarding house. Several days later, she had a new set of identity papers in the name of Jeanne Verdavoire.

That same night she placed them on the kitchen table in front of Miron.

"What's this?"

Sabine didn't speak. He would work out the answer himself quickly enough.

"Where did you get them? Never mind, I don't want to know."

"I had to have papers that would allow me to travel. The OSE has learned that Vichy is moving hundreds of Jews from Agde to Rivesaltes. I hope you understand."

"I can't say I'm happy about this, but I understand." The flatness in his voice didn't make his assurance sound convincing. "How much did you have to pay for this?"

"A hundred and fifty francs."

"Did OSE pay? We don't have that kind of money."

Sabine tried, but failed to hold his gaze. A wave of guilt rippled through her.

"Sabine?"

"I'm sorry, Miron. But we both know I wasn't ever going to wear that necklace your parents gave me. I should've asked you first."

"No need. It was yours to do with as you pleased."

The disappointment in his eyes belied his words.

"The pity is," he continued, "the necklace was worth at least ten times that amount."

Sabine hung her head. When finally she looked up at him, he simply shook his head, the movement barely perceptible. No more talking, then. The best thing she could do was to give him time to forgive her.

When she woke up the next morning, Miron was already outside doing chores. She waved to him from the yard, and she was relieved that he waved back. She wanted to talk to him, but the Red Cross truck was already screeching to a stop on the other side of the road. She thought it was a small miracle that Marius was able to keep it running at all.

She climbed in and said good morning.

"Not so good." Marius mumbled.

He was a stout man of few words, with almost no hair on his head, but a finely trimmed handlebar moustache of which he was exceedingly proud. Except for that moustache, he reminded her of a boxer because of the bluntness of his nose and the heaviness of his brow.

"What's wrong?"

"We're going to Rivesaltes today."

"So soon?"

He nodded. "Guards shipped several hundred two days ago. On cattle cars."

Sabine gasped, but Marius talked over her shock.

"It's about fifty kilometres, near Perpignan and the Pyrénées."

"So we're leaving the Hérault? Do we have authority?"

"We're going, aren't we?" He took the list of names from his shirt pocket and handed it to her without saying another word.

Sabine stared glumly out the window, barely noticing the

landscape—the distinctive stripes of planted vines, glorious fields of sunflowers, and then the arid plains leading to the foothills of the mountains. The low clouds that obscured the higher peaks matched their dark mood.

When Marius parked the truck outside the gates, neither he nor Sabine moved.

Rivesaltes was Agde multiplied, as bleak and desolate a place as they could ever have imagined. Rivesaltes was overcrowding, exposure to the elements, inadequate food and medicine, stench, filth, disease, and squalor behind barbed wire in a vast space. Rivesaltes was fifteen hundred acres of wind and the sorrow of thousands. It hurt the very soul to enter it.

"My god," Sabine whispered, and her voice wavered.

"No." Marius barked. "No tears. Get in, get out, we save as many as we can."

The guards here were different from those at Agde. Some of them smiled when Sabine held out her list in trembling hands. They enjoyed her fear. She turned away from them and approached the guards who had a vacancy to their expressions, as if all emotions had been scrubbed out of them. They barely looked at Sabine's list and they didn't count heads. That first day, she and Marius walked fourteen children through the gates of the camp, and smuggled a baby girl out by hiding her under a blanket.

Over the next few months, random deportations began from Rivesaltes to Drancy to camps in Poland, Austria, and Germany. There were whispers of starvation, of ghettos, of Jews shot in forests or worked to death in factories and salt mines. The fear and tension of those locked inside only worsened conditions. Listlessness and despair spread like another kind of infection.

Sabine's heart broke a hundred times a day in that place and was only put together piece by piece when she saw Marius giving a child a ride on his shoulders, or heard Léa singing to a group of bedraggled youngsters, or when she was finally home again with Miron who put his arms around her shoulders and hugged her to him and listened to every word.

MAURICE GERENSTEIN, THIRTEEN YEARS OLD

I REMEMBER THE PARLOUR in my Zayde's home. There was a long, polished table and tall wooden chairs with carved backs that looked like thrones. If my sister Liliane and I were good, he gave us sweets from a crystal candy dish.

Then one day, without warning, my Zayde fell ill. He was simply too weak to rise from his bed. My mother said his skin was so hot she was afraid the bed would start to smoke. When he died, my mother covered all the mirrors and hung black cloth over the windows. But it was a long time before she told me how he died.

My mother had a purple silk dress and a black cape with a fur collar and, for nights at the opera, gloves that reached to her elbow and closed with two pearl buttons. She had a pale blue embroidered shawl that smelled like her perfume.

When she had finally lost all of that, she pulled me aside and told me that Zayde had been attacked in the street by a gang of Nazis. They gave him a brush and told him to scrub the pavement. After several hours on his hands and knees under a hot sun, he'd asked for a drink of water and they made him drink the dirty soapy water from the pail, filled with grit and bird shit and shards of glass from smashed windows. Then they beat him and kicked him and left him for dead. He'd managed to crawl home, but never again got up from his bed.

"We are entirely alone and can trust no one now. This won't be an easy lesson to learn," mother warned me, "but probably Rivesaltes will pound it into your head."

When she was deported, she kissed me and told me to take care of Liliane.

Here, in Rivesaltes, Liliane wraps herself in mother's pale blue shawl every night, but it is ragged now, no longer beautiful, and we can no longer smell mother's perfume.

JACQUES, RICHARD, AND JEAN-CLAUDE BENGUIGUI, TWELVE, SEVEN, AND FIVE YEARS OLD

THE PHOTOGRAPHS OF MY FAMILY used to sit on the piano in our drawing room. I didn't like practising, so while I plunked away at the keys I was all the time staring at my favourite picture.

There is my father in a pinstriped suit too hot for the weather, sitting at a café table with a stylish woman, my mother, in a white dress and a straw summer hat. A carafe of wine stands on the table, together with the remains of a late afternoon meal. Sunlight streams down upon them through the branches of trees in full leaf, and the warmth of the season and the affection between my parents makes the image glow.

That photo was taken when my parents were engaged and before any of us children came along. My mother used to say: *That's a portrait of Marseilles at peace.*

She was born in Algeria, and always smelled of spices and tangerines. She swore she fell in love with my father at first sight, but all it got her was a perfect afternoon in Marseilles and four children. She was teasing, I think.

In the other photos, my brothers and I appear only gradually. I came first, just a baby with fat cheeks in what looks embarrassingly like a dress, sitting on my mother's lap. When I appear again I'm a head taller than my younger brother, Richard, whose head is always full of mischief, and Jean-Claude occupies the baby's position on my mother's lap. Last of all came Yvette, the only girl, as light and fragile as a baby bird, so little she still wears a lace bonnet.

I often thought about those photographs when my brothers and I were at Rivesaltes and I thought of them in words borrowed from my mother: *Those were portraits of a family at peace.* I remember them with ease, like someone who could play a piano without looking at the keyboard, picking out a tune last heard long ago.

MINA HALAUNBRENNER, EIGHT YEARS OLD

I AM WALKING WITH PAPA to the old Jewish cemetery. We go to be paying respects to my grandmother. He is telling me lots of stories about her. She baked best apple strudel in Austria. She was milking goats and she skis down mountains. But I'm little when she dies. I only remember her warm shawl. Is smelling like peppermint.

My mother was taking me to the synagogue for praying. A big wooden cabinet is home of Torah, the scrolls of our law, she told me. "What are scrolls, Mama?

"You'll see."

They are big sheets of paper on a wooden roll, like rolling pin for baking strudel. There are words on the paper and Mama says they're holy. She is liking to say that at night when the candles lit up the ceiling, it glows like heaven.

The day after the Nazis was burning the synagogue to the ground we are leaving for France. Mama says the resting place of Torah is nesting place for birds now.

Mama says if something bad happens or if some men are taking her away, I am not to be trying to follow her. That would make it more bad for both of us. Instead, I am to be staying close to my sister, Claudine. We can wait for her, but if she isn't coming we tell adult with kindest face we are orphans. Never to tell we are Jewish.

None of that happened. We are all sent together to Rivesaltes. The wind is never stopping here. Blows all the time and is cold. I see my papa sometimes behind fence. He is living in long shed. He shouts come close and I hear teeth chattering. His or mine?

At night, Mama, Claudine, and me sleep in same bed for

keeping warm. Mama gives us her blanket but in few days she is coughing all the time. Sometimes, Claudine pees in bed. She hates latrine. It makes her gagging, but soon straw bed smells bad too.

I was taught never ask God for things. Only be grateful for blessings. But I am praying to leave this place. I am praying my fate passes over me like angel of death at Passover.

LÉON REIFMAN, COUNSELLOR AT PALAVAS-LES-FLOTS

I REMEMBER WHEN SABINE AND MARIUS started bringing the kids from Rivesaltes to Palavas. I had been a medical student, but when my studies couldn't continue I volunteered to help the OSE and had been at Palavas with Léa Feldblum for about four months. All I could think was *the poor kids*. Their faces, huge eyes, and lips tinted blue from cold and hunger, could tear a person in two. They had nothing, only the clothes they stood in which were so filthy we didn't even try to wash them, just tossed them into the trash. One little girl, her name was Claudine, and she was four or five, a small, solemn creature with her hair in pigtails, had what might once have been a stuffed rabbit. She cried when we tried to take it away so Léa promised her she would try to "give it a bath" while the children were sleeping, but when she put it in the sink, a flotilla of bugs came streaming out of it, skittering over the surface of the water.

We talked in hushed tones above their heads, but these kids were already adept at reading the meaning of adults' whispers, *tuts* of the tongue, knit brows, sidelong glances, and hands over the mouth. We couldn't protect them from what they'd already experienced. When we sat them down for their first meal—small portions so they wouldn't get sick—we noticed more than one child slipped a piece of bread into their pockets. You couldn't blame them. For so long, they'd never known where their next meal was coming from.

Their first night at Palavas was always the most difficult. Some of the children had forgotten how to sleep in real beds, some were afraid of the dark, some were afraid to close their eyes in case, when they opened them again, they'd be back in Rivesaltes. Léa was so wonderful with them, so loving and comforting. I think she knew every lullaby ever written, in three or four different languages.

The resiliency of those children amazed me. Before too long, they'd be playing games, or putting their toes in the Mediterranean with squeals of delight, but those who had a brother or sister with them were always careful to keep each other in sight. Those who still had parents would ask to write letters to them.

Inspired by their bravery, I decided to approach the archbishop of Chambéry to explore the possibility of scattering some of the children among Christian institutions where they might be hidden from Vichy police. I met with a young priest who was very welcoming and I put my case forward as eloquently as I could. The priest responded with compassion and enthusiasm. He was sure that the Monsignor would agree to my request.

Just then, a large black car pulled into the courtyard: the Monsignor Costa de Beauregard himself had arrived. I repeated my request, careful to explain in detail the dangers faced by innocent children. I will never forget his response, or the cool superiority of its tone.

"But sir, how could you possibly expect us to mix Catholic children with Jewish children in our institutions?"

I begged him to consider the urgency of the times, and he grudgingly agreed to think over the matter and write me in a few days.

But I already knew his answer from the look of shame on the young priest's face. The look we traded was full of pity, his for the children and mine for him.

"That's it?" Léa said when I told her what had happened.

"A Monsignor is going to turn his back on little children with no explanation?"

"I'm sure he sees no need to explain to us," was my response.

"Perhaps one day, he'll be asked to explain himself to his god."

GILLES SADOWSKI, EIGHT YEARS OLD

I REMEMBER SITTING at the top of the stairs at night listening to the adults talking below me. My parents and my grandparents. I would scoot my bottom into the corner behind the stair rail and no one could see me. I liked the sound of their voices and laughter rising up. Like music.

I never thought I was being nosy. It was mostly boring stuff:

"That butcher is a cheat."

"The Rabbi's wife's having another baby."

"Gilles needs a new pair of shoes."

Stuff like that.

But then the voices changed. They were soft, like whispers, only urgent. I strained to hear. I could make out only words and sighs and bits of sentences. No one seemed to laugh any more.

"…Shouldn't stay."

"But where…?"

"I heard they…"

"Surely not … just rumours."

"…And children, too."

I didn't know all that was going on between my parents, but I kept an eye on them. They frowned a lot and my mother's eyes were often red and puffy.

You'd have to be pretty stupid not to know something bad was happening. My father wanted us all to leave Paris, but my mother just kept saying, *Where? Where can we go?*

One night my father came into my room and woke me. He looked worried, but he tried to sound cheerful and said we were going on a trip to the South.

"Look," he said, "I've packed you a little suitcase."

But I knew this was all wrong. Nobody leaves on a trip in the middle of the night. "Where's Mama?" I asked.

He just shook his head. "Mama won't come, but you must come. You must be brave." I didn't want to be brave and I didn't want to go, but he was my father and I loved him as much as I loved Mama. So I carried that cardboard suitcase for two days and three nights until we came to a place by the sea called Palavas-les-Flots and met a tall man with sandy hair.

"My name is Léon," he said. "I'll take care of you."

My father crouched down and hugged me. "I'm going back to Paris. There was a raid and many Jews were taken to the Vélodrome d'Hiver. I'm going to try to find your Mama. Do as Léon says, and God willing, I'll be back for you."

Many weeks passed, but Papa never came. I kept my suitcase packed, just in case.

MONTPELLIER, 1943

THE LAST TWO MONTHS of 1942 were as bleak as any Sabine could remember. Clouds and lightning raced across the sky from the sea almost every day. The sky was grey, and the ground was grey with the uniforms of the German soldiers who had swept south to occupy all of France, but for eight *départements* to the east of the Rhône. The newspapers printed pictures of troops crossing the now defunct Demarcation Line. Miron's parents were deported from Paris and Sabine had heard nothing from her family in months. The badlands of Rivesaltes were black with mud.

To add to the general gloominess, Sabine sensed that a remoteness had crept between her and Miron over the past few months. They had spent too much time apart. Even though she felt as if the events of her day were not real until she'd told him about them, he was still only an audience, not a participant in her daily life. She spent more time with Marius in his truck than she did with her own husband. Miron had withdrawn when he heard the news of his parents, not turned to her as he usually did for comfort. There were long lulls in their conversation and disagreements that flared into spurts of anger. Sabine felt like she'd failed him in some fundamental way, that she had become a different person without telling him.

At Landas, she and Miron had done so much together, scraped a farm from the dirt and planned a future. Perhaps the loneliness she often felt now was just the loss of that future and not the diminishment of love. That morning, despite the rain, Miron had left her to eat breakfast alone while he went outside to mend a fence. She waited at the window, watching him, sure that if he would only look back at her, her thoughts would be as transparent as the glass she stood behind, and they might begin together a different kind of mending. But Miron did not look up, and Sabine could not wait for him.

During a break in the downpour, she put on her raincoat and headed for the OSE headquarters in Montpellier, for she had heard rumours that the Vichy police had ordered releases at the camps to stop. Rumours came more quickly than radio broadcasts these days, transmitted mouth to mouth like life-saving breath, and the rumours were usually as true as they were bad.

When she reached the town and walked down eerily empty streets, a brush of rain fell across her face and she snapped open her umbrella. She heard a rattle of drops on the umbrella overhead and then a hand gripped her arm, pulling her into a doorway. She opened her mouth but before she could scream she heard a familiar voice.

"Don't go to headquarters. It's locked up."

"What's happening, Marius?"

"OSE's gone underground. There are soldiers at the door watching."

"What should I do?"

"Try our friend at the *préfecture*."

Before Sabine could even respond, Marius was walking away

from her on a mission to warn others. She changed direction and headed for the offices of the Hérault, hoping to find the fidgety young man she'd met so many months ago.

To her very great relief, he was still there, but occupied, according to his secretary, with no hint of the irony of the *double entendre* in her voice. Sabine took a chair in the outer office and some twenty minutes later heard herself announced, much to her alarm, as Jeanne Verdavoire.

As she entered Monsieur Fridrici's office, the secretary handed back her papers, her false papers, and closed the door.

The young man's mouth twitched to see the look on Sabine's face. "Madame Verdavoire," he teased. "You look remarkably like a certain Madame Zlatin I once met. But so many people come and go these days, I must be mistaken."

Sabine smiled, releasing the tension in her body, but the light mood of Monsieur Fridrici changed quickly. "Come, please sit. There's no time to lose. You know that OSE has closed its doors?"

She nodded.

"I have a friend, a *subpréfet* at Belley in the Italian zone." He picked up his pen and began writing, handing her a note. He opened a drawer and pulled out a sheaf of documents. "I also have a set of papers that will allow you and a number of children to travel. Do you understand?"

She nodded again.

"The Abby of Prévost is holding a number of packages for you. Do not leave them there long. A pleasure meeting you, Madame Verdavoire. *Bonne chance.*"

Sabine rose, as did the young man. They shared one last look at each other, direct and stripped of all pretence, one human being to another, and then Sabine turned away. She knew what she must do and hoped Miron would forgive her.

On the way home, she opened the note, memorized the name, Pierre-Marcel Wiltzer, and then dropped the scrap of paper into a sewer.

By the time she reached the farm, her hair was dripping with rain, the umbrella having buckled in the wind. For once, Miron was not outside, driven in by the weather, no doubt. She let herself into the warm kitchen, casting aside her wet coat and calling out for him, but he did not answer. He must be making an egg delivery, she thought, and set about fixing a simple lunch of omelette and bread. An hour later, she sat at the table, eating alone again, pretending she was not watching the clock.

Finally she was forced to admit to herself that she was staring at the minute hand of the clock so intently her eyes were beginning to water. It was so unlike Miron not to leave a note for her. The times were too dangerous for casual absences: a simple walk to a neighbouring farm or into the town market might lead to an inspection of identity papers. Sabine thought again about the stamp on Miron's papers: *Juif*. An inspection could lead to an arrest, and an arrest to deportation.

She stood up, shaking her head as if to shake off her anxiety, and walked into the living room. There was his book, cast aside, and his reading glasses. The floorboards creaked as she entered the bedroom and picked up his pillow from the bed. She pressed it to her face and instantly recognized his smell, warm and complex, slightly resinous. She straightened up and stood there indecisively. She told herself she was being foolish, but her instincts answered back that something was not right; some detail, out of place and alarming that she could not name but could feel, was gnawing at her.

She surveyed the room, turning slowly in a circle, and her eyes rested on the corner of a suitcase jutting out from under the bed. She knelt down and pulled it toward her, flicked open the latches. His clothes were folded neatly inside—underwear and socks, a couple of shirts, a sweater she'd knitted for him long ago in Landas, and under the inner lining of the suitcase, a thick envelope of French francs. At that moment, she heard a footfall.

She stood up quickly, like a child caught with her hand in the cookie jar, and turned to find Miron standing in the doorway. She felt like an intruder. She felt like a wife about to be betrayed. Guilt and confusion and anger were all mixed up together.

There was a pause, a hiatus in the whole progress of time, as they watched each other. The silence between them deepened, became cavernous. "What's going on?" Sabine finally asked, her voice more accusatory than she'd intended.

Miron walked toward her, then leaned over to close the suitcase, swinging it onto the bed and sitting down beside it. "Advance planning," he said. "Never be caught without a plan. I've been making arrangements. You might have noticed if your attention hadn't been elsewhere." He looked up and gave her the most open look she'd seen from him in a long time, something between admonition and apology.

She wanted to say a dozen things at once, the kind of words that would bring balance back into their lives and heal all the little hurts that had bruised their relationship, but instead she blurted out the most dangerous thing of all. "I have to leave Montpellier."

"Well, of course we do. That's what I've just been telling you. I've sold the farm, not for what it's worth, but at least in cash. If I'd waited any longer, it would've just been taken from us, confiscated by either Vichy or the Germans. We can stay until the end of the month, or leave tomorrow."

"There are things I have to do, places I have to go—the Abby of Prévost and the children's home at Palavas-les-Flots."

"I expected that, but this time, will you let me help? I can't be a farmer any longer, but I can still be a husband."

She laughed as she kissed him, a laugh that was something close to happiness.

"You haven't answered my question," Miron pressed.

"It doesn't need answering."

Sabine went to the monastery with its hunched shoulders and

black spires, exactly as she'd been told. She opened the heavy wooden door of the adjacent church and smelled the thick musty air, the smell of incense, dense and heavy, like spice cake on the edge of burning, layered over the odour of damp stone and the smoke from votive candles. She sat down in a carved pew, quietly waiting for someone to notice her. It was from her father that she had inherited her love of churches, but churches as works of art: no priests or sermons, just these great vaulted spaces filled with peace and prayers of yearning. She wondered if her father was dead and if she'd ever see him again.

A low, muffled sound, perhaps of a door opening or closing, caught her attention and she lifted her head to see a man approaching her. He was dressed in a monk's robe with no ornamentation other than a large cross. He was old but not weak looking, not diminished, and Sabine knew she was being scrutinized.

"I am the Abbot of Prévost," he said.

He shook her hand and took a seat beside her and began talking about the weather, the relentless rain, at least Sabine thought he was talking about the weather, though perhaps it was a metaphor for the bad tidings pouring down upon the country. There was an awkwardness in their conversation, as if they were actors who didn't quite know their lines or understand the point of the play.

"So the storm has finally come." The monk stared straight ahead at the altar, but was still watching her with his peripheral vision.

"We can always hope the sun will come out tomorrow"

"You're an optimist. I see nothing but clouds on the horizon."

This coded talk was giving Sabine a headache. She couldn't keep it up.

"I've come from Monsieur Fridrici," she said plainly. "I've come for the children."

"Ah, Monsieur Fridrici. There's a man with a clear conscience. He doesn't need to work at all, but took that job to try to do some good. His family's very wealthy, you know. They almost single-handedly cover the expenses of the orphanage."

"No. I didn't know. The children? How many are there?"

"We've been hiding four. Three boys and one little girl. We'd be glad to keep them, but we've been hearing rumours that soldiers will be requisitioned in the abbey. Sometimes it's hard to believe we pray to the same god. Tell me, Madame, do you know the Beatitudes?"

"I do."

"Well, then. The children are waiting outside in a car provided by the *préfecture*. Blessed are the pure of heart, for they shall see God. Take good care of them. We've given them some clothes and toys, and packed some food. The driver will take you anywhere you want to go. I hope your sun shines for you again."

"Thank you, Father," Sabine said. She didn't know if "Father" was the proper title, but it was all she knew. "And Father? Blessed are the merciful, for they shall be shown mercy."

From his sad smile, she could see that parting with the children was costing him some of his strength.

She walked to the car and opened the door and looked in at four little faces with huge eyes.

"It's okay," she smiled. "I'm taking you to the sea."

ALICE-JACQUELINE LUZGART, TEN YEARS OLD

MY AUNT USED TO READ fairy stories to me when I was little. She was a widow who once lived in Paris. She told me she liked to pretend, too. She imagined that all was not lost of the old world. On my seventh birthday, she gave me my own book of fairy tales. The author's name, *Charles Perrault*, was written on the cover in gold letters.

It was a beautiful book filled with marvels. Young men turned into snow-white swans. Kings and queens danced in a ballroom under crystal chandeliers. A beautiful princess slept for a hundred years in a rose-briar wood. My favourite was about a clever cat in fine leather boots. Puss-in-Boots tricked the greedy out of their fortunes.

I lived in that world of enchanted princesses, talking animals, and disappearing cats. I was happy there. But somehow the witches and wolves prowling the woods slipped out of the stories and into the everyday world. Perrault was full of warnings, too. If you somehow strayed from the path and the wolf got you, it ate you up and that was THE END.

It was only because I was with my aunt that the wolves didn't catch me. My parents were taken away and I couldn't go home again.

My aunt said we wouldn't be safe unless we travelled to the South. She placed me in a Christian orphanage where I could hide among other children. She sent me parcels and visited as often as she could. One day, the last day I saw her, she brought me a new Perrault book to replace the one I lost, but I didn't want it anymore.

I wanted to believe the world was different than it was, but there was just so much I could pretend. When one of the nuns who ran the orphanage told me I was being moved, I was frightened. I was being sent to another place I didn't know to live among other children I also didn't know.

When I saw Madame Zlatin for the first time, I thought she had a nice smile. She didn't look like a witch. But then I thought, how could you tell?

ISIDORE KARGEMAN, TEN YEARS OLD

A LITTLE PARISIAN BIRDIE told us not to go to the Marais that day, but I remember the noise of the round-ups. It rang in my ears for a long time, loud and harsh.

Achtung Judenaktion! Alle Juden Raus!

Germans yelling. Gendarmes yelling. Yelling in French and Yiddish. People wailing, dogs snarling, boots pounding, wooden doors splintering, and windows shattering. I held my hands over my ears, but it made no difference.

My mother and I were hidden in a Gentile neighbour's cellar, but the raid scared the lady so much, she told us two weeks later that we'd have to leave. Maman made no fuss. She just thanked the lady for hiding us and took my hand.

We walked along the edge of the Marais, watching out for the gendarmes. There were already new people living in some of the apartments where our friends had lived, but most of the apartments were boarded up. A lot of the doors and windows were wrecked.

Maman said we'd follow in the footsteps of my older brother who'd already found a safe route to the South. She sold some jewellery and the next day we were driven to a farm. I hoped we could stay there because the farmer had a big black dog with velvet ears and a wagging tail, but Maman said we had to keep going.

The farmer told us to lay face down in the back of his truck. There were holes in the bottom so we could breathe and he told us he would cover us up with ears of corn but we shouldn't move our faces because then the corn would fall through the holes and the Germans would know we were there. The corn felt heavy on our backs, but it wasn't too bad because we could see the road zooming by underneath us. We held our breath when the truck got to the border. We were waved through.

I thought we were in the clear then, but Maman held my hand and told me she would have to go on alone to find my brother and I was to wait for her at the orphanage.

I shut my eyes tight, but the tears came anyway. *Mon petit canard*, she called me. *Be a brave little soldier.* I liked holding her hand. I liked the weight and feel of it. When she let go, I felt empty.

It turned out that the orphanage was okay. The head monk said we were excused from mass. I don't think the nuns liked that, but they didn't dare cross him. I made friends with the other Jewish kids, Sami and Hans and Alice. We teased Alice a lot because she was the only girl, but I liked her because she could run fast. We were given books to read, good books about cowboys in America, and we had lessons so we wouldn't forget our sums.

It was only at night when everything was still and quiet that I would hear that shouting in my ears again and think about letting go of my mother's hand.

MONTPELLIER TO CHAMBÉRY, 1943

SABINE, MIRON, LÉA, AND LÉON sat at the long dining table at Palavas with a large map spread out before them. With her slender fingers, Léa traced the route from Palavas to Chambéry to Belley.

"We have safe passage to Chambéry thanks to Monsieur Fridrici," Léa said, "but we'll get no help from the Monsignor there. Léon has already tried and been refused. The OSE children's home in Chambéry is already too crowded, so we'll have to put our children in a village hostel until Sabine can make contact with her official in Belley."

"How many children are here?" Miron asked.

"Fifty-two at the moment." Léa read the dismay in his eyes. "It's true. We can't take them all with us on the buses. The American Quakers have visas for five of the youngest. Léon will try to take some of the others to the Protestant Mountain."

"What's the Protestant Mountain?" Sabine asked.

"A village called Chambon-sur-Lignon. The local minister, André Trocmé, has rallied the villagers behind him and they have refused to hand over Jews to the Vichy police. So far, they're holding their own against the Germans. I think Sabine and I can take forty children with us. Léon will take the majority of the rest."

"The majority?" Miron asked.

Léa smiled. "You're very quick, Monsieur Zlatin."

"Miron, please."

"Well, Miron. There are two older boys here, Théo Reis and Paul Niederman. We don't have any papers for them, and being older, they tend to stand out. Paul is especially tall for his age."

"I'll take them," Miron volunteered.

"But how?" Sabine countered. "You don't have travel papers, either."

Miron reached for the map again. "I know someone who can take us to Lyon. From there it's about thirty-six kilometres to Chambéry. We'll walk if we have to. Are the boys strong enough?"

"I think so," said Léon. "So, we all leave in two days, agreed?"

The four adults joined hands in the middle of the table, each trying to look confident so as to reassure the others.

Sabine and Miron did not go back to the farm in Montpellier. They stayed in a seaside hotel and stood on the balcony of their room to listen to the lapping waves of the Mediterranean, inky blue in the night.

"What happened to Léa?" Miron asked. "Why is she alone?"

"Her family fled from Belgium to Montpellier. The strain was too much for her elderly parents and they died within eight months of each other. Her brother and sister were deported."

"How did Léa escape?"

"Officially the OSE protected her and she has identity papers in the name of Marie-Louise Decoste. Personally, I believe she was spared because she's an angel mistakenly fallen to earth. She's devoted to the children."

Sabine suddenly reached out and grabbed Miron's hand. "I feel like something's going to go wrong," she whispered.

"It's not. It's not going to go wrong." He turned to take her in his arms and buried his face in her neck.

She closed her eyes and ran her hands over the muscles in his shoulders. Whether it was going to go wrong or right was not something either of them could control. They used to believe, long ago in Nancy, that they could shape the future, influence it with their own will, their talents and their decisions. She saw now how untrue that was. The future just happened. It was happening now, without the slightest regard for them, like the sun going down or the moon coming out or the restless motion of the sea, completely indifferent to the fate of human beings.

Sabine shivered in her thin coat and walked slowly through the narrow and hilly streets of Belley, looking for the *mairie* and the office of the *subpréfet*, Monsieur Wiltzer. It was March, but spring would come late in a mountain village. She could hear the rush of streams filled to the rim of their banks with melting mountain snow. The trees were still bare, black limbs etched across a fresh blue sky. The people she passed still wore winter coats and scarves, but she noticed they were unhurried, stopping to chat with neighbours, nodding their heads at strangers, something she hadn't seen in Montpellier for a long time. If there were Italian soldiers about, she didn't see them and no one asked to see her papers.

The *mairie* was at 11 Boulevard de Verdun, a pale yellow block of a building set among a series of white and grey façades with reddish-brown roofs. Sabine had telephoned and arranged an appointment once she and Léa had settled the children in Chambéry. She took a deep breath and entered the building, was directed to a hallway on the first floor, and knocked at a door left slightly ajar.

"*Entrez!*" a voice called out.

The first thing Sabine saw was the omnipresent portrait of Pétain whose influence extended even to this remote village and her spirits wilted a little. Then she turned and met the mischievous smile of a very pretty woman in her late twenties, with a sweep of blonde hair and wide-set green eyes.

"The portrait is *de rigueur*. Looks like a sour puss, I think. I'm Mademoiselle Cojean, Monsieur Wiltzer's assistant. You must be Madame Zlatin?" She had a slightly hoarse voice, laughter lurking in its undertones as if she couldn't wait to release it.

Sabine nodded.

"He's waiting for you. Go right in."

Monsieur Wiltzer rose from behind his desk and walked forward to shake hands. He was tall, in uniform, very official looking, but his handshake was warm. He looked to be in his mid-thirties, with a broad face and a rounded chin, dark eyes and hair, and a wide mouth. Not an especially handsome face, but a strong and appealing one. He seemed to be studying her as much as she was studying him.

"Please, sit," he invited, pulling out a chair. "Marie-Antoinette will bring us coffee. It tastes terrible but will be very hot on this chilly day. You've had a pleasant journey?"

"An uneventful journey is always pleasant these days. Thank you for agreeing to see me." Sabine could not help but stare at the unsettling Vichy uniform. "Monsieur Fridrici advised me to come. He said you might help." She paused, not sure how to go on, or how much to tell.

"Let me be very clear Madame Zlatin. I am in the employ of the Vichy regime, but I am a Frenchman first. My conscience is clear. How many children are there?"

"I have forty with me, and there are others, perhaps, in Chambéry."

The door opened and Mademoiselle Cojean entered with a tray. "Forty children," she echoed. "Are they all orphans?"

"Most of them. Some have been entrusted to OSE by their parents in the hope that they'll be saved from deportation. Now that the Germans have moved south we decided the Italian zone might be safer. Are the Vichy police active here?"

"Very," Monsieur Wiltzer replied. "Mostly running down false leads given to them by the Italians. Foiling Vichy is about the most fun the Italian soldiers have."

"But forty children," Mademoiselle Cojean spoke as if shocked by the number and Sabine didn't have the heart to tell her about the hundreds left behind.

"Well, then. We'll need a very large house. Drink up your

coffee and please bring the car around, Marie-Antoinette. There are a couple of places I'd like Madame Zlatin to see."

"Now?" Sabine asked, surprised and excited at the same time.

"Immediately," Monsieur Wiltzer said, reaching for his official Vichy hat.

PAUL NIEDERMANN, FIFTEEN YEARS OLD

MIRON ZLATIN TAUGHT THÉO REIS and me the fine art of moving without being noticed: fluid, unhurried, nothing jerky or out of pace with the crowd, nothing to catch the eye. He had a friend, an old farmer with a noisy pig, who kept the guards distracted all the way from Montpellier to Lyon on the local train that stopped at almost every crossroad. Théo joked that we could have walked to Lyon faster, but taking the market train meant that livestock—mostly chickens, roosters, and geese—were permitted. We were dressed as farmers, too, in work pants and rubber boots, berets pulled low across our foreheads. I was glad that pig stank to high heaven because as long as we stayed behind it, no one was interested in coming any closer.

The station in Lyon was noisy, grimy, and crowded. Trains seethed at the platforms, venting steam and the stink of carbon and sulphur into the air.

Just as Miron had planned, that pig got loose. It started charging across the platform, people leaping out of its way, soldiers bellowing at it, and in all the commotion, we slipped onto the train headed for Chambéry and sat in the end car as if we belonged there. Passengers crowded at the windows to cheer for the pig until it was finally corralled.

"Will they shoot it?" Théo wondered.

"No," Miron assured him. "Pigs are too valuable."

Doors banged and whistles blew. Slowly, like the hands of a clock moving, the train began to slide away.

No one spoke, not even Théo who liked to chatter. We knew

without being told that we were entering the most dangerous part of the journey and we wouldn't be safe until we reached the Italian zone. We passed through an alley of factories and warehouses and then a string of houses with peeling paint and broken windows. The scruffiest part of any town always seems to cluster around the tracks, but once in a while we saw a curtain or a burst of gardenias in a window box. Soon enough we reached open fields and patches of forest.

A half-hour or so somewhere east of Lyon, Miron opened his bag and passed out bread and cheese and one boiled egg to each of us. We were eating, the tension just easing from our shoulders, when the train came to a grinding halt at an unnamed station. The food I was chewing turned to sawdust in my mouth and I could barely swallow.

"Soldiers. Germans," Théo cried, looking out the window. "What should we do?"

Miron was up in an instant. "Follow my lead. Remember, don't run."

"Everyone out!" an officer shouted. "Line up! Get in line!"

People pushed and shoved along the corridor, some with bags, some without.

Queues formed, awkward shifting lines, and Miron made sure we were at the back.

Slowly, soldiers began moving down the line, snapping their fingers and calling for papers. My eyes were fastened on their boots. I couldn't seem to look anywhere else. The only things to see were those boots.

Miron touched my shoulder, and I forced myself to look at him and follow his gaze. He was watching a man ahead of us in the line. There was something unsteady about him that I couldn't put my finger on. I thought he was ill or maybe even drunk, but then, in a flash, I recognized the danger. Hunted. He was being hunted.

The officers drew closer to him, their words drowned out by the thunder of an approaching train on a parallel track.

As if in obedience to some unseen signal, the man suddenly lunged away from the line, raced diagonally across the platform and launched his body into the face of the oncoming locomotive. There was a silent flurry of limbs, a splash of red, and he was gone.

Time seemed to stop. All motion on the platform stilled.

Except for us.

We edged backwards to the side of the station house, slipped around to the back, and melted into the forest of pine trees. We lay on our stomachs and watched the locomotive continue to thunder by, a long line of rattling flat cars.

"Their loads are headed for the East," Miron whispered.

Théo and I knew what that meant—bound for the East and other, less sudden, encounters with death.

We didn't move. We listened to our own ragged breathing and the soldiers' voices that came and went in echoes until the night mercifully fell, turning the platform, the station and the forest pitch black.

IZIEU, MARCH 1943

SABINE COULD SEE THAT Monsieur Wiltzer was a good driver, obviously practiced on the twisting, mostly uphill roads in and around Belley. He was quiet, but smiled occasionally as Marie-Antoinette, leaning forward from the back seat of the car, pointed out the few highlights of the town: the fountain in the main square, the cathedral where Monsieur Wiltzer had married the prettiest girl in town, the house where the famous gastronome, Jean Brillat-Savarin, had once lived, and the *fromagerie* that sold the best cheese in the district. Sabine nodded politely in the appropriate pauses, but scarcely heard a word. She couldn't wait to see the kind of place Monsieur Wiltzer might find for the children.

On the outskirts of town, he stopped the car in front of a large but dismal building, a dull arrangement of grey rocks and arched windows, so darkened by soot as to be almost black. "This used to be an abbey house," he said. "What do you think?"

Gazing up at it, Sabine felt like a prisoner might while being led toward a cold glowering tower. Despite the building's size, it had a cramped, confined feeling and no grounds that she could see. She had hoped for a bit of space where the children might play. She bit her lip, stalling for time to find the right words and not seem ungrateful.

"Ugh. It would be like living in a quarry," Marie-Antoinette pronounced. "Whatever are you thinking, Pierre?"

Monsieur Wiltzer laughed. "I assume you agree with this condemnation, Madame Zlatin?"

"I'm afraid I do. Please, call me Sabine."

"And I am Pierre-Marcel, though my secretary accords me only half of that name while insisting on both Marie and Antoinette."

"Next house, please." Marie-Antoinette urged. "And this time I hope you have a house in mind and not a mausoleum."

They drove deep into the countryside, past lakes and waterfalls, into valleys tucked between steep rock cliffs and dense forest. As the road began to twist uphill toward the sky, outside the hamlet of Izieu, Sabine could feel her spirits lift with it.

Pierre-Marcel stopped the car at the end of a green tunnel of trees, on a small grassy hillock. "The road continues down and around to the side of the house, but I think this is the best vantage point. Ladies, please."

Sabine stood up and gazed across a wide expanse of green lawn that led to an old stucco mansion with a stone foundation, with moss growing up along the stones, and pale blue shutters at the tall windows. The white façade shimmered in the sun. She saw the long terrace and the fountain in the courtyard, the large barn and the granary. As she turned in a slow circle, the foothills of the Jura mountains folded in ribbons all around her. The sweep of the river was silver, the surface catching the light and fracturing it in a dozen different directions, bouncing it off the steep escarpments that scraped the sky. The air was crisp and clean. She could even smell the ice-cold river.

Sabine stood still and marvelled at the house of Izieu. Isolated. Peaceful. Protected. The sensation of space, of all things being possible, set her heart singing. This was the place.

"It was used during the summers as a kind of camp by a Catholic boarding school," Pierre-Marcel was saying. "I'm afraid there's no heating or running water."

"There is the river and the fountain. With a couple of stoves and some blankets we can always manage to stay warm." Sabine couldn't stop smiling.

"Izieu is very tiny, only six hundred people. You'd have to travel about fifteen kilometres to Belley for supplies, on twisting roads as you saw. Other than that there's only a winding path through the forest leading to the hamlet of Lélinaz. Across the river is the village of Brégnier-Cordon. You'd be pretty isolated," Pierre-Marcel warned.

"Oh, I know. Isn't it wonderful?" Sabine replied.

"Let's look inside," Marie-Antoinette suggested.

As they walked across the sloping lawn, the secretary slipped her arm through Sabine's and leaned toward her. "It's perfect," she whispered. "I knew Pierre wouldn't let you down. Don't let the uniform fool you. He's never taken the oath of allegiance to Vichy. He faked the flu for the formal ceremony, and when they sent officials to do it privately, he left the building ten minutes before they arrived. They still haven't caught up with him."

Pierre-Marcel climbed the front steps, fiddled with a set of keys, and after several tries released the padlock.

Sabine stepped inside, expecting the still air to be musty, and instead breathed in the scent of dried apples. She stood in a hallway that led to a flight of stairs in front of her and two large rooms on either side.

"Look at this," Marie-Antoinette called.

Sabine followed her voice and saw a large classroom fitted

with several school desks with hinged tops. Sunlight slanting through the windows lit up motes of dust that floated through the air like a thousand tiny specks of gold. Through the dancing light, she could already see rows of children with their heads bent over books. She would have to find a teacher and more desks.

Everywhere she turned she found surprises: a massive wood stove in the kitchen, long wooden tables where the children could eat meals in a room next to the front windows, a space large enough for a dormitory upstairs, an attic where beds could be placed for the older boys, even a room that might be used as an infirmary or an office, and next to it, a small bedroom for Léa. By the time she finished her tour, a cobweb had caught in her hair and her fingers were smudged with dust, but her eyes were shining.

Behind her, Pierre-Marcel cleared his throat and she looked around at him, her face full of anticipation.

He looked solemn. "I'm sorry, Sabine. But I've looked at the barn and it's a shamble. The roof sags, many of the stalls are broken. And the granary is just as bad. This place was built at the end of the nineteenth century. What kind of shape is the roof in? Who knows what kind of shape the electricity's in?"

"Surely all of that can be fixed. Just give me a month. My husband's a farmer. He can fix anything. Forgive me, Pierre-Marcel, but you haven't seen the internment camps. This place is a palace. We can plant a garden just over there," she added, pointing over his shoulder. "There are apple trees behind the house and wild berry bushes. And Miron, that's my husband, can set up a room in the barn as our bedroom. And best of all the children can play. Can't you just see them running across the lawn on real grass, and climbing the trees and gathering on the terrace in the evenings for stories?"

"I can," Marie-Antoinette answered. "I can see it."

Pierre-Marcel held up his hands, conceding defeat. "All right, Madame. It's yours."

"We'll call it the House of Izieu," Sabine smiled.

"We'll call it The Settlement for Refugee Children from the Hérault," Pierre-Marcel cautioned.

There was a shaking of hands, warm and two-fisted with Pierre-Marcel, and kisses on both cheeks from Marie-Antoinette, and the deal was done.

As the three walked toward to the car, Sabine looked back just as the clouds shifted, slanting the sunlight directly onto the front of the house. It shone in a warm, amber glow, inviting, beckoning. The land rolled away beyond the house and barn, fields and woods in rich and dark textures. The vision was so complete, so whole, she felt something inside her expand. *Home.* If a house could talk, that's what it would whisper, Sabine thought.

THÉO REIS, FIFTEEN YEARS OLD

AS SOON AS THE COAST WAS CLEAR, Monsieur Zlatin, he asked us to call him Miron, led us deeper into the forest. I say "led," but really we blundered. We couldn't see our hands in front of our faces, it was that dark. Still, he'd gotten us off that platform, so I would have followed him anywhere. After an hour or so of stumbling around, we stopped to rest. I sat on the cold ground and leaned against a tree, but whenever I closed my eyes I saw that train thundering by and that man leaping straight into it. I couldn't help wondering if I'd have the same kind of courage if I were caught.

The night magnified the sounds of night-creatures: foxes and owls and bats, maybe even wolves, all scurrying or scrounging or swooping for prey. It was unnerving. Nerves tightened and stretched and jumped at the merest and nearest sound. I don't think any of us slept. We were all listening for footsteps or dogs barking, sounds of the night-creatures that might be hunting us.

Finally the night grew paler and we could see well enough to walk steadily.

We must have gone about two or three kilometres before Paul asked Miron if he knew where we were going.

"To Chambéry," he answered.

"You know the way?" Paul sounded skeptical.

"I have a map in my head," Miron assured us.

"Well," Paul sighed. "Your map has taken us by this tree once before. I caught my sweater on it and you can still see the scrap of wool."

For some reason, beyond logic, we found this hilarious and we couldn't help laughing. There was nothing at all funny about being lost, but we laughed so hard we had to cover our mouths not to be too loud and Paul was doubled over, holding his ribs. Maybe it was the aftermath of what we'd been through or just our amazement at our luck.

"I wonder what happened to that pig," I said and that set us off again.

We sank to the ground right where we stood. Miron snorted, trying not to laugh too loudly, and that made us think he was imitating the pig. Pretty soon I had tears streaming down my face.

Miron sobered up first. "Look," he said. "I've no idea where we are, but I figure that unscheduled train stop must have been some kind of border between the German and Italian zones. We can't be more than ten kilometres or so from Chambéry. I did see it on a map once and I know it's southeast, so now that we can see, we can let the sun guide us. Chambéry is in a valley, so we'll likely have some climbing to do before we get there."

Miron still had some apples in his bag, leftovers from the meal we hadn't been able to finish on the train. We ate them before resuming our journey, sucking hard at the juice and trying not to think about how thirsty we were. We kept to the forest as long as we could, checking the sun frequently to adjust our direction. Eventually the trees petered out and we came upon a dirt road twisting steadily uphill. There wasn't much cover along the road and the landscape was rocky, but there were still pockets of forest scattered across the hills.

We went up and up and up until my thighs were burning. The palms of my hands were raw from the rocks, and my pants were torn at the knee and every few feet I asked how much farther we had to go until Paul started swearing at me. Miron's answer was always the same: Just up here, around that bend. The road had ended miles ago. What bend, I thought.

Late in the afternoon, I heard bells, not booming like church bells, but just a tinkling sound. I looked at Paul, wondering if he'd heard them too or if I was just going a little crazy from thirst.

Ahead of me, Miron stopped and waved at someone. It was a goat-herder, a young girl with a kerchief on her head, surrounded by twenty or so goats with strange golden eyes. After some conversation that I was too tired to overhear, she led us to her goat shed and invited us to join her for supper in her hut. Her name was Nicole and she gave us bread and cheese (goat cheese, of course) and plenty of water and directions.

The next morning we arrived safely in Chambéry, a pretty town. We passed a couple of Italian soldiers on the street and my heart hammered when I saw them, but they just walked on by. When we got to the hostel, Madame Zlatin kissed us all and asked me what happened on the journey. I told her we were saved by one girl, twenty goats, and one pig.

IZIEU, APRIL 1943

SABINE SPENT THE NEXT MONTH in a state of heightened excitement and a blur of activity. There was so much to do. With the money that she and Miron had been paid for the farm and help from the OSE, she bought school desks and books, mattresses and beds, dishes and cutlery, towels and blankets. Marie-Antoinette was invaluable—she knew every retail owner in the district and she swore they all owed her favours. After a quick conversation with the shopkeeper, the price Sabine was prepared to pay would suddenly be dropped.

Sabine went to Belley twice a week, every week. Marie-Antoinette would greet her, often with a large box of clothing—sweaters, pants, little dresses, underwear, shorts, and even bathing suits in all sorts of colours and sizes. Donations from her friends she would say, with a wave of her hand, but since almost everything was brand new, Sabine knew Marie-Antoinette was paying from her own pocket. Pierre-Marcel had a more difficult task. Ration cards and false identity papers. How he did it, Sabine never asked, but she knew he was putting his own position, and perhaps even his safety, in jeopardy.

One day Sabine arrived at the office to find a stout little man with a large moustache and the look of someone who thought himself important. His grey suit was impeccable, quite unusual for a country town and for the times: soldiers' uniforms were often far less shabby than civilian clothes. Sabine might have been properly impressed were it not for the black toupee that sat on top of his head like a crow. Her lips twitched and she dared not look at Marie-Antoinette, whose eyes, she knew, would be dancing.

"Madame Zlatin," Pierre-Marcel said solemnly, "May I present the mayor of Belley, Monsieur Tissot."

The formality of the introduction was enough of a signal to warn Sabine that Pierre-Marcel was not sure of the mayor's cooperation. Would he approve of a refuge for orphaned children if he knew they were Jewish?

"The mayor is interested in The Settlement for Refugee Children from the Hérault," Pierre-Marcel continued. "I've explained that you and your husband will be directing the home."

"*Enchanté*, Madame. An unusual name, Zlatin. You and your husband are from..."

"French citizens, Monsieur. May I say this is a beautiful town? You must be very proud of the work you do here."

Her flattery did not seem to warm Monsieur Tissot to her, though he stretched himself a bit taller. She thought he might come up to her shoulder on his tiptoes.

"How many children are you preparing for?" he asked.

"We think perhaps as many as thirty," Sabine deliberately underestimated.

"Thirty! My goodness. And how will you feed them?"

"They have French ration cards, of course," Sabine assured him, not looking at Pierre-Marcel. "And my husband is a farmer. We will grow as much food as we can."

"I see. Well I may visit on the day of your opening. What do you think?"

What did she think? She thought the immediate thoughts of a person who had something to hide: how to react, how to quell surprise, how to appear natural and casual. "You will be most welcome," she smiled.

"That's settled then. When do you hope to move into the home?"

"Our target is the first few days of May."

"Splendid. Until then Madame Zlatin." He bowed his head, said his goodbyes to Pierre-Marcel, and left.

Sabine and Pierre-Marcel looked solemnly at each other until they heard the outer door shut and Marie-Antoinette hurry into the office.

"What did he want?" she demanded.

"Just to feel important, I suspect." Pierre-Marcel said. "He likes to be consulted. But Izieu is too far away for him to be overly concerned."

"Why on earth did I invite him to visit?" Sabine wailed.

"You had no choice. To refuse him would have been far more suspicious."

"Could he actually prevent us from moving the children into the house?"

"No, no. He doesn't have that kind of power. He could ask some awkward questions, however. He's chummy with the

Italians, but there's not much danger there. It's just that I don't know how he would react if he knew the full story."

"If he knew that the children were Jewish, you mean. He certainly didn't like my surname."

"Don't worry, Sabine," Marie-Antoinette assured her. "Pierre and I will keep him busy here in Belley."

"And how do you propose we do that?" Pierre-Marcel smiled affectionately at his assistant.

"Well, I don't know off the top of my head, do I? But there must be dozens of ways. Think of a spring fête to celebrate, or drum up some kind of a parade. Maybe I could arrange for a broken water main or a downed telephone wire."

Pierre-Marcel looked at Sabine. "You think she's kidding, don't you? Never underestimate her. I've learned that the hard way."

But he was still smiling and Sabine could see that he found Marie-Antoinette marvellous.

MARIE-ANTOINETTE COJEAN, HEAD SECRETARY OF THE BELLEY SUBPRÉFECTURE

I REMEMBER THE LOOK that passed between Sabine and me, the kind of look that passes from one woman to another and asks a question about a man.

Of course I loved Pierre. I'd loved him since I was sixteen years old. He was handsome, tall, gentle, and kind, the stuff of every girl's dreams. I wanted him more than I wanted to breathe.

I used to trail far behind him and his friends when they went cycling on the mountain roads. He'd find me on my bicycle on his way back down the mountain and we'd ride home. I used to think hanging on to that bicycle was the only thing that kept me from floating up into the sky.

But then Pierre met Noelle and married her, and I grew up.

I loved a few other boys, but I never wanted to marry them.

I decided I wanted more. Maybe not more, but different. I thought women couldn't possibly make a bigger mess of the world than men had. I'm intelligent. Why not use my brains?

When the war came I was assigned to a post in the *préfecture*, and one day I looked up from my desk and there was Pierre, still marvellous, still vital, still married. My teasing, our banter, made for a fragile intimacy, almost fraternal. Why would I want to ruin such a rich friendship?

He has no idea. Men seldom do. If I were to unleash the depth of my feelings, the poor man would drown if he didn't first die of astonishment.

CHAMBÉRY, APRIL 1943

BACK IN CHAMBÉRY, the planning continued. Sabine arrived home to find Miron surrounded by half a dozen children, poring over what seemed to be some kind of map.

"What's all this?" she asked, finding a place to sit on the floor among the children.

The answer came from several voices at once: "It's a garden!"

Miron had made plans on paper for a vegetable garden— scale diagrams of the distance between rows of carrots that the children had coloured orange, streaks of green for runner beans, and red polka-dots for tomatoes. He'd even marked down his best guess for the angle of the sun at particular times of the day. The children who'd never lived on farms regarded these diagrams much as they might a pirate's map, certain that all the digging that had to be done would lead to some kind of treasure.

"What if it doesn't grow?" asked Jean-Claude.

"Of course it will," said his brother, Jacques.

"It will need sunshine and rain and fertilizer," Miron said.

"What's that?" asked little Claudette.

Sabine listened, trying to keep up with the names—she hadn't learned them all yet. Jacques and Jean-Claude had another brother named Richard, she remembered, and Marie-Antoinette had already found a family in Izieu to care for their baby sister, Yvette. Claudette's sandy hair was always in pigtails. She shuddered to think how confused she'd be when Pierre-Marcel gave her a set of new identity papers and the names of the children would all change again.

"Fertilizer makes the soil richer," Miron explained. "The best is cow dung."

Several children giggled and those in the know pinched their noses.

"Will we have a cow?" asked Isidore.

Sabine remembered picking him up from the orphanage with Sami and Hans and Alice. "Well, we'll have a barn. Why not a cow?" she said.

"Please, Madame Sabine. Tell us again about the house." Alice had scooted across the floor and now leaned against Sabine's knees.

"It's so white it shines in the sun. It has big tall windows that light up the rooms. There's a fountain and a huge yard."

"Is it a castle?"

"Oh, no. It's much better than that. It's a real home. You can sleep in real beds and have desks in your own classroom. And there's lots of room to play."

Sabine looked into the circle of faces surrounding her, suddenly conscious that the fidgeting had stopped and the voices had stilled. Some of the children just stared at her, wanting to believe her but not sure. Some of them studied their hands or twisted a strand of their hair, perhaps remembering other homes or other promises.

"And we'll all be together," said Max, who long ago had made Sabine promise that he would not be separated from his brother Herman, when she found them hungry and alone in a pension in Montpellier. "Brother with brother, sister with sister, brothers with sisters, right?"

"That's right. We'll all be together."

"Except that Madame Sabine and I will sleep in the barn," added Miron. "We'll be the ones picking bits of straw out of our hair at breakfast. Now who knows how to milk a cow?"

With that the children were off again, chattering and asking questions. Sabine slipped away and joined Léa who was busy preparing supper as best she could in the tiny kitchen of the hostel.

"I couldn't help overhearing. The children sound excited. Is there really enough money for a cow?"

"I think so. Miron and I have a bit left from the sale of the farm."

"That's what I mean, Sabine. You're putting everything you have into this place. What if it doesn't turn out to be all that you hope?"

"You think my hopes are too high, that I've raised the children's hopes too high? Don't worry, Léa. You haven't seen it yet."

With that, she changed the subject and pushed the niggling thought of the mayor of Belley to the back of her mind. There was so much to do. Miron would need lumber and nails and tools to build a bedroom in the barn. How many men could Pierre-Marcel find to help fix the stalls and the roof? She must remember to ask Marie-Antoinette to look for a suitable teacher for the classroom. And what about a cook? She sat down to make a list and didn't look up until she heard Miron clearing his throat behind her. "It's late, Sabine."

"What? Where are the children?"

"They're all asleep. Did you even eat supper?"

"I, no, I lost track of time." She suddenly realized how hungry she was. "Is there any left?"

"Time or food?"

She grinned. "Food please."

They crept into the kitchen without putting any lights on. Miron found her some bread and cheese and the small miracle of a glass of wine. The room was silent, but for the sound of her chewing.

"Don't look at me like that," Sabine said.

"It's too dark. You can't see my face."

"Believe me. I know exactly what your face is doing. It's frowning."

"You're pushing too hard."

"No, I'm not. We can't wait. We need to get them settled. The children need this."

She reached out for his hand, felt his fingers curl around her wrist, felt his thumb making small circles on her skin.

"I just want them to be happy again, my darling, for as long as possible, for however long it lasts. Is that so much to ask?"

He stood and pulled her into his arms and rested his cheek against her hair. *The stars and the moon*, he thought, but all she heard was, "Come to bed, now. Tomorrow you can start again."

There were inevitable delays. There was enough lumber to build a bedroom in the barn, but not enough nails. Pierre Marcel tore apart his own chicken coop to dig out the old ones, and swore he'd intended to donate his chickens anyway. Marie-Antoinette visited every farmer she knew and sweet-talked them into four more bags of nails. Several of her friends from Belley turned up to help with the hammering.

Miron set a date for the move and then stood at the window with Sabine watching the rain sweep through the town. It rained steadily for a week, while the mountain roads turned into tiny streams and became impassable. The children were restless and cranky, crowded into the hostel and bored with indoor games. Sabine received an urgent telegram from Léon Reifman advising her that he'd picked up a dozen more children who needed housing. When would she be ready to receive them? Léa fretted that one of the children, little Senta Spiegel, who barely spoke even to her sister, Martha, now had stopped talking altogether.

Sabine paced and studied the sky. Finally she saw the sun.

One day of sun and then another, then four days in a row of sun and spring winds licking up the moisture from the wet roads. Two school buses and four trucks lined up in front of the hostel. There was a flurry of running feet and last minute searches, telegrams sent and doors slamming and children lifted into the air.

The small, noisy convoy steered its way through the French countryside, gears shifting as it twisted its way up mountainside roads. The house was just past the next village, just ahead, just around the corner, and then, suddenly, there it was. The apple trees were in full blossom. The water in the fountain was crystal clear.

It was the sort of day that seemed sharply real, and yet not real at all. The children ran about the grounds, as if they couldn't believe their eyes. They whooped and hollered and peered into the barn and dipped their hands in the fountain.

When Sabine opened the door to the house, they stepped in one by one. Their eyes seemed huge in their surprised faces. They touched everything. They ran up the stairs and bounced on the beds. They tested out the rows of school desks and ran their fingers over the long tables in the dining area as if they expected these physical things to disappear at any moment.

Sabine knew what they were feeling: one life was ending and another beginning.

SENTA SPIEGEL, NINE YEARS OLD

WHEN I WAS FOUR OR FIVE years old, I thought people were only given a certain number of words to last their whole life. Once my words were used up I'd have nothing more to say. So I saved mine up. I had to say please and thank you, but I wasn't going to waste words on the weather when you only had to look at the sky.

At the camp we were sent to, my parents and my sister Martha and me, no words seemed to matter, not even *please*.

Madame Zlatin came to that camp and read out some words on a list. My sister took my hand and I said goodbye to my mother. My father was somewhere else in the camp where no words could reach him.

We went from place to place. Nothing was familiar. Martha spoke for both of us. I stored up the word *Mother*. I saved it, hoping I might use it again someday. If I wanted anything I could point, but everything I wanted was somewhere else.

Léa tried to get me to talk. By this time I was old enough to know there were endless words, but what did it matter? How many words were there for sorrow and what good would it do to let them out?

Then one day we were all piled onto a bus and we drove through the countryside. Everyone was chattering. I felt like I was on the bus with a flock of honking geese, all those words floating around and bumping into each other in the air.

"We're going to summer camp," Martha said, all excited.

I knew what the word camp meant. I thought she was crazy to be happy about it.

Then the bus finally stopped and I looked out through the window. My mouth formed an O. Everyone got off and started running about. I just sat there for a long time.

Léa came to find me. "Senta, are you okay?"

I smiled at her. "This is paradise," I said.

The words just flew out.

ESTHER BENASSAYAG, TWELVE YEARS OLD

I REMEMBER HIDING for a long time in an attic. The world was only whispers and tight corners, no speaking in full voice, hardly any talking at all. There was no going out, no feeling the rain or seeing the sky, no fresh breeze, no jumping or running, no laughing, no crying out loud. That was hard for Élie and Jacob. I had to hush them.

There was no colour but the faded shades of our dirty clothes.

No green of grass or blue of sky. No purple of twilight. The neon reds and oranges of shop signs, so bright the colours looked wet against the black of night, seemed lost forever.

Inside our attic, the moon was any globe of light, even one held in your hand, quickly snuffed out.

We were moles in a burrow, blind things.

The first thing I did when I came to the House of Izieu was run. Run with my mouth wide open, gulping in the fresh air, my eyes stinging from staring at the sun. Monsieur Miron took my hands and we spun in a circle until my feet left the ground and then we both collapsed in a dizzy heap, and I just lay there, panting and laughing and smelling the crushed grass.

At bedtime, I wore a white cotton nightgown. My hair was plaited and my face scrubbed clean. But I never fell asleep until I could search the sky and find the moon, just where it should be, high above me and huge among the stars.

MONSIEUR PERTICOZ, FARMER

I WORKED THE NEXT FIELD over from the Settlement for Refugee Children and thought it was only neighbourly to introduce myself the day they arrived. What a hullabaloo. There were kids everywhere, climbing the trees and running up and down the terrace. Cute little beggars. One little scrap of a guy couldn't have been more than three or four years old, still in short pants.

Miron Zlatin was the man in charge, him and his wife, Sabine. One handshake and I could tell he knew what was what. He had a farmer's hands, calloused, and not afraid of hard work. She was as tall as a man and wore pants like a man, too, but she was gentle as a lamb with those kids.

I asked right away if a couple of the older boys wanted work because I could use the help and I could pay in food. That was when I handed over the smoked ham my wife had packed in a basket together with a couple of bottles of wine and a big jug of sweet cider. Sabine thanked me very prettily and then Miron and I went off to talk to the boys and I met Henri and Joseph, fine strong lads.

I stayed a couple of hours and took a strong liking to Miron. He asked if I knew any one in the area who might be willing to join them as a cook and I recommended Philippe Dehan and his mother, Marie. They were refugees, too, from Paris, where they once ran a little bistro, and I thought they'd be good with the little ones.

When I got home my wife was full of questions. How many children, and how many adults, and did they seem like nice folk?

I just shook my head and told her that we shouldn't put any more ham in the next basket, no matter how nice our new neighbours were. "Why ever not?" she asked.

"You only need to take one look at them to see they're Yids. But a second look will tell you they're hungry. God knows what they've been through just to get here—all those little ones without parents. We'd best keep who they are to ourselves."

SARAH (SUZANNE) SZULKLAPER, ELEVEN YEARS OLD

I REMEMBER IN ANOTHER LIFE, there was a girl named Sarah. Her life was like one of those fairy tales her mother used to read to her in front of the fireplace in an apartment in Paris. Sarah's mother was kind and loving. Sarah's father granted her every wish. She had a dress as blue as the sky, and another as golden as the moon.

But one day an evil king came to rule the land. He had a thousand soldiers and they all raised their arms in the air when the king spoke. He shouted so loudly that even the earth seemed angry.

Silly Sarah thought that had nothing to do with her. She was happy in her own little world. When the king handed out yellow stars, she was stupid enough to think you got stars for good behaviour.

Then one night, bandits in black uniforms took away Sarah's father and mother and all her pretty things were stolen.

She couldn't think what she'd done to the king for him to punish her so. Maybe she was weak and greedy, like the king said when she finally listened to him.

People who used to be her friends didn't recognize her anymore. She ran to her teacher and he just shook his head. She ran to her cousins and they told her to hide. She ran to her rabbi and he told her to pray. She ran to the soldier and he told her to get on the bus. It took her all the way to Rivesaltes and she was smart enough then to know she was in hell.

Sarah could never have survived in that place. She was too spoiled. So one night she went asleep and woke up as Suzanne.

I'm a lot braver than Sarah. I pay attention. I watched this Red Cross nurse for days taking away other children. So I marched right up to her and said: "Take me."

She did.

At the House of Izieu, I became a wild bird, shaking the smell of Rivesaltes from my feathers. The other girl I used to be knew a story about an ugly duckling that transformed into a swan. Poor Sarah, she thought it was just pretend, but I know it's true. I'm that swan.

IZIEU, MAY 1943

THE FIRST DAY WOULD NOT have been complete without visitors. Monsieur Perticoz arrived from the neighbouring farm, a tall, rangy man in blue overalls with the weathered face of someone who'd spent his life outdoors. He brought a large basket of food and an even larger laugh and promised employment to some of the older boys. Within minutes, Miron was mining his knowledge of local growing seasons to put to use in his plans for the garden. Sabine watched the two men walk away in the direction of the barn and she couldn't be sure, but she thought negotiations were underway for a cow—and if the wishes of a little boy named Isidore came true—a dog, as well.

Marie-Antoinette and Pierre-Marcel were not far behind, their arms full of gifts. The children were wary of the Vichy uniform and kept their distance from Pierre-Marcel, but when he began to hand out little bags of striped peppermints, their suspicions seemed to vanish.

"I wish everything I'd brought today was sweet," Pierre-Marcel whispered to Sabine. "But I fear Mayor Tissot heard of your arrival and he's sure to show up at any moment."

"Nothing can spoil today," Sabine smiled. "Just look at the children and how happy they are. Their faces could melt the hardest of hearts."

She looked across the sweep of lawn and saw that the children were indeed beautiful, like blossoms in the still dreamed of garden, a bright gathering of different shapes and sizes, waving arms and legs, and bobbing heads of glossy black or mahogany or golden curls. Right in the centre of this laughing circle, the littlest of all, Coco, with his pretty mouth curved into a smile, was sound asleep in Léa's arms.

On the terrace Marie-Antoinette was holding court like a queen in a kingdom of children. She had dressed for the occasion, a white dress with embroidered violets all along the hemline and a violet shawl. Her hair gleamed pale gold in the sun as she leaned toward the upturned faces of her audience, keeping them spellbound with some story or rumour or scandal. You could never be sure what Marie-Antoinette might consider entertainment.

Sabine drew closer and saw that Marie-Antoinette was sitting on one of the gifts she had brought: a large pine chest with woodland scenes of dark glades, grazing deer, and fairies with pale wings painted on the sides. There was an elaborate looking lock peeking out from under the hem of Marie-Antoinette's dress.

"What's in that box?" one girl asked, curiosity trumping politeness.

The others joined in immediately. "Is it for us?"

"I'll bet there's toys inside."

"No. Look at the fairies. It must be magic."

Marie-Antoinette was delighted. This was just the reaction she'd hoped for. "It's a dress-up box," she confessed.

"What's that?" came a chorus of voices.

"You'll have to wait and see. It's for rainy days and special occasions only and Madame Zlatin will be the keeper of the key."

By late afternoon, the adults on hand had managed to corral all the children into the dining room for their first meal. Léa poured out cups of cider and Miron sliced the ham with a quick wink to Sabine. Hunger, after all, trumped the rules of kosher. Silence, and perhaps the first inklings of fatigue from over-excitement, settled on small shoulders as the children ate their sandwiches.

"You and Miron and Léa will never cope with this rowdy bunch," Marie-Antoinette teased. "You'll need help."

"Oh, but we won't be alone. Léon Reifman will likely be here by tomorrow. Paul and Théo are old enough to act as counsellors and Arnold Hirsch, who's travelling with Léon, has already been helping at the home in Palavas. Our neighbour suggested we might hire Philippe Dehan as cook. Do you know him?"

Marie-Antoinette shook her head. "I do not. But I know his mother, Marie. She looks like a raisin cookie, so perhaps that's a good omen for a cook."

"A raisin cookie?"

"You know—a round face, kind of soft and doughy looking, with little black eyes like currants or raisins."

"Really, Marie-Antoinette, your imagination..."

Sabine was about to say more when her sentence was interrupted by a sound from the courtyard, a kind of rushing sound like a sudden wind, or the sound of a moving car, which was exactly what it was.

Miron and Pierre-Marcel stood up and Sabine motioned them to join her in the courtyard.

She thought it must be Léon arriving early, but when she opened the door she felt her stomach jump with nerves.

Mayor Tissot was standing by his car, staring up at the house. Sabine thought his eyes were like two grey stones on a winter beach.

Pierre-Marcel greeted the mayor politely, if not cordially, while Sabine introduced Miron. Their conversation opened, as conversations between two uneasy strangers often do, with banal comments about the weather. From there, the group slid into silence. They were awkward with each other. Sabine was nervous, and the mayor seemed stiff, as if his smile had been applied with a brush, like a quick coat of paint, as ill fitting as his toupee.

"Would you like a tour of the house?" Sabine finally offered.

"It seems a bit crowded right now."

Sabine swung around to see what the mayor was looking at—a dozen little faces peering through the dining windows and a dozen more through the classroom windows. Up above, noses were pressed against the dormitory windows.

"It seems I've come not a moment too soon," the mayor continued solemnly. "Something will have to be done."

He turned his back to them and began to retrace his steps, returning to his car. Sabine watched him nervously, unsure of what he was going to say or do next.

At that moment, the door opened and Marie-Antoinette swept into the courtyard with Coco in her arms.

"Mayor Tissot. How lovely to see you. This is Coco, the youngest of the children."

Coco stared at the mayor and the mayor stared back. The boy had curly black hair that sprang all ways and asked to be ruffled. With the unpredictability of children everywhere, he suddenly smiled, a wide, beatific smile.

Sabine swore she saw the light change in the mayor's eyes.

"My, what a beautiful boy," he murmured and then, when he reached the trunk of his car, he heaved out a huge bushel and thrust it into Miron's arms.

"Seed potatoes," he said. "You'll need to start a garden. And for you, Madame—" his head disappeared for a moment as he plundered the trunk once more, "two sacks of flour, one of sugar, a little salt, and a whole pound of butter."

"Why, Mayor Tissot, you haven't been dallying with the black market, have you?" Marie-Antoinette teased.

"No. Oh no," he replied, immediately flustered. "Just a few provisions my wife and I had set aside. I'll see about getting more."

"You've already been so generous," Sabine assured him. "Thank you, Mayor."

"Generous, no. No, Madame. I've been blind. I didn't understand. There have been rumours, but I didn't know. About the children, I mean. I didn't—"

"I know."

He bowed stiffly, and Sabine thought he suddenly looked old, and then he was gone.

When the children were finally all tucked in and Léa was singing lullabies, Miron and Sabine waved goodbye to Pierre-Marcel and Marie-Antoinette and carried their lanterns into the barn. Their light triggered the rustling and whispery sounds of small creatures scurrying for darker corners, and disturbed at least one owl. It flapped its wings at them in annoyance and then sailed away above them, its shape briefly silhouetted by the moon.

The ceiling of their bedroom was the floor of the hayloft, and though they both had to duck their heads, the space was cosy enough.

Sabine sat hunched on the bed with her arms around her knees. She smiled, cat-like and content. "We've done it," she whispered.

Miron stretched out beside her. "We've only just begun. But we've done enough for today. Do you realize how cold it is in here?"

Sabine ran a hand through his hair and kissed his forehead. "I'll keep you warm," she promised.

OTTO WERTHEIMER, TWELVE YEARS OLD

STRANGELY, BECAUSE A LOT of bad things have happened, what I remember best is standing in my mother's kitchen on a summer's afternoon. I'm maybe four or five. My mother is mixing a large bowl of fruit bread. She stirs in the sugar and the candied fruit peel and covers the bowl with a towel to give it time to rise.

But I can't wait.

I lift one corner of the towel, dip my finger in the sweet yeasty dough and lick it. Then I dip my finger in again.

I can still taste that sweetness in my mouth. I can still see the sunlight shining through the pots of geraniums on the kitchen windowsill. I can hear my mother walk into the kitchen behind me, her shoes on the wooden floor.

She laughs and swats my hand away from the bowl. "Good things are worth waiting for," she says.

I guess she was right because I sure waited long enough for the House of Izieu.

Bad things don't take any waiting for—they just pounce on you like a cat on a mouse, like my father turning the wrong corner and running into an identity check and being dragged away.

But here I am in this big old house in a bed of my own with a pillow. My cousin Fritz is here, too, just beside me, a piece of family.

We had ham for supper, something I've never tasted before and it sure tasted good. Monsieur Miron has promised to take us on a hike through the mountains when the summer comes.

So I'll wait here for you, Mother, however long it takes. And if you want to swat my hand for eating ham, well, that'd be the happiest day of my life.

MARTHA SPIEGEL, TEN YEARS OLD

WE ALL SLEPT TOGETHER in the upstairs room at Izieu, boys on one side, girls on the other. Real beds, with sheets and blankets and soft pillows. It made me feel safe to hear all that breathing around me.

In the camps, my little sister, Senta, had nightmares. I knew why. I would shut my eyes to try and sleep but I'd see ghosts. They'll jump out at you and try to grab you. I'd sit straight up like a poker. When I opened my eyes, I would see shadows on the ceiling that looked like witches crouched in the trees. Senta saw them, too. When the wind rattled the walls of the barracks, I couldn't think of anything but demons and skeletons trying to get in and snatch us.

Mother told Senta to settle down and not make things worse than they had to be. She tried, but someone's dress hanging up to dry in the night was a ghost waving in the dim light. She'd wake everyone up with her screaming. She stopped talking, even in the daylight.

Her nightmares went away in Izieu.

Madame Sabine said it was because of all the fresh air and exercise, but I think it was because of Léa. She sang to us, and when she leaned down to kiss our cheeks, her hair smelled of lily-of-the-valley.

One day I heard Madame Sabine call Léa an angel.

I think she was.

I imagined her standing outside our door in a circle of pale golden light with feathery wings to sweep away any terrors that came by in the small dark hours.

Then in the dawn, she folded up her wings and put them away so no one else would guess her secret.

But one morning, I woke up very early and surprised Léa coming up the stairs while I was going down. She had a feather in her hair, a small, curly white feather. When I pointed to it, she pulled it out and smiled at me and put a finger to her lips. I never told anyone that, not even Senta.

RENATE AND LIANE KROCHMAL, TEN AND EIGHT YEARS OLD

WE REMEMBER HOW SURPRISED we were at how big the house and grounds were at Izieu. We'd never been any further than the end of our village street until we were sent to Rivesaltes, which was ugly and crowded, but here the air was fresh and wide fields surrounded us. We could see the line of the horizon and we tried to imagine what lay beyond it.

We often played in the fields where everything smelled green and sweet. There must have been a dozen different kinds of wildflowers that we could never remember the names of. When they grew in patches, we thought they looked like puddles of colour—scarlet, cornflower blue, butter yellow, and the palest shades of pink.

Sometimes we would play a secret game. If the night was very mild, we would sneak outside. We would lie on our backs in the grass and stare up at the stars. We would choose the brightest one or the closest one and then blink once and be gone.

We'd travel right up to that star and look down at Izieu and France and the whole wide world. We were newly born creatures of the sky.

There was room to breathe up in the stars, and no Nazis either. We thought this must be how angels view the world. We'd imagine looking down and pretend we could see our old house. But after we'd floated around a bit, we always wanted to come back to earth because that was where our mother would look for us. She wrote us letters and told us to be brave.

We were always together. *Two peas in a pod,* Madame Sabine said. We always knew what the other was thinking and we dreamed each other's dreams, and we smiled at each other every morning when we woke up because those dreams were always of home and that tiny village street we'd left so far behind.

HANS (JEAN) AMENT, TEN YEARS OLD

FRIDAY NIGHTS MY MOTHER would place a veil over her face and move her hands in graceful circles over the candles. We ate chicken flavoured with parsley and thyme, and broke open hot loaves of bread.

When we were forced to flee to Belgium, we were hungry most of the time. But when my brother, Alfred, and I were granted visas for America, my parents insisted on celebrating with big bowls of *coq au vin* at the inn where we were staying. That was our last meal together.

The very next day, the Nazis invaded Belgium. My father went into hiding and my mother became very ill. I never got to see America, though I sometimes still dream of it. The OSE took in my brother and me and after many months, we came to the House of Izieu.

I remember breakfast on that first morning—porridge with honey and warm milk that tasted so sweet and familiar. It was like holding a piece of home in my mouth. I pretended to have something in my eye, because I didn't want Alfred or anyone else to see that a bowl of porridge could make me cry.

Our mother was suffering from tuberculosis and she was placed in a sanatorium called L'Espérance, not far from Izieu. We wrote to her almost every day.

Some things Alfred explained to me because he made a big deal of being six years older than me. Some things were left unsaid. Sometimes we'd just sit under a tree together not talking at all, just breathing in the smell of fresh grass. Just the two of us, blowing dandelion puffs into the air, feeling the sun on our skin, remembering when there were four of us.

LÉA FELDBLUM, TEACHER-COUNSELLOR

FINALLY, THE CHILDREN were all asleep. I crept into the dormitory and watched them for a while. The room was crowded, all flung limbs and linens, a leg dangling off a bed here, an arm there. Sabine and I did our best to group them by age—the five five-year-olds in one corner, the seven eight-year-olds in another, and so on—but that plan soon broke down, as siblings gravitated to each other. I didn't blame them for wanting to cling to what they knew. They'd been shunted around for months, some of them for years.

My own bedroom, close by, was an oasis, but I never got used to Sabine and Miron sleeping in the barn. They sank everything they owned into this place, and what a place. I doubted her, but Sabine was right.

When I first saw the House of Izieu, I had the sense that the boundary between dream and reality was becoming too subtle, almost invisible. Heaven had suddenly fallen to earth, though much of that earth was still dangerous and broken.

I lay in bed and listened to the blissful silence of sanctuary. And when I heard footsteps, I just smiled and pulled back the covers so that little Émile Zuckerberg, in jumbled pyjamas and a bird's nest of blond curls, could climb in beside me. He has been a part of me ever since I found him, alone and crying, in Rivesaltes. He is not my child, but I love him; I love all of them, as if they were. Children know love when they see it.

With Émile's head on my shoulder, I looked out through my window at the unencumbered sky: no uneven roof tiles, no spires, no telegraph poles strung together with sagging wires, no guards, and no barbed wire, only dense clusters of stars of every size.

The river flowed underneath the moon, and the rivers of my heart flowed with it.

IZIEU, SUMMER 1943

THAT SUMMER THE MOON WAS GOLDEN.

Sunlight was glorious. A bird was a wonder.

The House of Izieu was bustling and alive, filled with the whoop and holler of children roaming free, the sounds of games and laughter, and beneath it all the liquid music of the river, swollen from mountain springs and rushing to find the sea.

In the river meadows, alder, brambles, and wild roses formed a magical tangle for playing hide-and-seek. There were wild strawberries for picking, apple trees for climbing, marshy pools for wading, and river ponds for swimming. While the older boys pulled fish out of the river, grey herons and swifts circled overhead. This was *la France profonde*: ancient, luxuriant, generous, and remote.

Every day had its routine and its surprises. Mornings began with trips to the fountain where the children washed their faces and then gathered around long tables next to the kitchen for bread and bowls of hot cocoa. There were lessons in the schoolroom, followed by chores: beds made, dishes washed, chickens fed, the cow milked, and the garden weeded. If the day was fine, lunch was often eaten on the terrace or simply on the grass beneath the nearest tree. There was a quiet hour, when the littlest ones might nap, except for four-year-old Coco who started every quiet hour with the chant "No *nap*. No *nap*." The older children read to each other, or drew pictures, or wrote letters to parents, or cousins, or siblings, or aunts, or whomever was left of absent family.

Then the children were set free to play and the surprises began. There might be swimming or hiking, tree-climbing or skipping. Some of the children collected all sorts of things: rocks from the river in the shape of bears or lions, every kind of feather, and pinecones of all sizes. By nightfall, their pockets were crammed with treasure. Others brought Léa and Sabine fistfuls of wilting wild flowers, or used the shells of acorns as miniature teacups, or fashioned dolls from sticks and the blossoms of hollyhocks.

That summer was a good one for blackberries. Some of the bushes were taller than the children and covered in sweet, ripe fruit. The little ones filled their pails easily and came home with lips stained purple from blackberry juice.

Surprises also came in the shape of people and animals. It seemed, at least in May, that someone or something new came every day. Léon Reifman arrived with eight more children dressed in layers of patched, cast-off clothes, like a row of tiny scarecrows. Léon took one look at the house and announced he would be delighted to stay on as a counsellor. Monsieur Perticoz rambled across the field leading a brown cow, followed by a bounding, long-eared cocker spaniel. Renée and Paulette Paillarès came all the way from Montpellier with a tent and a goat, prepared to stay for the whole summer. They also brought four-year-old Diane Popovski, long ago rescued from Agde by Sabine, and adopted by the Paillarès family.

Perhaps best of all was the arrival of the cook and his mother. Philippe Dehan was dashing—tall and well proportioned with broad shoulders and thick black eyebrows that gave him a ferocious air. A lock of hair, black as coal, danced on his forehead. Most surprising of all, he wore an eye-patch, perhaps a souvenir from the war that was to end all wars but had failed to do so. Several boys nicknamed him the pirate at first sight. The cook's mother, Marie, was stout and dignified, as dignified as a woman could be with a face that did, indeed, look like a raisin cookie. She wore a white kerchief over her hair and, unlike her son with the mysterious past, was as open and welcoming as her smile.

Philippe immediately took command of the kitchen, slamming around pots and pans, and hollering for more wood to fire up the huge cooking stove. The bravest children hovered in the doorway to watch him, while the most timid peeked out at him from behind the nearest skirt. Marie acted as sous-chef, washing and chopping vegetables from the garden, and setting the table.

When the moment came to taste the first dish, a thick fish stew, Philippe stood in the doorway of the kitchen and watched with his arms crossed over his impressive chest. The children lifted their spoons with some trepidation, but the herb-scented smell of the stew was enough to make mouths water. Soon there was nothing to be heard but the clicking of spoons and the scraping of bowls. Philippe smiled, a huge grin that revealed a quick flash of gold.

"Look! He has a gold tooth," one boy whispered to another. "He really must've been a pirate."

Nodding and smiling, Marie gathered up the empty bowls, the older children quick to help her. Then everyone gasped as Philippe brought out a large, rectangular cake, placing it on the table with a flourish.

"My specialty," he announced. "Gingerbread. But don't get used to such spoiling. It's to celebrate my arrival."

As he carved up the cake, placing warm chunks of it on plates, Sabine sidled up to him. "You have a soft heart, Philippe," she whispered. "Don't worry. I'll keep your secret."

After supper, if the night was fine, everyone gathered on the terrace for stories or songs. The cousins Fritz and Otto had once lived in Germany and knew the *Der Struwwelpeter* stories—a boy sucks his thumb and has it cut off by a tailor with a giant pair of scissors; another refuses to eat his supper and starves to death. These were quickly declared to be horrid little stories, banned from the terrace, but, happily, Alice knew all the stories from Charles Perrault, and she could recite her favourite, *Puss in Boots,* almost word for word.

When Léa read aloud, her stories were soothing and gentle to match her voice, but if Marie-Antoinette were visiting, which could be anytime because she had no need of an invitation, the readings became theatrical performances and her stories resembled impromptu radio plays. Her voice could be low and raspy for talking bears, or high-pitched for the squeaks of field mice, or sugary for good fairies, or rough and hoarse for the cackles of witches. The small children, sitting on her lap or gathered at her feet, listening with rapt concentration, needed the wonder of Marie-Antoinette's stories almost as much as they needed air to breathe.

The songs were most often of the sort that everyone could join in on—*Frère Jacques, Alouette,* and *Au claire de la lune.* But if Barouk-Raoul Bentitou chose to sing, everyone else listened. He sang the street music from the old Casbah in Algiers, songs of love, joy, misery, and everything in between. His twelve-year-old voice was pure and clear. Sometimes it swelled and at other times softened, pulling at hearts. When he sang, Sabine thought of birds wheeling in the setting sun, of rolling waves, and of sparks dancing up into the air from a bonfire on the banks of a river on the edge of the world.

During the long summer nights, the children's feet, bare on boards, constant as rain, moved up and down the hallways and the stairs. Every bed and every room was full and no one wanted to be alone. The children's voices echoed in slow, drowsy spirals through the house.

Up in the attic, at the very top of the House of Izieu, Paul Niedermann and Théo Reiss lay down in their narrow beds. Théo was Paul's best friend and confidante but he had never needed to make that explicit, because both of them took it for granted. "If we're sharing a room," Paul said, "I need to know: do you snore?"

"No. Do you?"

Paul shook his head. "Do you suffer from nightmares?"

"Sometimes. Don't you?" Without waiting for the obvious answer, Théo changed the subject, or rather returned to the subject that was never far from his mind. He was a lovely, dark-eyed teenager, and part of him was lonely all the time, a young, hungry part. "Tell me. Do you know anything about girls?"

"Almost nothing."

"It's Paulette, you see. When I'm around her, I feel like I'm all elbows and knees."

"Ah. Well, there's one thing my mother told me once. She said men should treat women with tenderness."

"What does that mean, exactly?"

Since Paul didn't really know, his answer was short. "Go to sleep, Théo."

There was always a time in the night when everything finally went silent—when the children were sleeping, or pretending to sleep, when the chickens stopped scratching, and the cow stopped lowing, when the wind stopped blowing, and the fir trees were flat against the dark sky.

Alone in their separate space, their makeshift bedroom in the barn, Sabine and Miron often talked about how the children had altered their lives. To be in love with the children was to understand how alone they had been as a couple without them. It was to know that if they were ever to be without them again, the gap left by their absence would be unbridgeable, a yawning sorrow beyond fixing. Yet they were irresistible, these children, and they could no more stop loving them than they could stop loving each other.

ARNOLD HIRSCH, SEVENTEEN YEARS OLD

I REMEMBER MY LAST IMAGE of my parents. My father was bearded, dressed entirely in black, in a heavy overcoat and hat. My mother stood next to him, leaning against his arm and sobbing. They were standing on the train platform, waving goodbye to me with white handkerchiefs.

As the train carrying me to the South pulled away, they grew smaller and smaller, more and more indistinct, and their despair reinforced my premonition that I would never see them again.

My father was never boastful or unkind. He sang at the piano, and gave ferocious hugs that lifted my mother and me right off our feet. As a little boy, I tried in vain to copy him in every way.

My mother believed that laughter healed most wounds of the heart, and for anything else she recommended a remedy of chicken soup served with a spoonful of cod liver oil. She single-handedly drove away my fears and cares.

At Izieu I learned to face my fears on my own and I cared for the little ones. I helped them organize their games and made sure no one was left on the sidelines. If they were tired, I carried them on my shoulders. If they were sad, I gave them hugs that lifted them off their feet.

As the days came to an end, when the western horizon glowed a warm orange, I cuddled them on the terrace. We waited for the sky to darken and searched for shooting stars, and talked into the night.

I missed my parents, but when I emulated their kindness, I felt the distance between us shrink, and the space I kept for them in my heart overflowed. This was the peace I found at Izieu.

FRITZ LÖBMANN, FIFTEEN YEARS OLD

THE COOK'S ARRIVAL was the trigger for endless speculation. Maybe he had to flee Paris because he had poisoned a Nazi in his bistro, or maybe he'd had his eye poked out by a jealous husband, or maybe he hadn't lost an eye at all and the patch was a cunning disguise to hide a criminal past. Unlike the younger boys, I didn't believe for a minute that he'd been a pirate, but he must have been hiding something or he wouldn't have come here.

We're all hiding here.

I read a book once about a wild boy who got lost in the Black Forest where the wolves found him and took care of him. They licked him clean, and brought him meat to cook on an open fire, and when the nights were cold, their fur kept him warm.

I love that story. I remember wildness: running through the forest, my body buzzing with energy, leaping up for the joy of it with a mouthful of freedom to shout out. We're all wolf cubs here, roaming the woods and the mountain trails like wild things.

Of course, the real wolves are the Nazis. I never understood their hate, but I understand how it can leak out from a black heart into the light of day. It begins with muttered insults behind your back, with gravestones toppled over in Jewish cemeteries, with Dirty Jew scrawled on a shop window, and with synagogues on fire. When those eyes are on you, following you, watching you, tracking you, it feels as real as a fist punching you in the back.

That's why I love the House of Izieu, far from those tracking eyes. The forest is a thick curtain, and the rocky escarpments are like a fortress. It's the best hiding place I ever found.

BAROUK-RAOUL BENTITOU, TWELVE YEARS OLD

EVENINGS ON TERRACE ARE BEST. On fine nights whole house is coming there to tell stories and sing. Music is in my blood, Paulette Paillarès says, and I guess she's truth because at Izieu I am singing all the time. Humming when brushing my teeth, and whistling on hikes in woods. I am tapping my feet to tunes I hear while we are eating. In evenings I open my mouth and music of Algiers pours out.

People are asking me about Algeria. I don't have much to tell them. I am really little when we are leaving our town for

Marseilles—most I remember hot skies going on forever, and sand in my food and hair. And camels. They only look silly standing still. When camel in motion, moving on long legs over desert, in place where they are born and belong to, they as handsome as ancient kings.

Never sure where I belong, so music my father and brothers taught me is home. They arrested in Marseilles when Nazis burst into café where we play for money for food—my father on *mandole*, Maurice on conga, and André on flute. I shake the *Yoruba*. I am being taken, too, only waiter grabs my shirt and stuffs me behind bar. Many months later the waiter, name also Maurice, writes letter to Madame Sabine and she is bringing me here.

So yes, I am singing. Old folk tunes of Bedouin, songs of love from Casbah. I sing father's hands on steel strings of *mandole*. I sing percussion of brother's heart on conga, and I am singing André's lips on flute. When I am hearing pure notes and feeling my body swaying in rhythms, I belong again. To them.

JUNE 1943

THE RIVER WAS NOT like the sea. It never threatened or boomed. Sabine grew to love the glass smooth calm of the evenings when the river reflected the silver and blue tones of twilight.

From the terrace, she had an unobstructed view of the vista of mountains, river, and sky, cast by the evening light in a uniform blue. A thinly drawn line of darker blue, the horizon, appeared very near, as if she could reach out and touch it. She liked this delineating border and the feeling it gave her of being encircled, contained, even embraced. It was what she loved most about living here in this forgotten corner of France. She could live here in the moment, and immerse herself in the everyday. She could experience the world through the eyes of a child.

Hours earlier, she had watched Léon take a group of children down to the river to feed the ducks that lived in the reed bed along the river's edge. He was an excellent swimmer, sleek as an otter. Suddenly he dove into the water with a quick fluid grace that barely disturbed the surface.

The surprised children jumped in the air and clapped as he emerged. "Do it again," they shouted. "Do it again."

Sabine had laughed and returned to her chores until she felt a tug on her skirt and looked down into the worried face of five-year-old Sami Adelsheimer.

"What's wrong, Sami?" she asked.

"There's mermaids with green hair in the river."

"Mermaids? Well, that I'd like to see." Sabine took his hand and he led her to the river, or as close to the river as he wanted to be.

"There," he pointed to the spot. "See? That's green hair."

"Those are just weeds, silly."

"They don't look like weeds. We helped Monsieur Miron pull weeds in the garden. They didn't look like that."

"These are river weeds."

"Are you sure?"

"Sure I'm sure."

"It looks like hair," Sami repeated, not convinced.

"I'll pull one out for you," Sabine offered. "The weeds have long fronds that wave in the currents."

She slipped out of her shoes and waded into the water and tugged at one of the plants until she had pulled it free. "See? Just a plant, not hair."

"Is it slimy?"

"Just a bit." Sabine held it out for him and Sami quickly backed up.

"Aren't you coming into the water?" she asked. "There's nothing to be afraid of as long as Léon is here to watch you."

"Maybe tomorrow," Sami said and then ran off as fast as his legs could carry him.

Sabine would have been content to spend every hour with the children, but she would often leave without saying where she was going or when she'd be back. Two or three days might go by, with no news from her, and then suddenly she'd reappear with a new set of identity papers for some of the children, or a suitcase full of flour bags, or another child.

Her trips were often to Belley. Pierre-Marcel was more than a protector of the House of Izieu. He had become a true friend, a man immune to corruption and vanity, with a weakness for defending the needy with artful and clever subterfuges. And Sabine was certainly needy. She needed ration cards and more food than she could buy legally; she needed clothing, and identity cards without the *Juif* stamp for the children, and she needed to find a teacher and a doctor. Above all, she needed people she could trust and she found all of that in Pierre-Marcel and in his loyal assistant, Marie-Antoinette, from whom he seemed to be inseparable, despite his abiding love for his wife, who was expecting their second child.

From the relative safety of the *subpréfecture* office, that pair kept a close eye on the restlessness of the bored Italian soldiers and the nosiness of the Milice, and kept track of any grumblings, suspicions, or slurs from the townspeople of Belley and all the tiny hamlets nearby.

"How is Léa?" Marie-Antoinette asked.

"Knee-high in children," Sabine smiled, "and loving every minute of it. Yesterday, she had them make paper boats and race them across the water in the fountain. Huffing and puffing was allowed to speed the boats along, so it was a wet and wild affair."

"And Philippe and his mother?"

"Performing marvels with whatever vegetables or fruits we manage to harvest and whatever fish or canned goods we have. The children are beginning to fill out and their cheeks are turning pink."

"You might try selling some of your vegetables in the weekly market in Izieu," Pierre-Marcel suggested.

Sabine raised an eyebrow, "Is that wise?"

Pierre-Marcel nodded. "Take a few of the younger children along. Let the villagers see that there's nothing to be afraid of. If you are too separate from the village, people will become curious and tongues will start to wag. Also, when the summer ends, you might think about placing some of the twelve or thirteen-year-old boys in the boarding school in Belley where they can get proper education. In the meantime, I'm still searching for a teacher from among the closest villages who might be willing to make the daily trip to Izieu."

Marie-Antoinette saw the concern on Sabine's face. "Don't worry. Any boys who come to the school in Belley will be my special friends. They'll be treated well. Oh, and please tell the Benguigui brothers that their little sister, Yvette, is growing like a weed. She's the darling of the family that's taken her in."

"Any luck yet with finding a doctor?" Sabine asked. "Léon Reifman has a sister who's a doctor, but she has a child and aging parents. I think she'd gladly come to stay, but it's a question of room. And I still get letters from desperate parents asking for placements for their children."

"You can't save them all, Sabine," Pierre-Marcel cautioned. "And speaking of letters, be careful that the ones the children write mention only Christian holidays because we can't be certain that their mail won't be intercepted by the Milice. There's one man I know you can trust, a Doctor Albert Bendrihem in Glandieu, near Izieu, but be careful. Only go there for very serious problems, ones that you can't manage on your own with your nursing training. He's a kind man, but he's suspected by the scoundrels in the area to be a 'Jewish' doctor. Whether that means he himself is Jewish, or that he is willing to treat Jews, I don't know. I only wish it didn't matter, but in the meantime, he has whatever protection my office can offer."

In the silence that followed this speech, Marie-Antoinette looked at the solemn faces of her two friends and wished she could find some miraculous remedy for their troubles. Their faces reminded her that for all the protection offered by the

House of Izieu, its very existence was still precarious. Since she had first begun working with Pierre, and then again when she had met Sabine, she had wondered what motivated some people to be full of goodness and mercy, for no personal gain and at considerable personal risk, while so many others bent their heads and knees to fanaticism and the cruelty it spawned. We know so much, she thought, about what motivates people to be evil, and so little about what motivates them to be good. She looked down at her empty hands and knew she had no cure to soothe her dear friends' spirits, but she smiled and offered what she could.

"By the way, Sabine, I've been collecting children's books from some of the citizens of Belley. I've got *The Magic Egg, Eskimo Grasshoppers, The Forest, The Musicians of Bréme,* and *April's Fish.* I'm still looking for stories of cowboys, but you can take home what I have."

When Sabine returned from her necessary journeys, she was always relieved to see Miron with his sunburned cheeks, affectionate smile, unshakable inner strength, and certainty that they could solve any problem together. When she told him that Pierre-Marcel had suggested that trips to the market might be used to barter vegetables and smiles for meat and goodwill, he set about at once to fashion a mode of transportation for the children. It took the form of a large cart, a long contraption with four high wheels, pulled along by a single horse borrowed from Farmer Perticoz. The bottom was made of three wide boards. The sides were ladders fixed at angles to the bottom. Miron sat on a board fixed across the ladders and filled the cart with straw, carrots, tomatoes, cabbages, beans, and half a dozen or more excited children.

The trips to the market became a weekly excursion. In addition to the vegetables there were wild strawberries and rhubarb to sell in May, cherries and courgettes in June, pears and raspberries in July, and blackberries and blueberries in August.

The younger children took turns accompanying Miron, who, as Sabine said, was the only one brave or foolish enough to drive the cart, but he never had to worry about the children's behaviour because they all loved the trips and knew that if they weren't unfailingly polite and helpful they would lose their chance to go to the market when their next turn came.

First to pass by the cart was always Marie-Antoinette who rode her bicycle all the way from Belley to Izieu. The Spiegel sisters, Martha and Senta, adored her and ran into her arms. Sometimes she had hard candies hidden in her pockets for the children to find, and sometimes she helped one or two of the Benguigui brothers, especially five-year-old Jean Claude, slip away to visit their little sister, Yvette, living with a village family.

Before many weeks had passed, almost all the villagers looked forward to the arrival of the cart from the Settlement for Refugee Children from the Hérault. The poor little orphans, as they were privately referred to, won the villagers' hearts. One day, the butcher would discover he had an extra bit of meat to trade for strawberries, and a bone for the cocker spaniel named Tomi. The barber had a cousin nearby who grew artichokes. They weren't his wife's favourite, but perhaps the children would enjoy them. The baker had six loaves that hadn't risen to his liking and it would be a shame to see them go to waste.

One week, one beautiful girl, only eighteen, leaned her bicycle against a tree and watched from a distance. She had a letter clutched in her hand, and she had a wish. She counted eight children between the ages of five and ten. How could she possibly know anything of their loss? These children were not the same as her little brothers. Their world was not the same as hers at all. She caught the gaze of the tall, sunburned man with the wary eyes who always accompanied them, and looked away quickly.

Miron was fully aware of her presence. Indeed, it would have been difficult not to notice her lithe figure and her dark

Italianate curls cut into a shapely bob. The last two weeks in a row she had watched the children and leaned her bike against that tree, yet she had never approached the stall nor spoken to anyone. He looked again and thought he saw a wrinkle of doubt on her pale oval face. Was she waiting for someone, he wondered? Was she waiting for him?

At that moment their eyes met again, and the young woman took a deep breath and stepped forward.

Miron crossed the ground between them quickly. "Can I help you?"

"Monsieur Zlatin?" she asked.

As soon as he nodded, she began to speak rapidly, giving him, she hoped, no time to turn down her request. "Hello. I'm Marcelle Favet. I've a letter here from Monsieur Wiltzer. I'm a teacher, that is, I want to be a teacher. I want to help, maybe for the summer, until a more experienced teacher can be found."

Her rehearsed speech had left her cheeks red, and she thrust the letter at him as if it were a small, dangerous animal.

To her dismay, Miron didn't open the letter, but slipped it into his shirt pocket instead. "Do you know Monsieur Wiltzer?" he asked.

"I do. I know his wife very well. She's my godmother."

"And you want to teach at the Settlement?"

"I'd like to try. I live near Izieu. I could come every day."

"Have you seen the house? It won't be an easy journey on your bicycle—mostly uphill and on dirt roads."

Marcelle shook her head, but insisted she was strong.

"I've seen you watching the children," Miron continued in a gentler voice. "It won't work if you're frightened of them."

"Frightened? Oh, no, Monsieur. How can little children be frightening?"

"It won't work if you feel sorry for them, either."

Marcelle blushed and looked down at the ground. She felt she'd been caught out, that this man had quickly measured the distance between their two worlds and judged it to be too far.

She saw that he'd drawn a line he thought she couldn't cross. But there must be a way over, a way through. She believed that people could move beyond the limits of their known world. Why else was there music, poetry, imagination, or prayer?

She raised her head then and looked him in the eye and her voice was lovely, clear and strong. "Give me a chance. Everyone deserves a chance to learn, to try. Perhaps lines are not real, only drawn from the inside out."

Miron stood perfectly still. She had surprised him, touched him.

He reached for her bicycle, took a few long strides, and swung it up onto the cart. "Come on, then," he called back over his shoulder.

Marcelle paid no attention to the route, surrounded as she was by the children. Some of them were shy and only looked up at her through their eyelashes, but some of them asked questions right away. *What was her favourite colour? And did she like games? Could she whistle? Did she like having short hair?*

She looked away from them at a point in the road where a person could look down and see the house and the shape of the landscape and get a sense of what it felt like to be there. The house fitted so perfectly into the contours of the countryside that it appeared to have grown there naturally, like a tree.

She reached for the nearest little hand and held it in her own. She was no longer uncertain or hesitant. That moment was past.

NINA ARONOWICZ, TWELVE YEARS OLD

MY DEAR AUNTIE,

I am very happy to be here. There are beautiful mountains, and from high up you can see the Rhône flow by and it's so pretty. Yesterday we went for a swim in the river pool with Mademoiselle Marcelle. She's our summer teacher, but she plays games with us, too. One time, when we'd finished our sums, she let us make paper planes and fly them outside to see whose would go the furthest. We wrote messages on the flaps, like Be Brave or Wish on the Moon or Shout Out Your Name or Eat a Carrot. Once all the planes had landed, we each had to pick one at random and try to guess who'd written the message. Sometimes that was easy because the boys are messier printers than us girls, and Théo just wrote down Paulette because he's sweet on her. I wrote Be Brave because that's what you always tell me in your letters.

Did I mention that Mademoiselle Marcelle is very beautiful? Her hair is black and her eyes are violet and sometimes she wears pants instead of dresses. One day she asked us what we want to be when we grow up. Esther is the smartest and she wants to be a scientist like Madame Curie, and Suzanne wants to be a dancer, and Mina said she wants to be a nurse. I said I want to be Mademoiselle Marcelle and everybody laughed.

I'm fine here and eating very well, three meals a day, and sometimes snacks. Whenever anyone gets a parcel with sweets or biscuits, we all share.

I hope to see you again very soon. While I'm waiting, I'm hugging you as hard as I can.

Your loving niece, Nina

LATE JUNE 1943

ON MARKET DAYS, Sabine used one of the long dining tables to spread out the account books and search for money between the lines. Any relatives of the children still at large sent money when they could, and there was a monthly allowance from the OSE. These funds barely covered expenses. So Sabine was more than grateful for donations from friends she'd left behind in Montpellier, especially Berthe Mering who she'd met when they both worked for the Red Cross.

She was writing a thank you note to Berthe when she heard the sound, a whispery, broken sound that she recognized immediately as a child crying. Knowing Léa or Paulette or Marcelle would be close by, Sabine opened the window a crack and bent her head to the open space.

Mina was trying to console her little sister, Claudine, who was cupping a pile of feathers in both hands. "Don't cry, Claudine. It's just a dead bird." This pronouncement made the tears fall faster and Claudine made a little sobbing sound.

"Look. I'll tell you what. Give the bird to me and we'll bury it. You go down to the river and get the prettiest stone you can find. We'll have a ceremony."

"What's a ceremony?"

"You know. We'll wrap the bird up and put it in the ground. Then you place the stone on top and we'll say a prayer. I'll make up a poem, if you like."

"All right. What'll we wrap it in?"

"I'm not sure. How about your sock?"

Claudine yanked off her shoes and one sock and held it up to her sister who took it and slipped the bird inside. "See?" Mina said. "Now the bird has its own little blanket."

"Is this a Jewish bird?"

"Of course."

"Then we must put handfuls of dirt on the body before the stone can go on."

"Oh, you must remember when we buried Bubbe. Yes, we'll do that first."

Sabine watched Mina dig a little hole under a tree with a rock. Pretty soon Marcelle crouched down beside her. "What are you doing, Mina?" she asked.

"We're having a burial for this bird. Claudine found it and started to cry."

"May I watch?"

"Okay. Here's Claudine now. That's a pretty stone. Isn't it lovely, Marcelle?"

"Very."

The two little girls bent their heads over the bird in its grave and then sprinkled handfuls of dirt on top. Mina smoothed over the surface and Claudine placed the stone.

"Now the poem," Claudine demanded.

Mina stood up and spread her arms, full of the solemnity of the occasion.

"Here you lay, unhappy bird. Here in the ground and not the sky. Worms will get you. Your bones will dry. And so we say Goodbye, Goodbye."

"Oh dear!" Marcelle exclaimed, as Claudine burst into tears again and Sabine tried not to laugh out loud from behind the window.

"Let's try that again, shall we? Now, let me see. How's this? Rest in Peace, O lovely bird. Your wings are still, but soon you'll fly, high above in Heaven's sky. Goodbye, Goodbye."

"Oh, that's much better. Don't you think so, Claudine?"

The little girl nodded and stared down at her bare foot. "I'm missing a sock now."

"C'mon," Mina said, leading her back to the house. "You can have one of mine."

Sabine turned back to the accounts. She didn't have any money, but she felt richer than she'd ever been.

To celebrate summer and the longest days of the year, when the golden light of the setting sun often traced a tattoo of shadows across the terrace, the children planned a very special event. A fête, with skits and songs and dancing.

Sabine had supposed some sort of play was inevitable as soon as the first rainy day had come and the children had begged her to open the marvellous chest that Marie-Antoinette had brought them as a house-warming gift. When the key finally turned the lock and the lid was flung open, there were exclamations all around for the chest was filled with costumes. There were striped pants and spangled vests, forest green cloaks and scarlet capes, turbans and feathered hats and tiaras, and long ruffled skirts in shades of wine-red and topaz. There was even one pair of gauzy wings made from starched lace, an inky-blue feather boa, a witchy-looking wig, and, at the very bottom of the chest, a slender flute of polished wood with silver keys.

There was also immediate chaos. All the children wanted to try something on *right away,* and several children wanted to try on the same thing. There was tugging and shoving and shouts of *No, me!* And *Not fair!* Sabine felt trapped in a sudden whirlwind of unleashed desire and uncontrollable children with flailing arms and fierce expressions.

Philippe came rushing from the kitchen, took one look and ran back to the kitchen for a ladle and a cooking pot that he used as a makeshift gong. After several ringing bangs, hands dropped, mouths closed and silence drifted over the room like an icy rain. Philippe glared at the upturned faces staring back at him, each trying to look more innocent than the next. "Who are you lot, then?" he growled. "And what have you done with my good children?"

Esther, slim and graceful with grey eyes, took the lead and stepped forward. "We're very sorry, Monsieur Philippe. Aren't we?" She looked around, but no one else budged and she had to poke her brother, Jacob, in the ribs.

"Oh. Ouch. I mean, yes, we're all sorry."

"Yes, yes, yes, we're sorry," the remaining chorus chimed in, except for one anonymous voice that pleaded, "Please, don't take the chest away."

"All right," Sabine had steadied herself. "Everyone into the classroom. I want you to sit quietly and think about the best way to play with the costumes so that everyone gets a turn."

There were a few audible groans, but of course the children did as they were told. They rested their chins on their hands, and scratched their heads and dangled their legs, but from this rather glum beginning the idea of the Summer Fête was eventually born, and to make it even more exciting, the exact content was to be kept from all the adults in the most cross-your-heart-and-hope-to-die secrecy, with the exception of Marcelle, who promised the children time in the classroom to rehearse, and Marie-Antoinette who could be counted on in a pinch for extra props.

For the next few weeks, there were whispers in corners, sudden halts to conversations whenever an adult appeared, and giggles behind the closed classroom door. If, amid this tumult, any of the adults noticed that Théo and Paulette were spending hours together, their interest soon passed because there was always something else to attend to in a house busy with fifty or sixty children.

Théo was in a constant state of shy paralysis. A strand of dark hair hanging over Paulette's forehead made all the difference in the world, as did the slightest glimpse of a collar bone above the top of her summer dress. He wondered how no one else seemed to notice the flawlessness of her skin, or the bottomless dark of her eyes, or the lightness of her voice.

At first, Paulette showed no signs of being aware of the effect she had on Théo, and she treated him with the same sunny kindness she happily bestowed on everyone.

Yet, if the slightest opportunity arose—say the chance to pass the salt or bring Paulette a glass of water—Théo would seize the moment, planning to charm her with his manners and pay her pretty compliments. But when she looked at him and smiled a polite thank you for the water, he found his throat had gone so completely dry that he could not say a word. Instead, he drank down the water himself in two noisy gulps.

Paulette lifted an eyebrow at this piece of rudeness, and Théo, blushing furiously, rushed to the kitchen for another glass. In his brief absence, Paulette, who was as quick-witted as she was pretty, pieced together a previous series of longing glances and shy smiles into a clear picture of love sickness and decided she was more than flattered. She was interested.

When Théo returned with another glass, Paulette's knowing gaze made him so dizzy his hands shook and he spilled a bit of the water, and in his nervousness to mop it up, finally succeeded in knocking over the entire glass. Water flooded the table, and scarlet flooded Théo's cheeks, and while the other children at the table leapt up to avoid getting wet, Paulette whispered into Théo's ear that she'd like to go for a walk with him later.

After that fortuitous accident, the two were inseparable. Théo felt he was the luckiest boy on earth, and Paulette believed that every word he spoke was poetry. Perhaps theirs was only a summer romance, but their youth and circumstances infused it with an intensity that even the youngest children could sense.

They pestered Théo with questions.

Is she your sweetheart?

Are you going to kiss her?

Whenever Paulette passed by, they chanted *Paulette loves Théo* and made kissing noises with their lips.

They were thoroughly annoying.

Eventually, Léa put a stop to all the teasing. She gave her blessing to the yearnings of the two young hearts, because compared to the danger of the real situation they found themselves in, a stolen kiss or two seemed nothing to be worried about. She only wondered in which corner of a crowded house, or in which corner of an uncertain future, this couple would ever find shelter.

RENÉE PAILLARÉS, COUNSELLOR

MY SISTER, PAULETTE, fell in love with Théo Reis that summer. At first, I couldn't believe it and I placed my hand on her forehead to check for fever. He seemed so clumsy and he was always chattering. He ought to have remained a pest, and he would have, if he hadn't been so beautiful. You had to give him that. He wasn't as tall as Paul Niedermann, but then no one was. Théo had a wonderful smile and sad eyes. Sad underneath, I intuited. And though Paulette sparkled when she was with him, I tried to warn her. It wasn't a good time to fall in love with a Jewish boy. At our age, I thought it would be a disaster to meet *the* one because it would be the wrong time and it would end in sorrow.

She just looked at me like I was the crazy one, and she had a point after all, because here we were at the House of Izieu. My family had taken in little Diane wholeheartedly, and we'd be taking her home with us at the end of the summer. Loving someone meant you didn't see the danger, or rather, you saw it, but chose to see past it to a world where difference wouldn't be a matter of life or death.

Théo writes letters to his mother, but he confessed to Paulette that he misses her so much that he sometimes tries to invent reasons to love her less. All the children wrote letters to someone. I was glad, though, that Diane was too young to write to her family, because sometimes, when I watched the other children writing letters, I was overcome by the sadness of it—pages and pages filled to the margins with their longings and hopes spelled out in tiny handwriting or slanted printing to parents who would, in all probability, never survive the war.

Paulette was more resilient than I was. She flung her heart open to joy, searched it out, and laughed at the shadows that made my chest tighten. She fell in love enthusiastically, as if the world would welcome it, and never looked back, or should I say forward.

JULY 1943

SABINE CONSIDERED LÉA to be indestructible, which was why it took her so long to realize how ill she was. Her skin had turned a chalky white and her hands trembled as she tucked the children into their beds.

Sabine touched Lèa's hand and felt the fire of the fever racing through her friend's body. Immediately, she shouted for help from Renée and Paulette and the three of them virtually dragged Léa down to the river to dowse her in cold water. Then they removed all her clothes and rubbed her body with towels, wrapped her in blankets, and put her to bed.

"I'll stay with her tonight," Sabine assured the young sisters. "But perhaps you should sleep in the dormitory instead of in your tent. I don't want the children to be frightened."

None of the adults slept that night, with the exception of Léa who dreamed so deeply that Sabine feared she was slipping into unconsciousness. Having employed every skill she possessed as a Red Cross nurse, Sabine finally resorted to prayer and the slim chance of divine intervention. She whispered Léa's name a thousand times, counted every sigh, and observed every fleeting expression.

Outside Léa's bedroom door, Léon paced. Miron ran up and down the stairs with cups of tea that Marie insisted on brewing even though Sabine refused them all because she would not cease her scrutiny of Léa's face even for the second it would take to raise a cup to her lips. Sometime after midnight, Marie gave up and convinced Philippe to begin preparing a huge vat of chicken soup, which was the only cure she knew for illnesses that came in the night. Paulette and Renée enlisted the help of Théo, Arnold, Henri, and Paul, and together the teenagers told the children every story they knew and rocked the little ones in their arms until they felt like leaden weights.

In the morning light, Léa was breathing shallowly, her eyes tightly closed, the lids dark smudges. Her skin was now white marble. Sabine looked upon the woman she loved for her selfless life and her unwavering strength, and feared that Léa's poor body might simply evaporate into the close air of the sickroom before she could count to ten. The swiftness of the fever shocked her and she knew what she must do.

Sabine called for Léon, who entered the bedroom so quickly he almost ran her down. "I'm going to fetch a doctor. Stay with her."

Without another word to anyone, Sabine pedalled her bicycle all the way to Glandieu, near Izieu. She had no memory of the journey afterwards for her head was filled with the ceaseless repetition of the doctor's name given to her by Pierre-Marcel and the urgency to find him.

She must have looked wild from her ride for some of the villagers in Glandieu turned away from her, but eventually an old woman selling flowers pointed to the home and surgery of Dr. Albert Bendrihem. Sabine would not take the seat offered by the young receptionist, choosing instead to pace the small waiting room.

Finally, he appeared. The doctor was an affable looking man of about fifty, almost completely bald with bifocals that magnified his pale brown eyes. As soon as he had ushered her into his office, Sabine blurted out all of Léa's symptoms and begged him to return with her to the House of Izieu.

"This house is The Settlement for Refugee Children from the Hérault, is it not? The one Monsieur Wiltzer told me about?"

"Yes."

"And he also told you about my—shall we say, my reputation here?"

"Yes. That doesn't matter."

"I'm afraid it does matter, Madame Zlatin. The young receptionist you met is my son. No one else will work for me. If you bring your patient here, indeed if you bring any children here, I'll gladly treat them. But do you really want me to travel to your front door? I fear my movements are being carefully noted, exactly by whom I don't know or care as long as they do not wear the uniform of the Milice."

"Léa wouldn't survive the journey. She is the very soul of the House of Izieu, doctor. What can I do?"

"Save her. You were a nurse? I'll give you what medicines I can, but you must administer them. Put her on an intravenous drip. Don't let her get dehydrated. Do you have a telephone? No, of course you don't. Send a quick boy to the village if her symptoms change. Right now, I'd say she has pneumonia and possibly a viral infection. I'm sorry, Madame Zlatin, but we mustn't put the whole Settlement at risk."

Sabine nodded her assent, but she couldn't bring herself to speak. She gathered up the equipment and the medicine she'd need and flew back to Léa's bedside. When she ran into the house, she couldn't help but notice that every room and hallway smelled like chicken soup.

Over the next three days and nights, Sabine became an expert in tracing the slightest signs of improvement in the patient. She stroked her hair and pressed cool cloths to her forehead. She adjusted and readjusted the intravenous drip, and breathed in the odour of medications on her skin. Miron and Léon took turns at Léa's bedside and ordered Sabine to sleep, finally hauling in an extra mattress because she refused to leave the room. When exhaustion overcame her, she sank onto the mattress and watched the light fade, filling the space with shadows, blurring the objects in the room, and transforming Léa's face into a pale blotch on the pillow.

On the fourth morning, Léa opened her eyes and asked what day it was. Sabine was euphoric for she knew that her friend had come back to her from the land of everlasting dreams. The good news galloped from room to room, triggering a collective sigh as if the house itself had begun breathing again.

Strict bed rest was ordered, and the children, clamouring for visits, were only allowed into Léa's bedroom in pairs, and only allowed to stay as long as it took to deliver their tiny bunches of wild flowers or get well cards coloured in crayon.

Sabine asked Léon who the fastest runner was among the boys and he nominated Isidore who was always racing about with the cocker spaniel that seldom left his side. "Take him to Glandieu, please, and have him run to Dr. Bendrihem with the good news. It's the house with the blue door."

That night, as Sabine settled down on her makeshift bed, she heard a lovely sound. Since Léa could not sing to the children, they sang to her, French lullabies in high, wavering tones. The music of their sweet voices flowed through the house, soaking into the wooden floors, coursing up the white walls, lapping against the windows. Sabine fell asleep, rocking gently in a sea of song.

The next morning, under a pale, blue-white sky, Sabine walked down to the road through the fields. She passed the postman and smiled, knowing how excited the children would be to get mail. But she already had a letter of her own, and she was taking it to Belley to show Pierre-Marcel.

When she arrived at his office, she was disappointed not to find Marie-Antoinette, for her cheerful welcome always made Sabine feel lighter, as if her troubles were no more than a puff of smoke she could blow away.

"What? No Marie-Antoinette today?" she asked when Pierre-Marcel came to greet her.

"She's off running a mysterious errand. Don't be surprised if it has something to do with an upcoming Summer Fête. Come in, come in. How can I help?"

"I've brought you a letter I received several days ago. Why don't you read it first, and then we'll talk?"

Pierre-Marcel smoothed out the page and began to read:

Dear Madame Zlatin,

I have your name from a dear friend in Montpellier, Berthe Mering, and she has told me of your refuge in Izieu.

I am sure you have heard many stories of struggle, so I will spare you mine, except to say simply that I have a daughter, Lucienne. She is five years old. We are utterly alone.

If you could welcome us both, I would do any sort of work— cooking, cleaning, mucking out the barn, fieldwork—anything at all. I could help with the other children as Berthe tells me there are many.

If you do not have room for two, I beg you to take one. Lucienne is a good little girl. She takes up very little space, except in my heart. Please accept Lucienne.

Awaiting your response and wishing you well,
Mina Friedler

Pierre-Marcel folded the letter. When he looked up at Sabine, his face was grave, an expression of genuine sorrow darkening his features.

"How many children are at the house now?" he asked softly.

"This would bring the total to sixty-two. Plus seven adults. I don't count Renée and Paulette Paillarès, or Marcelle, because they'll be leaving at the end of the summer. Léa has volunteered to share her room with Mina Friedler and we can always squeeze an extra bed into the dormitory for the child, but it seems a lot to ask of you. More IDs to manufacture and more ration cards."

Pierre-Marcel waved his hand, as if producing these documents that risked his office and his life was no more than swatting a fly. "We found this shoved under the office door. Read it." He pushed an envelope with a smudged address across his desk.

Sabine opened the single folded page inside and stared at the words. *Some of the children at the Settlement are Jews.*

She ran her fingers over the words, as if she could erase them. When she looked up, Pierre-Marcel was staring out the window. She studied his profile, the muscles of his jaw tight. "When did you get this?"

"Two days ago. I showed it to Marie-Antoinette. She was angry. She wants me to hunt down the sender and put the fear of God into him or her."

"Can you find out?"

"Not even Marie-Antoinette can do that. I can think of at least fifteen or twenty people capable of such a denunciation."

"As many as that?" Sabine whispered. The betrayal of a child was so immense she didn't have enough room for it in her chest. She could scarcely breathe. Surely it could be no one in Izieu itself. The neighbours had adopted the children, the farmers had welcomed their labour, and the shopkeepers regularly gave them apples and treats to make up for their misfortunes.

Pierre-Marcel tried to reassure her. "Look, Sabine. These are people who spy on their neighbours and raise the alarm whenever someone gets a better piece of meat at the butcher's than they do. The Italians don't take them seriously."

"And the Milice?"

He didn't answer her, but neither did he look away. "It's cause to be careful."

"I wasn't careful. I went to Glandieu to see the doctor. I had to. Léa was ill. Oh, yes, she's recovered now, but for a while it seemed her life was in the balance. I went in a rush, and I asked people in the village for directions."

"Perhaps that's it, then. Someone watching the doctor and making assumptions that anyone who goes to him must be Jewish. No one followed you on the journey home?"

"No. I'm sure of it."

"Then this denunciation is just vile speculation. There's no proof. But, Sabine, some of the older boys can easily draw attention because of their height. The Milice, and even the gendarmes, are ever mindful of the push to send workers to Germany. We need to think about smuggling them out of the area. I'm thinking of Paul Niedermann and Henri Alexander. Will OSE help? I think Léon should also think about leaving."

Sabine nodded her agreement, but she felt numb and not even the return of Marie-Antoinette, with a sealed box that was to be delivered directly into the hands of Marcelle, could lift her mood.

All the way back to the House of Izieu, she kept hearing Pierre-Marcel's warning until the world outside thinned to nothing and all she could see were ugly words scrawled on a sheet of paper.

When Sabine delivered the parcel from Marie-Antoinette, Marcelle's wink finally made her smile, and soon she settled down by the window with a bowl of soup. She watched as a group of children returned from their hike. It had started to rain while they were out, a sudden downburst while the sun went on shining, and Paul was holding his sweater over the little ones' heads like a tent. They laughed and walked without the least bit of hurry and it came to her that they were at home and unafraid.

Somewhere, maybe on the forest paths, or on the terrace, or in the barn with the animals, or under their pillows at night, they had set aside the ache of not belonging, the quiet hungering for home. It was beautiful, this place, this peace.

Sabine wished that the moment would go on forever. The rain would keep falling, the sun shining. The dog would keep wagging his tail, and the circle of boys laughing. How was she ever going to tell Paul he must leave?

MINA FRIEDLER, MOTHER

I REMEMBER THE ROAD to the House of Izieu was hard earth. It twisted ahead of me and out of sight. The leaves of the bordering trees made an arch above, and even the still air was tinted green.

I smiled down at Luci, my Lucienne, and squeezed her small, sparrow-boned hand. Hair the colour of wheat. Eyes like a deer's. The sunlight poured like water through her pale hair. The delicate spray of freckles across her cheeks and nose looked like a tan. I couldn't remember the last time she'd laughed.

Finally we came to a curve in the road where we could look down and see the house in the distance. For a moment, the hot sun blazing on the white walls and the windows made the whole house shimmer and blur slightly as if it were a mirage, an illusion, or perhaps a block of shining ice just beginning to melt.

I slowed my steps. I needed more time to arrive here fully. I knew how quickly one world could disappear and be exchanged for another. The memory of my husband was a dark flame coursing through my blood. His loss was an empty hole, as raw as the socket of a tooth.

As one world unravelled, another rose. As one door closed, another opened. But, oh, to see behind the closed door just once more.

I knew that when I stepped through this new door, everything I had imagined about the House of Izieu would vanish and what was real would rush in to fill that space.

"What is it, Maman?"

"Nothing, my pet. Don't you think the house looks grand?"

Luci nodded silently, but then she suddenly pointed. "Look. I see children. And I see a cow."

A brown cow. Nothing could be more solidly real than a cow.

"Come, Luci. Let's meet the children. This is our home now."

CHARLES WELTNER, NINE YEARS OLD

I LOVE ALL THE ANIMALS BEST. I always wanted a pet when I was little, but my mother said that Budapest wasn't a good place for dogs, because they love to run through fields and chase rabbits more than anything in the world. When I asked for a cat instead, she swore they're nasty things. They'd scratch your arms and legs if they were cornered.

There are lots of animals at the House of Izieu. White birds swing through the sky over the river, and ducks with bright green feathers nest in the river grass. The sparrows settle in the trees at night and chatter, like the girls here do when they tell stories to each other.

If the night is very still, I can hear the jingle of goats' bells in the hills. And sometimes the hoot of an owl.

Most of the animals belong to Farmer Perticoz. On market days, he lends us his big, broad horse with powerful legs to pull the cart. He's the colour of the caramel apple that my father once bought me at a fair, and though I can't reach his nose, I can pat his sides.

At Farmer Perticoz's barn, there was a litter of kittens once, balls of black and orange fluff that weighed nothing in your hands. I held one to my cheek and its fur was like silk. They licked milk from my fingers with their rough little tongues, and they didn't scratch, not once.

Our own dog at Izieu will roll about on the ground with you. Tomi, that's his name. He leaps into the air to catch a stick, and whenever he gets wet, he shakes his whole body from head to tail and a spray of water spins off his fur. When he's tired, he finds a lap to lay his head on.

But my favourite is our milk cow, a plain brown cow with deep, dark eyes and long lashes. She has a soft mouth that I pet when I feed her handfuls of grass. She loves being scratched and talked to. I put my arms around her neck and tell her stories of my mother. And sometimes, when I'm lonely, I just lean against her flank with my arms stretched across her back, and rest there for a long time. She doesn't seem to mind. That cow knows all my secrets, and all my dreams, and when I look into her tender eyes, I swear she understands them all.

I trust animals more than people. Animals don't care where you come from, or whether you're Jewish or Christian. They only want people to be kind to them.

JOSEPH GOLDBERG, TWELVE YEARS OLD

I REMEMBER THAT the House of Izieu allowed me to raise my head and see again.

Before, I kept my head down. The world only existed from the waist down, an endless procession of cracked pavement and litter in the sewage drains, anonymous shoes and stockings, trouser and skirt hems, and later, shiny jackboots. Who would want to look up and risk seeing something terrible in the world? Don't look, and what you don't want to see is invisible. I was always moving, trying to find solid ground amidst the constant shifting around me.

At Izieu, I look up and the grey world is suddenly flooded with colour. I had never imagined how many shades of green there are and I try to paint them all: the thick evergreen of the pine forest, the silvery green of the moss, the coppery green depths under the trees, the glossy, luminous green of the river in a rainstorm.

Madame Sabine guessed my dream, as if I had spoken it aloud. It happened that she was in the classroom that first day of school. We sat in neat rows and we were given new pens to write with and fresh paper.

I remember staring at the blank page, so clean, so pure, so full of promise. I didn't want to make a mistake and have to scratch something out. I was afraid the ink would leave a blotch on the perfect page. So I didn't risk any words.

Instead, I took from my pocket the last of my pastel crayons and drew a long-beaked bird with translucent green feathers.

"You have a gift, Joseph," Madame Sabine said. "Follow me."

She led me out to the barn and asked me to wait while she disappeared into her bedroom. She came out with a large artist's box and placed it in my hands. The lid was carved with the letters Y and Z. "My initials," she said. "My father called me Yanka. I, too, wanted to be an artist. This is yours now. Use it well."

The box was filled with paints. My mind was flooded with all the images I could colour into life. My heart was bursting. I wanted to shout my thanks from the rooftops, but my throat was too dry. I felt Madame Sabine's hand on my arm. "No need for words," she smiled. "You and I have discovered a common language."

I paint almost every day now, every brush stroke filled with the kindness of a woman whose father called her Yanka.

JULY 1943

THAT NIGHT THE RHÔNE HAD a silvery shine, as if the moon had fallen right down to its depths like a cold white stone.

A small sound on the periphery of her dreams woke Sabine.

"Miron? Why are you dressed?" she murmured.

"Sorry. I didn't want to wake you. I won't be gone long."

Fully awake now, Sabine sat up in bed. "Where are...?" Her voice trailed off as she saw the grave look on his face.

"I know some people who might be able to help with Paul and Henri. Pierre-Marcel is right. We need to help them get away."

People? What people, Sabine wanted to ask. The villagers, Farmer Perticoz, the invisible Resistance?

"So," she said instead, "you've made this decision without me."

He didn't reply.

"I'm not surprised," Sabine sighed. "If I can help, you only need to ask."

"I won't ask. It's my duty to protect you."

"That's what I knew you'd say. But if the day comes when it all goes wrong, I'll stand by you, and that's not my duty. That's my choice."

Neither of the Zlatins knew that Léon, waiting for Miron in the doorway of the barn, heard every word. For a moment, he was afraid for them, afraid for himself. He had tried to forget that the world was still treacherous. But the Zlatins' strength astounded and inspired him. He squared his shoulders and followed Miron into the blackness of the forest.

Sabine could not fall back to sleep. She lost herself in a memory of Miron playing with some children in the late afternoon sun. Tall and narrow, he was running with a group of boys, then turning and crouching down to encourage Coco who charged toward him with all the determined clumsiness of a four-year-old. As Coco ran into his arms, Miron had straightened up, hoisting him above his head. She could still hear Coco's shrieks of laughter, and see Miron's flushed cheeks, his skin smoothed brown from the summer sun.

Where had her love led him? To happiness, she was sure, but also to uncertainty, to risk, to danger. She had cluttered the simple life he'd always craved. Would he be asleep right now in his own bed, if not for the problems she always brought to him with the expectation that he would find a way? Maybe he would be dreaming of leaving this place and planting a garden on his own land someday, or maybe that was her dream for him.

At first, she thought the faint sound of crying she could hear was her own. But it was not.

Sabine wrapped a blanket around her shoulders and left the barn. For a moment she heard only the throaty chorus of frogs. Then the crying came again, softened to a kind of whimpering. She followed it to the side of the barn and saw little Max Leiner curled into a ball, knees tight against his chest, arms tight against his knees.

"What's this?" Sabine whispered, crouching down. "What's wrong?"

The story leaked out slowly, in ragged sentences. Some of the other children had received letters that day from mothers or fathers or aunts or cousins, but there was no letter for Max.

"Something bad has happened to Mama," he sobbed, the words coming out in wet bursts. "And then that new girl came. Luci. And she was holding her mother's hand, and it's not fair."

No, it wasn't fair. She couldn't lie to him. She couldn't take away his loneliness. She was overcome with the desire to protect him from what he already knew. "My parents are lost to me, too," she said, and the moment the words were spoken she knew they were true. "But I keep them here in my heart and so I know they are always with me." She tapped Max's heart. "What do you keep here?"

He lifted his tear-stained face and stared at her with his dark eyes.

She nodded encouragingly, swept a curl from his forehead. "Tell me about your Mama."

For a long while, Max said nothing at all. The two of them sat side by side on the ground, leaning against the side of the barn and listening to the murmurs of the night. Frogs again. A splash in the river, maybe from a fish. The secret movements of rabbits in the long grass. Sabine's thoughts drifted up into the sky, and she wondered about all the parents longing for their children, and all the children longing for their parents and all of them staring at the same moon and yet as scattered as the stars.

When Max finally spoke, his voice was thin and reedy. "She has soft hair. I used to curl it around my fingers. She has a favourite blue dress. She used to take my hands and dance with me in a circle. She loves cats and we had a big tabby with a long, feathery tail."

"Max, would you like to have a cat?"

"Could I?"

"Tomorrow, we'll visit Farmer Perticoz's barn. You can pick out your very own kitten. Come now, try to sleep."

"I want to sleep with you."

Sabine tucked him into bed, pulling the blanket up to his chin and then lay down beside him. Max put his head on her shoulder. His hair smelled like apples and fresh hay.

"Max," she whispered. "Do you think you can forgive Luci for having her mother with her?"

"I'll try."

"Good boy."

The day of the Summer Fête finally arrived at the House of Izieu, noisily, with children running up and down the stairs and into the dining room to gobble down breakfast and out to the terrace to begin the decorating, all of them lit up from the sparks of anticipation shooting through the air.

"They're going to wear themselves out before noon," Sabine commented.

"We can tell them all to take naps," Léa suggested.

"Good luck with that," Léon laughed.

"Don't worry," Marcelle smiled. "We have rehearsal in the classroom after lunch. That will settle them down."

Philippe and Marie looked at each other and shrugged. Something light for lunch then, they thought, to settle nervous stomachs.

Piece by piece, the terrace was transformed. Several bed sheets slung over a line of rope became curtains, upon which Joseph had painted an enchanted woodland scene of forest animals. Homemade paper lanterns, coloured in shades of deep rose and pink so they would glow when met with just the right angle of the sun, were fastened all along the balustrade. Several boys tied torches into a nearby tree so their light would shine upon the performers when the time was right.

Meanwhile, sixteen children, one by one, cheerfully reported to Marcelle that the clouds were breaking up and the sky was turning blue. Most of the others fretted that rain would spoil the festivities. The optimists won. The sun shone, and the day was glorious.

While thumping, stomping, giggles, shushing, and other mysterious sounds emanated from behind the closed door of the classroom, the visitors began to arrive—Farmer and Madame Perticoz, Pierre-Marcel and his wife, Noelle, the prettiest girl in Belley, and not least, Marie-Antoinette with a huge picnic basket. Blankets were spread on the lawn for the audience, and as Sabine took her place, leaning against Miron, the low sun cast a golden net over the terrace.

The curtains opened and Marcelle stood before them. She looked dramatic and amused in a long white dress and embroidered shawl. Her black hair was dressed with honeysuckle and roses, and pulled back in a simple knot that bared the curve of her neck. "Welcome," she said, "to the Summer Fête . Tonight you will see a series of scenes and performances presented by the children of the House of Izieu. We begin with the Procession of Thanks to the Garden."

From the back of the terrace a group of children marched forward solemnly and formed a line across the would-be stage. One by one, they stepped forward.

"I'm Tomato," shouted Coco. He was covered head to foot in a billowing red cape, pillows obviously stuffed underneath to give him a round shape, and his cheeks were two circles of scarlet.

Alice, tall and thin as a willow slip, in a long purple skirt and carrying a basket of berries, stepped forward more decorously than Coco had. "I am Plenty," she smiled, her dimples flashing.

There was Carrot and String Bean, both clothed in the appropriate colours, and then Sigmund Springer with a halo of gold foil spread his arms wide. "I am the Sun," he pronounced proudly.

"I'm Tomato," interrupted Coco.

"Shush. We already know that," Sigmund whispered, though his words were lost in a burst of hilarity from the audience.

Squash and Potato appeared, holding a jumping but silent Tomato between them, and then Senta turned a full circle in a billowy, shimmering shawl of blue. "I'm Rain," she announced.

Finally, little Élie in a black sweater and yellow skirt, with black wings attached to her back, passed up and down the line touching each vegetable with a golden wand. "I'm Population that makes the garden grow." There was a murmur of incomprehension, followed by a quick whisper from Sigmund, and then Élie tried again. "I mean Pollination — that makes the garden grow." After she spoke everyone bowed and the audience clapped enthusiastically, while two boys closed the curtains.

There was banging and jingling from somewhere at the back of the terrace, and then Marcelle appeared again. "We now present two folk dances, a French bourrée and a Flemish mazurka."

The source of the banging quickly became clear: upturned pots from the kitchen and wooden or metallic spoons. The drummers managed a beat, followed by children clapping or jingling with tambourines, no doubt delivered by Sabine herself in a mysterious package sent by Marie-Antoinette. The dancers of the *bourrée* moved hand-in-hand in a circle that sometimes collapsed into its centre and then expanded again. The skirts of the girls twirled, and the boys wore sashes that were once ordinary towels. The pace gradually quickened, until the girls' skirts were a swirl of colour and several dancers were so dizzy they began to stagger. The end of the dance was a triumphant shout.

The older boys and girls took the stage in a more dignified mazurka that required partners, accompanied by Barouk's flute playing. Léa counted the couples—Paula and Max-Marcel, Maurice with his sister Lillian, Nina with Majer, Arnold with Martha, and petite Renée with tall Paul—and, of course, Théo who had jumped at the opportunity to put his arms around Paulette. Soon she was laughing at Paul trying to crouch down to match Renée's height. When he finally got tired of stooping, he simply picked her up and she finished the dance two feet off the ground.

"Intermission," Marcelle announced on the last note of Barouk's lively tune.

Some of the children scurried back to the House for a costume change, while others joined the audience on the lawn, casting enquiring and hopeful glances at Marie-Antoinette's picnic basket. Everyone, adults included, cheered when Philippe emerged with large pitchers of lemonade and Marie passed around glasses.

Twilight was deepening into a dark blue, and the air was perfumed with the resin of the pines. Sabine felt like a fresh breeze had swept away her worries. She reached for Miron's hand and held it tight, as Marcelle reclaimed the stage.

"Act Two begins with the Procession of Heroes." At Marcelle's cue a double line of the youngest children emerged from the house, each carrying a large, lit candle, their flames bobbing up and down like fireflies.

"Candles? Where did they get candles?" Sabine whispered to Miron.

"I suspect Marie-Antoinette has been squirreling away votive candles from her church in Belley. Best not to ask."

The honour guard of the Procession of Heroes took up their place on the stage. They were dressed in red or white or blue to represent the colours of the French flag, and each little face beamed with pride. There was Claudine in her trademark pigtails, Émile with his mass of blonde curls, dimpled Sami, shy Jean-Claude whose brothers, now up in the tree working the "spotlight," cheered him on. The last of the five-year-olds was little Luci, whose mother's eyes shone as she watched her daughter laugh and take her place among new friends. Six-year old Liane and seven-year-old Marcel filled out the group.

Next, the Heroes stepped forward from the shadows at the back of the terrace. First came regal Esther wearing a golden tiara, playing the role of Queen Esther, of course, the Jewish heroine who was honoured at Purim for saving her people from their enemies. Then, dark-haired Paula appeared in a white blouse and red skirt as Marianne, the embodiment of French spirit and liberty. Joan of Arc shone in a silvery dress to represent her armour, and had never looked as happy as Rénate did in the role. Arnold Hirsch made a magnificent and handsome Moses with a hefty staff, and Otto made the audience gasp as Joseph with his coat of many colours. Lucky Gilles brandished a slingshot as David, and Léa suspected that was one prop that would never be relinquished. Each of the Heroes told their story under the light shining from the trees, ending each speech with a bow or a curtsey or, in one case, with the shooting of a green apple aimed at Miron who caught it in one hand in mid-air.

With the help of the older Heroes, the children placed their candles along the balustrade and then merged with the audience to watch the final performance of the night.

Barouk blew a cascade of plaintive notes on his flute and, seemingly from nowhere, ten-year-old Sarah, *Suzanne* she always insisted, stood before the audience in a simple white cotton shift and bare feet, her straight blonde hair pulled back in a single braid.

Suddenly what had been a coltish child with too-long legs, a dandelion of a girl, metamorphosed into a magical creature, limbs swaying in graceful, fluid motions, her face transformed as she lost herself in the music. She arched her back, stretched out a leg and cast a spell, extended an arm above her head and enchanted. She leapt up on invisible wings and seemed, for an ephemeral moment, to float in space without gravity. An arabesque. A plié. The musician and the dancer in perfect harmony.

The beauty of the dance transported the audience and unleashed something in Sabine, words rising whole and perfect from somewhere deep in memory in the shadow of another house when she had promised her father she would stay true to herself. She felt hope wash over her like a caress.

A final graceful turn and then, as suddenly as it had begun, the dance was over. Suzanne folded herself up on the floor of the terrace as neatly as a cat. The performer had vanished and the little girl was back.

There was thunderous applause, and several children ran to Suzanne to hug and congratulate her.

Everyone agreed the Fête had been a triumph and now it was the adults' turn to reward the players.

Philippe and Marie appeared with huge platters of chicken legs and potato salad and, finally, Marie-Antoinette opened her picnic basket and handed out almond cakes with white sugar frosting.

It was one of those heady summer evenings that seem to linger and stretch out endlessly, when bedtime is suspended and all the rules, like brushing your teeth and folding your clothes, are abandoned, and things seem to teeter on the edge of wildness, giddy with full-throated laughter and lit up by stars.

MAX-MARCEL BALSAM, TWELVE YEARS OLD

THERE IS SO MUCH TO DO at Izieu, lots of boy things that my brother Jean-Paul and I love. We used to live in Paris and knew nothing of the countryside until we came here. We were skinny at first—most Parisians had lost weight because food was even scarcer than kindness—but we grew strong with all the activity.

I'm the best tree climber. From my hiding place in the leaves I can see Jean-Paul and my best friend, Majer, looking for me. I have to cover my mouth to choke back a giggle. I am a sparrow in a tree with my eye on a worm, or maybe a squirrel spying a nut.

Léon taught me to swim. No one is allowed to swim alone. The river is fresh, bracing against the skin, but full of sly currents and weeds. I love it anyway. I love the cold shock to my body, and the way sound thickens when my head is submerged and I can open my eyes to the crystalline green of the surface just above me. We crawl out onto the riverbank, barefoot and barelegged with hair like waterweed dripping down our backs.

There are hikes almost every week. Philippe packs us sandwiches and we carry water and go for miles. Majer and I are older than many of the other boys, so we quickly figured out that the hikes have a purpose other than just fun. Monsieur Miron wants us to know the forest paths and all the best hiding places, just in case.

Then came the Summer Fête. Majer and I were dead set against it. We thought putting on costumes was silly stuff for girls. And dancing? Really? But Majer's little brother, Coco, was so excited, and Marcelle cleverly promised time away from schoolwork for rehearsals, so that sealed our fate.

I have to admit that I was kind of mean to Paula when we started practising the mazurka, but she had such an earnest face under a mop of dark brown, very curly hair that she gradually won me over. On the day, I was actually excited, but convinced it would rain.

Then the sun came out and the terrace was transformed into a stage. We were all transformed, just like Marcelle promised we would be. The dancers were spinning, their arms upraised and the girls' skirts belling out like moons, and the music and the swinging and the swaying made me want to clap and tap my feet and laugh out loud.

I was, I am, that happy.

GEORGY HALPERN, EIGHT YEARS OLD

DEAR PAPA,

I am fine and hope you are, too. The weather has been warm and we go on hikes on Thursdays and Sundays. We have a pretty teacher and we do composition, maths and French history. I am good at reading and like it best of all.

Last week we had a fête and it was really fun. We all got to dress up and I was a carrot in the first performance to give Thanks to the Garden. I was dressed in orange from head to toe, and had green feathers attached to my hair for the carrot top. My friend Gilles played the hero David and he got a slingshot as a prop that he sometimes lets me play with. We tried to shoot birds with little stones, but Léa warned us that if she found just one stunned bird the slingshot would disappear forever. So now we just shoot at leaves and each other.

Thank you for the package you sent. Madame Sabine says to especially thank you for the money hidden at the bottom that she says she will use to buy food and warm clothes for the winter. I liked the colouring book and paints. We pin our pictures up in the classroom, which has maps on the walls and four big windows.

At night before I go to sleep, I think of Vienna and pray that we might all be together there again under the linden

*trees. You and me and Maman. Do you still have your mous-
tache? Sometimes I can't remember everything about your
face, so please send me a photo. I am ending this letter with
100000000000000 kisses.*
   Your son who loves you very much,
   Georgy

AUGUST 1943

THERE WERE DAYS IN JULY when fierce thunderstorms turned
the sky purple and shook the firs on the mountainsides. In a
city far away, Benito Mussolini was deposed and arrested, and
the Italian soldiers in foreign lands grew restless, tasting the
bitterness of disillusionment.

   One day at the market, in the midst of a sudden downpour,
Paul Niedermann ran for shelter under a convenient shop
awning and found himself huddled next to a gendarme.

   Without turning his head to look at Paul, the gendarme spoke.
"You're still at the Settlement? Don't come back to the village.
You must get away from here. The Milice will be looking for
you. Tell Miron it's time."

   Before Paul could utter a word, the gendarme turned and
entered the shop, closing the door firmly behind him.

   Tall as he was, Paul felt dwarfed by desolation. He had come
to love Izieu and his friends there, especially Théo. He had
already said goodbye to his mother in the Rivesaltes Camp.
He had said goodbye to his brother, Arnold, who'd left for
America with the Quakers. And now yet another goodbye was
to be wrung from him.

   As soon as the marketers returned to the house, Paul delivered the gendarme's message to Miron and then sought out
Théo. The two friends climbed into their attic bedroom to
make promises. They would see each other again. They would
find each other after the war, because someday the war would
end. They would never forget the pig squealing through the

Lyon train station, or the outline of the mountains at dusk, or the shine of the river. They would never forget the times they talked each other to sleep, imagining their futures. Théo tried to give Paul his most precious possession, a small knife, the very one he had used to carve his and Paulette's initials in a heart on the attic beam, but Paul refused to take it, saying he mustn't have any sort of weapon in his possession in case he was arrested.

At dusk, Miron knocked on the door and handed Paul a pair of heavy boots and a jacket. "You can take what you can carry. Léon is going with you. You won't be alone."

Paul and Théo shook hands silently, eyes memorizing each other's face. It was as close as they could come to expressing the emotion that threatened to overwhelm them.

I'll come back here someday, Paul vowed, and his certainty gave him courage.

He followed Miron across the sloping floor of the dormitory where the youngest children were already sleeping, down the stairs that dipped in places from decades of footsteps, past the huge wood-burning stove, and the children's paintings in the classroom, with its shelves crammed with books, and photos tacked to the walls. He could hear the voices of the children who were still allowed to be up drifting towards him from the terrace. He felt his chest tighten.

While Miron and Léon headed to the barn, Paul stopped for a moment at the edge of the garden, and scooped a bit of earth into his hand, the good, rich earth of Izieu that had fed and nourished him. When he stood up, there was Sabine, her features slightly blurred in the gathering darkness.

She saw the look on his face and tried to make light of his imminent departure. "Look, I've made you something to eat."

It was a Jewish mother's natural first thought and it made him laugh. He held out his arms and hugged Sabine so hard she felt as if she might snap into pieces.

"Be safe," she whispered, kissing him on both cheeks.

He was saved from having to respond by the cocker spaniel, Tomi, who pushed a wet nose into his hand. He caressed the dog's velvet ears one last time and then turned to join Miron and Léon at the edge of the forest. The house looked bare in the moonlight, the trees more navy than green, the grass bleached grey.

A few kilometres into the beech woods, they left the familiar paths and began to file along a barely visible trail, Miron in the lead, then Paul, then Léon. A guide emerged from the darkness and spoke softly to Miron. There would be no more talking. When the trail disappeared completely, swallowed up by brush and rocks, they began to climb upward. The guide took his bearings from marks carved on tree trunks and eventually from spots of paint on the rocks that would be nearly invisible in the daylight, but that shone under the moon.

They climbed for hours, without stopping and without meeting a single human being. They were alone in a cold solitude, and Paul was sure he could smell water.

Finally, they reached a curve of river where the trunks of birch trees stood out under the moon like solid bars of silver in the night. Paul could discern another guide waiting for them in a clumsy looking shallow boat.

"This is where we part," Miron said. "There's a forgotten pass between two border checkpoints on the other side of the river. Friends will help you into Switzerland."

They embraced and then Paul and Léon stepped into the boat. For them, for now, the House of Izieu was a memory.

By late August, the air was swimming with light. Two more teenagers, Henri and Alfred, soon said their goodbyes and followed Miron through the forest to the secret river pass. Paulette and Rénee packed up their tent, and two teenaged lovers bent their heads in sorrow. Marcelle kissed all the little ones and promised to return the very next summer.

Gradually, the long hot days and thundery showers were replaced by mornings that smelled of apples and chimney smoke, and mist that drifted over the river.

A five-year-old stretched out her hands to catch a falling leaf.

IZIEU, WINTER 1943-44

THAT AUTUMN THE MOON WAS ORANGE.

The countryside was redolent of wild thyme and sage, and glowed in wine reds and rusty yellows. Leaves swirled in lazy circles through the air and fluttered to the ground, carpeting the lawns and the terrace and riding the waves made by children's hands in the fountain. The last of the milkweed drifted slowly across the river, while the shadows along the rocky mountainsides were choked and violet.

The youngest of the children were beginning to forget what their parents looked like and how their voices sounded, and so they were free to make up what had been forgotten.

The postman faithfully came and went, and one day Max jumped for joy and ran into the arms of Sabine. "I got a letter," he crowed. "Me too, this time. My very own letter from Marcelle."

"And what does she say?" Sabine smiled.

"She says she misses me. She says I must work at my sums so that I don't grow up as a dimwit. And she says she will write to me every week so I never have to be sad again on mail days. And there's a P.S. If I'm very, very good, she's going to send a parcel."

"Lucky Max. You can start being very good by helping to pick apples. It's harvesting time."

"We didn't have to harvest in Mannheim. We lived in the city."

"Well, do you know the story of the grasshopper and the ant? The ants work all summer and fall to store away food for the winter so that when the snow comes, they'll have lots to eat. But the grasshopper only plays and realizes too late that he'll be hungry all winter. Would you rather be an ant or a grasshopper?"

"Oh, I'd rather be a grasshopper, but I'll be a smart one."

Max ran off to help and Sabine watched him fondly. It was so kind of Marcelle to remember him. She'd had a golden touch with all the children who missed her lightness of heart and, not incidentally, her inexperience in the classroom. The day of her leaving had been full of tears, and her popularity had complicated the day of the new teacher's arrival, for of course Pierre-Marcel had kept his promise and had sent along a fully qualified and experienced schoolmistress.

Gabrielle Perrier had a serious face, with a nose and chin that were a little too sharp, and an inclination to make rules she expected to be obeyed. Her dark eyes glistened like Spanish olives, the eyes of someone who can spot mischief before it even happens. There would be no paper planes in her classroom and no notes passed from desk to desk. The thought of swimming in the Rhône made her shudder.

But Mademoiselle Perrier, never just Gabrielle to the children, was not unkind. When she entered the classroom that first day, she was greeted by a rush of whispers, like a wave rippling across a pebbled shore. She didn't take offence during art class when the youngest students all drew pictures of Marcelle, painstakingly explaining how pretty she was. She refused to play tag with the boys after lessons, but thanked them politely for their invitation. Nor was she particularly discouraged when she came upon Martha, reading a tattered copy of Victor Hugo's *Les Misérables*.

"Are you enjoying your book?" she asked.

"It's for school, isn't it?" Martha replied, as if that fact settled the question once and for all.

Mademoiselle Perrier smiled a little tightly, but she persisted. She knew the children had had too many goodbyes in their short lives. She gave praise lavishly where it was warranted, and drew upon great reserves of patience when it was needed. She had no desire to win their hearts, but every intention of improving their minds.

GABRIELLE PERRIER, SCHOOLMISTRESS

I REMEMBER THE GHOSTS of the House of Izieu. Oh, I don't mean spooky shapes drifting like fog in the hallways, or spectres hovering inches below the ceiling sending chills down your spine. I mean the melancholy ghosts of lost families. All the children have these kinds of ghosts, lost loves that had once taken a specific shape, or had a certain smile, or a particular tone of voice.

I can always tell when a ghost is visiting. A way of looking without seeing will come into a child's eyes. A way of walking will bend a child's neck, or slow a child's steps. There is often a whiff of lavender in the air, the scent of nostalgia and melancholy.

It's not that the children aren't happy. They are. They are giggly and spontaneous, full of curiosity and adventure, and sometimes saucy, like children everywhere. The atmosphere of the House is cheerful and relaxed.

But there is an undercurrent. I call it a haunting. I think it is the presence of the ghosts that helps forge the close bonds among all the people who live here. Sabine and Miron are brother and sister to Léa, and they have adopted Mina who seems to be everywhere, willing to do everything, from helping me in the classroom, to mucking out the barn, to harvesting the garden. And the children adore gruff Philippe and his sweet old mother who always seems to have a white kerchief around her head and a child on her lap and a story on her lips about naughty Paris in the days before the war.

But it is the children who surprise me most. There is something heart-stopping about them. I never see a fight. Oh, a childish spat maybe, or a flare of temper, but never a fight. And no bullying, either. They've had enough of that. Whether alone, or with brothers or sisters or cousins, they are attuned to each other's moods and needs. If they go for a hike, Arnold is there to pick up any stragglers. If they choose teams for a game, they choose in groups of three or four so that no single child is ever picked last. If tears are shed, you soon hear Barouk singing some merry tune, or see Théo pulling funny faces or standing on his head, anything to turn the tears into laughter.

When lessons are over, I stand in the doorway and watch them burst from the house, running down to the edge of the river across the sloping lawns, calling out to each other, laughing, sweaters flapping, without slowing down or perhaps even noticing their terrible vulnerability.

SIGMUND SPRINGER, EIGHT YEARS OLD

I REMEMBER WHEN the new teacher came, and we were cross because she wasn't at all like Marcelle. On the very first day of lessons, she told Jacob Benassayag and me we couldn't sit beside each other any longer because we talked too much. So I had to move and sit beside a girl. At recess I complained to Marie, who always made me feel better, but that day she told me that if I stuck out my bottom lip any further, a chicken would nest on it. "Stop pouting," she said. "Give the new teacher a chance."

I guess we were kind of mean to Mademoiselle Perrier that first week. There was a lot of eye-rolling and heavy sighing when she asked us to do anything. Gilles took out his slingshot and pretended he was going to shoot at her when her back was turned, but we started to laugh and somehow she guessed what he was up to and took the slingshot away. Mina whispered to me that the teacher had eyes in the back of her head.

At recess, she won't play with us. She'll just go for a little walk, or maybe stay inside and mark our compositions.

But one day when I couldn't solve my division problem, she knelt by my desk and showed me how to do long division and carry the numbers forward, and I feel pretty good that I can do it on my own now. When she hands me back my composition on my favourite animal, I see she's drawn a little star on the top. We kind of warmed up to her, I guess. And I think she is relieved that we've stopped talking about Marcelle, all except for Max who has such a crush on her because she writes him letters.

We're all pretty involved with Philippe and Marie's rush to harvest anything we can eat in the winter. Harvesting, they call it, even though I grew up in Vienna and the closest I ever got to harvesting was watching my mother make jam. Mademoiselle Perrier gives us whole afternoons off to help in the kitchen and we help make jars of applesauce, some of us peeling, some chopping, some stirring, and some scooping the sauce into jars. Claudine is only five and she can't do much except steal slices of apple. We've nicknamed her Little Squirrel because her plump cheeks make it seem she's hiding apples in her mouth. Pretty soon I notice Mademoiselle Perrier is up to her elbows in applesauce without a word of complaint, and when she sees me watching her, she smiles.

After that, she was just part of the House, and I overheard Jacob tell her he was sorry for saying her face was like the Jura rock cliffs.

HENRI GOLDBERG, THIRTEEN YEARS OLD

HARVESTING TIME at the House of Izieu is the best time, because I love working on the farm and watching all of spring and summer's labour finally bearing fruit. We rake the sweet-smelling hay into stacks and laugh when bits of it stick in our hair and all over our bare skin. We pick the fodder corn that will keep the horses and cows fed in the winter. Madame Perticoz brings baskets of food out to us as we work in the fields, meat pies and jugs of cold cider. I worked with Farmer Perticoz almost every day of that summer, but at harvesting we are joined by Monsieur Miron and most of the older boys. We stand shoulder to shoulder, and Farmer Perticoz makes a great ceremony of thumping us on the back for an honest day's work.

I love everything about the farm, even the things that drive my brother Joseph crazy—like the wisps of hay that get up his nose, or the thick, acrid smell of the barn, or the sweat that trickles down your back as you bend over a shovel digging potatoes. I love the smell of freshly turned earth, and the wide-openness of the fields, bright green and biscuit-coloured under the August sun, turning shades of russet and sepia as the air grows chillier. Joseph makes me notice the colours because he wants to paint them, but I just lap them up. I just want to be part of them, part of the landscape.

When Joseph and I lived in Paris with our parents, I used to love the fall markets around *Les Halles*: a heaving, hollering place, busy with buyers, bargains, and rats. There was stall after stall heaped with thick ropes of garlic, pyramids of blushing pears and apples, mounds of potatoes and curly-leafed cabbages, and glossy aubergines. I always talked to the farmers. I wanted to know how long it took to grow an aubergine, how many pumpkins made up a patch, which apples were for eating and which for cider, and how many kinds of squash were there, anyway.

When September arrives, I have to go to school in Belley. Marie-Antoinette has arranged everything and I can't disappoint her, but my heart will always be on the farm. Well, *les carottes sont cuites*, as the saying goes, but I'll sneak back here every chance I get. Farmer Perticoz is always happy to see me. He'll wink when his wife scolds me and calls me a naughty truant. Then he'll take me out to the barn and we'll talk about the planting for the spring, or chop logs, or maybe polish the bridles for the horses, and he'll give me a swig of his homemade wine. In a day or two, he'll take me back to school, but I bet he'll never say goodbye because he'll know that in a few weeks, I'll be back.

SEPTEMBER 1943

IT WAS A GORGEOUS MORNING. Behind the clouds, the sun had begun to rise, turning the clouds orange-grey, like fire behind smoke. The clouds gradually thinned, wafting away to expose deep blue patches of sky. In a castle far away where Benito Mussolini was being held captive, German soldiers mounted a daring rescue. The Italians rebelled and signed an armistice with the Allies. The Germans responded by swarming into the French Jura like highly trained Dobermans, pushing the traitorous, treacherous Italians out. The earth shook from German boots, dogs howled, and bells fell silent. The Occupation of every inch of France was now complete.

For a few days, Sabine and Miron told themselves it didn't matter. The House was so well hidden. The road from the village of Izieu to the house was overgrown and untended, deliberately so. The children all had new names on new sets of identity papers. The snows of winter would choke the mountain roads, turning them into icy slides. Surely the mountains and the twisting roads and the distance from Lyon would protect them.

The war would not last forever. Another winter would seal the frozen fate of the Germans on the Russian Front. Allied planes were hammering German cities. Americans and Canadians had taken Sicily and were even now churning their way up Italy from the South. Everyone knew, even the children, that there was going to be an Allied landing in France, and the rumour went around that it would be a massive invasion of British, American, and Canadian soldiers fighting shoulder to shoulder. It was difficult to imagine such a majestic force massing so far away, tensing its muscles to strike, and even more incredible to believe that it would actually arrive.

But this was daylight courage. At night, a sob burned in Sabine's throat and she swallowed it angrily. She would need to be stronger than this in the months ahead, she told herself, for there was much to be done. At night, she rehearsed her plans with Miron.

"We have to *do* something. Maybe move the children somewhere safer." Sabine looked across the bed at Miron sitting with his elbows on his knees.

"No place is safe now. We can try to move some of the older children across the border, but the danger will be greater without the Italians to help us."

Sabine climbed over the bed to him and rubbed his back. Then she circled him with her arms and leaned her head against him. "We've got to think. There must be a way to protect them."

They were both prone to thinking their way out of predicaments as if the combined force of their intellects could control an unpredictable world.

"We might have to split them up," Sabine sighed.

"That will break their hearts. Let's not rush to any decision and in the meantime pray for snow to block the roads."

"Tomorrow I'll go into Belley," Sabine decided, for if reason failed her, she was sure her friends there would not.

They were quiet for a while, lying now in each other's arms, curled together.

"Germans *here*," Sabine suddenly gasped.

"I know."

They took what comfort they could in each other. They were in this together, come what may. They both loved the children with a lion-like force. Whatever distance might appear between them evaporated when Barouk sang or Joseph painted or Coco learned a new word. The children delighted them in myriad ways every day. They had built the House of Izieu together and the only person in the world who felt as much worry as Sabine was right here by her side. She wanted to keep the children together, but knew that would be a dream too far.

The next day, Sabine sat in Pierre-Marcel's office looking braver than she felt. She'd seen no soldiers, but the swastika flying over the municipal offices had shaken her. Marie-Antoinette welcomed her warmly, but she was ill prepared for her friend's news.

"Léon Reifman is back in France."

"What? How? Why?"

Pierre-Marcel shrugged. "There was chaos at the borders when the Italians retreated. Some wanted to cast their lot with the Germans, some wanted to get away from them. Anyway, Léon has new papers, Swiss ones, and he's on his way now to Le Chambon-sur-Lignon."

"The Protestant mountain?"

"Indeed. He thinks he might be able to map out an escape route and take some of the children from Izieu to Switzerland."

"Which ones? How will he choose? How can I choose?"

"I'm guessing that would depend on the route, if he finds one. How rigorous it would be, how fit or agile the children would have to be and so on. You're going to have to face it sometime, Sabine—splitting up the children."

"Yes. I know that, but so soon?"

"Well, not today or tomorrow," Marie-Antoinette assured her. "We'll wait to hear back from Léon. In the meantime, he's contacted his sister, Suzanne. As you know, she's a doctor and she's willing to move into the House of Izieu so long as she can bring her young son."

"I think it's a good idea," Pierre-Marcel interjected. "Should you need a doctor now, it would be dangerous to approach Dr. Bendrihem again."

"Yes. Of course. We'll make room for them somehow. But what will the German occupation mean for you? And for this office?"

"Vichy still exists in theory, though the strings of the puppets are now exposed for all to see. I'm guessing this office will lose some of its authority or at least be put under some form of scrutiny."

"You mean no more extra ration cards or sets of papers," Sabine guessed.

"I think that's probably the case. But, Sabine, the people of the French Jura are no friends of the Germans. They will still turn to me and to Marie-Antoinette as their leaders, and that may be to our advantage. They know what we stand for, and more than ever, I think they'll stand with us."

"Here's something that will cheer you up." Marie-Antoinette spread a map over the desk, ignoring Pierre-Marcel's attempts to move his papers out of the way. "See if you can find Izieu."

It took Sabine several minutes to do so, even though she knew where to look. Very small towns appeared in very small print.

"As you know, the Germans are headquartered in Lyon. That's almost ninety kilometres away over mostly dirt roads, and you'd need to have a map. Sad to say that over the last few weeks there's been a nip in the air, and people all over the French Jura have had to burn their maps just to keep warm."

She looked up, very pleased with herself, and deliberately knocked Pierre-Marcel's arm just as he was taking a sip of water. The glass slipped from his hand and Marie watched as the liquid spread slowly over the map, soaking into the paper.

"Oh dear. I'm so clumsy. Sorry, Pierre. Let me clean this mess up."

Marie scrunched up the map into a soggy ball and winked at Sabine. "I'll just get a rag to mop up the desk. Excuse me a moment."

Pierre-Marcel stared after her retreating figure before turning to Sabine. "She's incorrigible," he said flatly, shaking his head.

"Thank goodness," Sabine replied, finally laughing. "Oh, I know they have maps in Lyon, but that performance certainly made me feel better. You will take care of her, won't you? Make sure she doesn't do anything rash in front of the Germans."

He bowed slightly. "I'll do my best. She's her own woman."

"That she is," Sabine said, thinking to herself that Pierre-Marcel truly didn't have any idea how complex Marie-Antoinette really was, her abiding love for him both unresolved and unacknowledged.

Once a month there was a celebration with a single birthday cake, because with forty-four children now in the House of Izieu there wasn't enough sugar in all of France to mark each child's day individually. This month, Philippe had made an apple cake with honey from one of the neighbouring farmers, his last handful of brown sugar dusting the top.

Suzanne Reifman and her son, Claude, arrived in time for the birthday celebration. Her hair was dark and thick, but as she turned away from Miron to greet the other adults, he saw that it shone with glints of red in the sun.

"She's very pretty," Miron whispered to Sabine, as if he hadn't been expecting that.

"I'd say she's confident, even brave. You must be, to be a woman and qualify as a doctor. Léon hasn't told us much, but I know she lost her husband right at the beginning of the war and yet she's kept that child safe."

Ten-year-old Claude had curly hair like his uncle Léon, and a big grin on his face as he spied the cake.

The seven children born in October got the first slices, and afterwards opened handmade cards written by the other children. Marie peeked at the messages and saw they were all variations on a common theme.

My dear Suzanne, I wish you a very happy birthday, and hope next year, you'll be with your parents.

Dear Georgy, I'm writing this little note to make you happy on your birthday. Hoping you rejoin your parents, and the war gets over.

Dear Lilianne, HAPPY BIRTHDAY. I'm wishing that on your next birthday, you'll have your parents back.

Dear Théo, On your special day, I know you must miss your parents, and Paulette, too. I hope you see them soon.

To my dear friend Esther, My warm wishes for your twelfth birthday. You are a good big sister to Élie and Jacob and your parents will be proud of you. May you be with them soon.

Dear Paula, I wish you a happy day and know your parents do, too. May all your future birthdays be celebrated with them by your side.

Dear Herman, Best wishes, little brother, on your tenth birthday. I made this special drawing of a tiger just for you. Keep it forever.

When the last crumb of cake had been eaten, Phillipe and Marie pushed the long dining tables under the window to make a space for storytelling, for it was too cool now in the evenings to linger on the terrace.

"Tell us about Paris," Nina urged Marie.

"Oh, Paris was wild in the twenties. We used to go to Montmartre to watch the ladies from the Moulin Rouge. They wore nothing but feathers with spangles on their—"

"Marie!" Miron cautioned.

"As I was saying, spangles on their dresses. We called them the Queens of the Night because some of them were—"

"Oh, look," interrupted Miron. "Here's a book from Marie-Antoinette about the legends of Belley. Why don't you read to the children from this, Marie."

Marie glared at Miron but took the book anyway. "Oh, this one sounds good," she began. "The old folk of Belley tell tales of an enchanted lake. They say that at the bottom of this lake there was once an old convent and that on certain nights the lights of the convent still glimmer."

"Lights wouldn't work under water," Hans protested.

"These are enchanted lights. And on certain windy days, the waves on the lake look like nuns' wimples."

"What are wimples?" interrupted Senta.

"You know, those things they wear on their heads. Now, do you want to hear this story, or not?"

"Story, please," several children said at once, nudging the interrupters.

"All right, then. It says here that on very silent nights, if a person listens closely the sound of chapel bells ripple up from below the surface of the water."

Marie looked up sharply, but though several tongues were bitten the children remained silent.

"Cattails and white water lilies with pink centres encircle the lake and its glassy circle reflects the sky, as if it were the very mirror of heaven. Young girls have been known to dive into the lake in search of the convent, novitiates in search of God. They never return.

"But once, a young girl from Belley disappeared into the lake and she *did* return several days later, only she had no memory of where she had been, or of what she had seen, or even of her name. For a long time afterwards, people insisted they saw her in a dress as white as ice walking through the fields at night to dip her fingers into the lake water and, if you were very quiet and didn't move at all, but stayed low to the ground by the lake rushes, her dress might brush against you as she passed and you'd be blessed from that day forward."

Marie closed the book and looked up from her reading.

"What happens next?" Nina asked. Her blonde hair was so fine that wisps of it always escaped her braids and floated about her head.

"That's the end of the story," Marie said.

"Well, that's very unsatisfactory," Nina insisted. "We ought to know at least if the girl ever remembered anything."

"No. That's the nature of legend," Esther argued. "We're

meant to wonder. There are mysteries in the world that can't be explained."

"Well, there's no mystery here. That's just a superstitious story," Nina complained, "meant for people without a brain in their heads."

"Satisfied?" Marie asked, as she handed the book back to Miron.

MARIE DEHAN, COOK

OH, THE STORIES I might have told those children. Some of them thought my son was a pirate. The truth is my son is too handsome for his own good. Women used to hang about our bistro in Paris like stray cats, but instead of shooing them away like he should have, he'd take them dancing and break their hearts.

Oh, the Parisian ladies adored him all right, but it wasn't in his power to grant even the smallest of their wishes, because Philippe can only love men.

When one poor, obsessed woman learned his secret, she hit him with a bottle of champagne she'd planned to use to seduce him, which is how he lost his eye, and which seemed as good a reason to leave Paris as any, especially with the Nazis growing too fond of his food and more and more suspicious of his fatal attractions.

Sometimes running away means you're headed in exactly the right direction. So we ran to the Jura where I spent my girlhood. There's nothing like it—the fresh scent of the countryside blowing into your lungs, and a fresh start. Fields of wild narcissi in the spring, and huge forests of beech, oak, chestnut, and every kind of evergreen. There are men here who can spot a violin tree hidden among hundreds of others. The famous Stradivarius violins come from spruce trees that grow slowly, in a straight vertical up to the sky.

We hadn't been here hardly a month before we ran into

Philippe's old friend, Perticoz. He told us about the Settlement and before we knew it we were running into the arms of these children.

They sure can make a racket with their wild games of kickball and tag. The mix of accents when they all begin to talk at the table can make your head spin. German, Austrian, French, Polish, Belgian, Algerian, and Romanian. It's like eating with a huge flock of different kinds of birds, blackbirds and starlings and gulls and swifts, all singing at once, the verbal chorus of Europe.

But they can be quiet, too, the darlings, as quiet as mice, as silent as cats on padded paws. They do well at their lessons, because schoolwork, in comparison with living, is so much easier. They're not intact in the way other children are. There is a surface, and then a gap between it and their inner lives, shattered like broken cups.

In them, I recognize my son, who lives with that same gap, and who finds among them, uncomplicated love.

CLAUDE LEVAN-REIFMAN, TEN YEARS OLD

I NEVER LIKED THE DARK.

I remember my father, a good Catholic, used to ask the archangel, Gabriel, to protect us from storms and woe. That was one of his favourite words, *woe*, and he would say it like he was talking to a horse to make me laugh. One night, after a heavy rain, there was a golden light in the sky.

"See? That's Gabriel," my father said. "He's made of light."

He went inside then, but I stayed and watched the light fade and knew the angel had turned away from us.

My father was arrested the next morning, in the hours before the light returned.

My mother and I vanished and our lives were full of woe— my father's word but he wasn't there to make the truth of it lighter. I look for the sun in my mother's face, but it is full of clouds, and for a long time she only wore clothes the colour of night.

Then after many months, my uncle wrote to us and arranged for us to come here, to the House of Izieu. I call it the House of Light—sunlight, moonlight, the shimmer of the stars, the sparkle of the river.

That first day, my mother and I stood by the window at sunset and watched the sky turn soft red and orange, melting into gold.

"Look," my mother said, smiling and pointing at the flood of colour. "The wings of Gabriel have come back to us."

I never really believed in Gabriel, but *something* has come back to us. For the first time I realize a memory can make you happy, instead of sad.

LILIANE GERENSTEIN, ELEVEN YEARS OLD

I ADMIT I TOOK A LOT of the blessings of my old life for granted. I went to a fancy school. I had lovely clothes. Gifts fell at my feet—a silver hairbrush from my father, dolls with porcelain faces and velvet dresses from my aunties. On one birthday, my mother knit a blanket for me that was so white and soft she said when I fell asleep I would dream of baby lambs in spring meadows.

All of that is gone now and I should have paid more attention.

I learned to be grateful for things at the House of Izieu. It's like a summer that stretches on forever, only with lessons. It's a gift that appears out of thin air when you least expect it, like a star you've been staring at, but only gradually see in the centre of your sky.

We have group birthdays at Izieu and when my month came, Philippe baked us a huge apple cake. Before I might have complained I was getting pretty sick of apples—applesauce in the mornings, apples for snacks, even apple slices in the soup once—but I loved that cake because I knew Philippe had stayed up until midnight to bake it for us. And I got cards from all my friends they'd made themselves and decorated with bits of old ribbons or leaves or feathers, and I think they are every bit as nice as silver and velvet.

I often wonder aloud to Léa what twist in my life path brought me here. Was it pure luck or God? I told her that when I was little, I used to look for God, for signs. Since God is Light, I thought he might be easier to see on rainy days when everything is reflected in water and I would hunt for a flash, or a shine, or something shimmering somewhere. Léa always listens and this is what she taught me: you've got to be on the look out for luck, just as much as for God. You've got to be ready to grab onto luck before it gets away. So, at the House of Izieu, I hold on fast.

NOVEMBER 1943

THAT WINTER, THE MOON WAS WHITE.

A cold wind pushed against the windows and through the trees, shaking the branches. The sunlight, when it appeared from behind clouds, was thin and brittle.

The barn was freezing. Sabine and Miron clung to each other under a huge pile of blankets while their breath curled like smoke into the frigid air. "Should we move the cow into the bedroom to help keep us warm?" Miron suggested.

"Better for us to move the bedroom into the house," Sabine replied.

"It was a joke. Where exactly would we sleep in the house? On the stairs? On a mattress in the classroom?"

"All right. I see your point. We don't need the cow. Just think of something warm."

Several silent minutes passed.

"Miron? Are you thinking about palm trees and sandy beaches?"

"No. I'm thinking about snow. Lots and lots of snow, making the mountain roads impassable and the House of Izieu unreachable."

But the next day, and the day after that, everyone at the House of Izieu was talking about snow under clear and heartless blue skies. Those children who had grown up with snow became self-appointed experts, while the youngsters who'd never experienced it clamoured for information.

"What is it feeling like?" asked Barouk.

"Soft when it's falling and hard when it's packed," Otto declared.

"Packed? Why pack snow?"

"Not in a suitcase, silly. The best kind of snow will hold a shape. You can pack it just by scooping up handfuls and pressing your hands together. That's how you make snowballs. Or we can make snowmen."

"Snowball fights!" Fritz shouted. "We can have teams. Boys against girls."

"No, you can't," Sabine warned. "You boys outnumber the girls."

"Do snowballs hurt?" Élie worried.

"Nah," Fritz promised. "They break apart when they hit you and you'll have a thick coat on and won't feel a thing."

"There are other ways to play in the snow, Élie," Sabine promised. "You can make snow angels. I'll teach you how."

"But if you stick your tongue out and touch it to anything metal, you'll freeze right there and have to wait until spring to get your tongue back," Majer said gleefully.

"Majer," Sabine glared, while Élie quickly covered her mouth, "promise me you won't try that."

"When I was a boy in Russia," Miron said, "it was the custom among some people to roll newborns in the snow to harden them against the ferocity of winter." This announcement was met with an uneasy silence.

"Thank you for that, Miron." Sabine said finally. "Since we have no newborns that's not a custom we need to worry about."

"Is snow very, very cold?" Jean-Claude wondered.

"Well, yes, all at once. But a single flake will melt in an instant and no two flakes are exactly alike and each flake is beautiful," Miron said, trying to make up for his old mouldering tale about Russian babies.

"My father once gave me a snow globe," Sabine remembered.

"What's that?" Richard asked.

"Imagine a globe made of clear glass. Inside the globe, there was a miniature house surrounded by fir trees, the tallest one topped with a tiny gold star. If you shook the globe, snow would whirl around the forest and then fall gently to the ground."

For a moment, Sabine wished that miniature house could be the House of Izieu, tucked safely inside a glass globe.

"Why didn't the snow melt?" Richard asked, interrupting Sabine's thought.

"Oh, it was just pretend snow. White sand or tiny bits of paper."

"Well I wish the real stuff would come soon." Richard pronounced.

"Me too," several children sighed at once.

The frost came first, tracing lacy patterns on panes of glass. The light at the mouth of the barn was crystalline, as if miniature particles of frost were suspended in it, sharpening the edges of the door and brightening the air. When Miron and Sabine rose and walked across the lawn toward the house, the grass was stiff and crunched beneath their feet. The turned over earth of the garden lay exposed to the cold, and became as solid as cement.

The next night brought ice, glazing the branches of the trees, and transforming them into glistening sculptures. In the morning, Pierre poured kettles of hot water onto the handle of the stone fountain's pump to loosen the icy grip of the deep freeze, while the children watched the steam rise in cloudy ribbons and snapped icicles from the balustrade of the terrace.

The day before the storm came, the sky was purple and smelled of wind, though the air was perfectly still.

"It's coming," the children whispered to each other.

At first, the snowflakes were slow and lazy, white moths floating down to land on upturned cheeks and outstretched tongues. The children exclaimed and wondered, their faces flushed and their eyes bright, cold and happiness conspiring to make them look so beautiful.

Then the wind stirred the flakes into a white, whirling mass, until the sky was thick and churning. The children ran inside and stood at the windows, watching the world rapidly disappear.

A long season of enchantment began. Nothing was as it had been before. The snow seemed to alter the contours of the land, creating new valleys and ridges, turning the tallest of pines into stately white pillars. The light had a bluish tint, casting mauve shadows. The cliff faces softened, the roads vanished, and the pinnacles of the mountains glittered so brightly Miron had to shade his eyes to look at them. He reached for Sabine's hand and squeezed it tightly. He could almost feel her body loosen as the tension in her muscles relaxed. The House of Izieu was buffeted, impervious. Snow had become its armour.

Farmer Perticoz raided the storage in his barn for sleds, and the children, bundled up in an assortment of mismatching boots, coats, mittens, and scarves of every colour, ploughed through the snow to the top of the hill that overlooked the house.

Arnold, on his stomach with little Sami on his back, steered the first sled from the highest point, down the steepest slope, at alarming speed. Sami, screeching and laughing, finally fell off, tumbling down the last two feet. He was up in a flash, already scrambling back to the top of the hill as fast as his short legs could pump. As the sliding, whizzing, and shrieking filled the morning, the older boys showed the younger children how to steer by leaning or dragging their boots in the snow. Soon the slope of the hill was as slick as a glass slide.

As the days passed, snow angels decorated the meadows, and snowmen patrolled the terrace. Trails of footprints on pristine snow looped in aimless circles of play, or disappeared into newly carved tunnels, or drifted down to the green river, its edges brittle with ice.

There were thrilling sleigh rides with Farmer Perticoz and dozens of snowball fights, star-flooded nights and ice-blue skies. November was hot soup and toast, coats steaming near the wood stove, and dreamless sleeps under warm blankets.

In December, trails of wood smoke from the chimney guided the postman on his skis to Sabine's front door, where he placed a parcel and a letter from Pierre-Marcel, written on official stationery, in her hands.

Dear Madame Zlatin,
I hope all is well at the Settlement.
As Christmas approaches, I am pleased to inform you that the good citizens of Belley, Izieu, and several neighbouring villages have donated a sum of money and goods (here enclosed) to help the refugee children celebrate the festive season.
Obersturmführer Werner was most impressed by this generosity.
Thank you for your invitation to attend your Christmas Eve dinner. While Obersturmführer Werner sends his sincere regrets, I will be most pleased to attend.

Sabine read the words not written as intently as the words that were, and carried the letter to Léa.

"Clearly, your friend is warning you. The Germans have learned of the Settlement and believe the children are Christian, no doubt with Pierre-Marcel's encouragement. We must have a public Christmas. I think we should also assume our mail is being read."

"Exactly what I thought. But what will the children think?"

Léa's face brightened as she thought of a solution. "We'll

tell them that Christmas will be like the summer pageant, a kind of play. And we can still celebrate Hanukkah privately, with a special meal, and later, stories at bedtime. What's in the package?"

"Flat tins of sardines, a kilo of sugar, some butter, seven packs of colour pencils, eight knit sweaters in various sizes, and a one hundred franc note."

"Good. I'd say we're off to a promising start."

And so began the celebration of a very public Christmas at the House of Izieu. When Miron drove a sleigh full of children to the market, they wished everyone they knew, and plenty they didn't, *Joyeux Noël*, for each child had learned the phrase in French to perfection. They thought it was outrageous fun to chop down a fir tree, drag it into the house, and decorate it with paper stars and strings of dried apple while its boughs dripped melting snow onto the classroom floor. The office of the *subpréfet* of Belley received forty-four Christmas cards, all with the obligatory drawings in children's crayon of Christmas trees, angels, jingle bells, holly, stars, wreaths, mangers, shepherds, Three Wise Men, or *Père Noël*.

Sabine wrote letters to everyone she knew in Montpellier, and soon packages began to arrive and were quickly hidden in the barn. Philippe, dressed for an expedition to the north pole, skied into town for supplies, or perhaps not to any town but to some secret cache or contact, because Sabine never saw a single receipt despite all the boxes and bags he brought home and carefully hid in the larder or behind innocent jars of homemade applesauce.

"Where did all this come from?" Sabine finally asked.

Philippe's only reply was a wink.

"What do people eat at Christmas?" she wondered, "and will there be enough for guests?"

"Leave all that to me," Philippe assured her.

So invitations were sent to all the friends of the House of Izieu. As the day of the party drew closer, Sabine dreaded the departure of Mademoiselle Perrier whose return to her own home for the holidays meant that lessons would be suspended at a time when the children were already fizzing with excitement. She suddenly felt like that old woman living in a shoe with so many children at loose ends she didn't know what to do. But, as it turned out, the children were no trouble at all, disappearing into the classroom behind closed doors, busy with their own seasonal conspiracies.

Plans and schemes were everywhere. Miron spent all his spare time in the barn and came to bed covered in sawdust. Pieces of thread were tangled in Léa's hair and she had the pink eyes of a white mouse from sewing so late into the evenings. Meanwhile, Mina and Suzanne neglected their daily chores to indulge in a sudden passion for knitting.

Sabine thought everyone had gone crazy letting themselves be caught up in a pretend Christmas because all these tidings of hope and mercy would surely vanish in an instant if a single jackboot crossed the threshold. She had little tolerance for the gaudy fuss of the holiday, and found the whole enterprise disquieting. What were they thinking, hidden Jews performing Christmas like some kind of play? She couldn't help but feel that the natural order of things had been turned upside down. She felt twitchy, like an animal before a storm, and expected nothing less than disaster.

But Sabine was wrong. When the eve of Christmas finally arrived, Pierre-Marcel in full dress uniform and Marie-Antoinette in a fur-lined cloak arrived with it, pulling up to the house with a flourish in a horse drawn sleigh filled with presents, the three boys who attended the boarding school in Belley, and the lovely Marcelle. The children were drawn to her as though she radiated light, and she greeted every one with a kiss or hug or handshake, depending on their age or preference. The reunion made the house so warm it seemed the air was turning to mist, and the younger children hopped from foot to foot, giddy with pleasure.

While Miron greeted Madame and Farmer Pericoz, Pierre-Marcel drew Sabine aside and whispered that his wife, Noelle, and Mayor Tissot had arranged the best surprise of all, a dinner for the German officers stationed in the area which would keep them full and drunk and listless for days to come.

There was an hour of carol singing, a bit ragged because the children didn't know most of the words, and the adults were distracted by the siren call of smells wafting from the kitchen. Then, finally, it was time for the traditional meal, *le réveillon de Noël*, served proudly by Philippe and Marie, with a few menu substitutes necessitated by circumstance. A simple duck pâte took the place of *foie gras*, and grilled sardines stood in for more luxurious seafood. But the roast capon with chestnut stuffing could have been the star of any French table, followed by the best cheeses of the Jura, *Mont d'Or* and *Morbier*.

Five-year-old Émile's mouth formed a perfect 'O' when he saw what Philippe had prepared for the final course: seven *Bûches de Noël*, rolled cakes in the shape of Christmas logs covered in chocolate ganache, enough for everyone to have a slice of their own.

After dinner, everyone crowded into the classroom where the desks had been pushed against the walls and Pierre-Marcel took charge of the distribution of presents, beginning with his own offering of bars of chocolate for the children. The treats had cost him a small fortune and a stab of conscience because he'd been forced to pretend that the unsavoury characters that had sold it to him were not part of an outlawed black market ring. Despite all his trouble, he was still upstaged by Marie-Antoinette who unveiled a carton of four-dozen oranges, a fruit so rare in the dead of winter in the midst of war that it might just as well have been exotica from another planet. Her laugh, when she saw the look of amazement on Pierre-Marcel's face, was as close to the peal of a Christmas bell as anyone in the Jura was likely to hear that night.

The children received their gifts with enthusiasm. The knit bears and rabbits with button eyes were fiercely hugged, and the rag dolls were instantly rocked. Théo had carved small squirrels and birds for the youngest children and a cat for Max, while Léa had embroidered scarves for the older girls. There were paints for Joseph, sweaters for the older boys and, from Farmer Perticoz, the promise of a piglet for Henri. Sabine's surprise for Théo was a letter from Paulette that had arrived two days ago from Montpellier still smelling faintly of roses.

No one wanted the pretend Christmas to end because it had turned out to be the real thing, provided religion, which had caused so much trouble in the world, was set aside. Even Sabine believed that night that the world might be saved after all, if only all children were treated tenderly. But when Marcelle found Coco curled up and sound asleep under one of the desks, his cheeks sticky with melted chocolate, the guests knew it was time to leave. When Léa and Mina finally put the children to bed that night, they smelled of cake crumbs and sugar.

A few hours later, all the goodbyes said and all the dishes done, Miron turned to Sabine. "Did you have a good time tonight?"

"Best Christmas ever," she replied.

"You've never had Christmas before."

She laughed, a full-throated musical riff. It had been a long time since Miron had heard her sound so happy. "Come. Let me show you what I've been working on in the barn."

They crossed the lawn hand-in-hand and Miron led her to a gleaming wooden sled for the boys and a multilevel dollhouse for the girls.

Suddenly, Sabine felt like a teenager again, impulsive, unpredictable, and drunk on mischief. "Let's take the sled for a run," she coaxed, "before we set everything up for the children."

So, while the House of Izieu slept under a Christmas moon, Sabine and Miron went sledding, swooshing down the sloping lawn, landing in a tangle of arms and legs, and kissing the snow from each other's face.

It was sometime in mid-January, after the House had settled back into its comfortable routine, when little Jean-Claude Benguigui first called Miron *Papa*. Miron crouched down and put a gentle hand on the boy's shoulder. "You know I'm not your father, Jean-Claude. I'm sure your real papa misses you."

"But I don't remember him. And Yvette calls her new family mama and papa."

For a moment, Miron didn't know what to say. For many of the youngest children, the war stretched backwards into their earliest memories and forward into their unknown futures. How do you tell a five-year-old that the people who shielded him from the world, the people he trusted most, hoped to turn him over one day to parents who'd become virtual strangers?

"You must talk to your older brothers, Jean-Claude. They can tell you stories about your father to help you remember."

"But I don't want to remember."

"Why? Why don't you want to remember your own father?"

"Because he might not come back. If I remember and he doesn't come…"

"I see. We all share that problem here. But I promise you that someday, whether your father returns or not, you'll want to know all about him. Even your baby sister will want to know."

Jean-Claude looked hard at Miron. It was clear he'd heard this advice before, but he was too young to understand that those memories that cause misery could also bring consolation. Adults often spoke in riddles. He shrugged, looking entirely unconvinced. "In the meantime, can I call you Papa? You're not going anywhere, are you?"

Miron smiled. "I'm here to stay. But call me Papa Miron, just to keep the record straight."

Jean-Claude nodded and ran off, seemingly content with their bargain. But Miron was reminded of how fiercely children live in the present. Time was suspended for them at the House of Izieu where all that mattered was cocoa at breakfast, lessons in the morning, and if the day was fine, maybe a hike or a game on the lawn. Maybe the war would last forever, or maybe it would end tomorrow.

The adults, however, were aware of distant concussions and smudges of smoke in the peerless blue sky. The Allies were coming, and the Germans were going. The ending was inevitable, but Miron prayed for sooner rather than later.

Though the weather began to soften, February was not a kind month. When Georgy caught the flu, Jacob slipped into the infirmary to show him his new comic book, and a few hours later Jacob kissed his sister, Esther, good night. Esther read a bedtime story to Rénate and Liane, and by the next morning, half the children were flushed and feverish.

Suzanne Reifman moved quickly to quarantine the infected children in the upstairs of the house, but the virus proved difficult to contain and seemed immune to Marie's hot chicken soup, even though it was guaranteed to lift the spirits and drive sickness from the body. Several children gagged on the broth and before nightfall several others had begun to vomit.

"I need help," Dr. Reifman declared. "I need real medicine."

Sabine and Miron agreed it was too risky to send a child alone to Dr. Bendrihem in Glandieu because German soldiers could be anywhere. Sabine set off alone, while Miron readied himself for a trip into the mountains to confer with Philippe's mysterious contacts.

It took hours to slog through the snow, and by the time Sabine reached the village, she was exhausted. She took shelter in a café from where she could see the doctor's blue door and ordered a cup of faux coffee to give herself time to recover from her journey. Through the window she watched three German soldiers on a slow patrol along the street, but no one entered or left through the doctor's door.

An hour crawled by and Sabine knew she couldn't delay any longer without drawing the attention of other customers. How many cups of bad coffee could one woman drink? Her plan had been to enter the doctor's office with at least one other person to seem less noticeable, but apparently no one else in the village had so much as a minor cold to complain about to a doctor.

She rose to her feet just as the waitress who had been serving her approached. "Sit down," she whispered. Sabine sank back onto her chair, for her legs were suddenly weak.

"Your bill, Madame," the waitress said in a louder voice. "Just check the total."

As Sabine scrambled for change, she read the words written under the addition, *Meet me at the back door.*

The waitress swept up the coins and the bill. "Thank you, Madame." Her face and her voice gave away nothing.

Sabine had no choice but to leave the café. Should she trust this stranger or go straight to the doctor's office? As she entered the street, her eyes were riveted on the backs of the German soldiers. Could she reach the doctor's door before they turned around? Acting purely on instinct, Sabine ducked down the alley and found herself at the back of the café.

The waitress was a thin woman, tall, though not as tall as Sabine, in a faded print dress and a black coat. She stared at Sabine with hooded, storm-grey eyes. "Follow me."

"Wait. Who are you?"

"A friend. Keep up unless you want to be arrested."

Shaken, Sabine followed the woman down the alley and through a maze of lanes to the back door of a small, ramshackle house. "In here," the woman said, holding the door open for Sabine.

The interior of the house was full of shadows, as ominous as the overcast sky, and Sabine dreaded crossing the threshold. At that moment, someone inside lit a candle, and in its halo Sabine could make out the face of a young boy, a boy recognized from somewhere. "Hurry up, please. It's starting to rain," the waitress urged. "This is Gérard, the doctor's son. His father was arrested in January."

The door swung shut behind Sabine and she could hear the turn of a lock.

"I recognize you," the boy said. "You came to see my father once. You're from the Settlement."

"You are?" the waitress said. "Thank god. I'm Lucie Feiger. I've been hiding Gérard ever since his father was taken by the Gestapo. If you'd approached the doctor's door, you would've been taken, too." She lit another candle as she was talking. "I'm afraid we can't turn on the lights. The front of the house has been boarded up. So far, the Germans think it's vacant. My husband was also rounded up. This is where we lived."

The bad news broke over Sabine like a cold wave. "What happened?"

Lucie glanced at Gérard and then back at Sabine. "Another time. Can you help us?"

There would be no medicine found here for the children, and no travelling back to them until the weather cleared. At least the hideaways were dry inside the house, and Lucie had food from the café. While the rain poured down, while the wind rose in the east, Sabine would think of a plan, she'd have to, because she could no more abandon a child in need than she could stop the rain with just a wave of her hand and fly back to the House of Izieu.

In the end, the rain began to melt the snow, and Sabine's return journey, though cautious, was easier than she'd supposed.

"I've brought no medicine," she told Suzanne, "but at least we have more help with Lucie and Gérard. How are the children?"

"Rallying slowly, but the sisters, Rénate and Liane are gravely ill, weakened no doubt by their months in Rivesaltes. Perhaps Miron and Philippe will have more luck."

"They're not back?"

"Not yet."

It was midnight, and the wind was battering the trees, when Miron finally appeared at the mouth of the barn. His face was pale and his hair was drenched from the rain. His eyes, usually so expressive, telling Sabine all she needed to know about what he was feeling, were empty and dark. He looked exhausted, and without asking any questions, she took his face in her hands and kissed him.

He responded eagerly, but then rested his forehead against hers. "A man was killed," he murmured.

"A soldier?"

"A resister. We buried him, but there'll be questions. Shots were fired and we heard dogs."

She wanted to tell him to stop talking, that she shouldn't know about this, but it was as if he had something inside him that had to pour out.

"I think Philippe knew him. I had to drag him away from the grave. It was all I could do to get him back home. That big man, Sabine, he sobbed like a boy."

She put her arms around him, felt him shudder. He leaned into her and pressed his face into her neck. "We brought back the medicine," he murmured before falling into bed.

Sabine lay awake for a long time watching Miron sleep, listening to the inevitable melting of the snow, knowing that their dream of keeping the children together was coming to an end.

Montpellier was grimmer than she remembered. The leaves of the palm trees were a bleached-out green. The streets were grubbier. The faces of the few people she saw on the street had an ashy cast. Coils of barbed wire were strung along the beaches like thorny snakes. Only the sea was unchanged, an impervious, arrogant blue.

There were many more soldiers here than in the Jura, but even they looked dispirited. With her false identity papers, Sabine travelled unchallenged. At first, she found it astonishing that other people judged her to be calm and capable even though she was still spiralling from the arrest of the doctor, and she guessed this was because of how she looked: tall, almost mannish, with a plain and solemn face. She seemed as utilitarian as an old pair of brown shoes a bit worn down at the heels as everyone's were because the war had eaten up most of what the world had to offer, including leather. With her hair scraped back, and no make-up to soften her square face, she could be mistaken for a nun, maybe, or a head mistress, but certainly not as a woman with secrets to hide. And so, Sabine kept her secrets to herself and few suspected she had any to tell.

She went first to her good friend, Berthe Mering, the soul of charity who lived in a small house well below her means in order to avoid drawing attention to her fortune. A devout supporter of the Red Cross and the OSE, she greeted Sabine with open arms and bad news. "The headquarters of the OSE in Chambéry was raided two days ago by the Gestapo and the staff were rounded up," she said. "The entire organization has gone underground. This must be the work of Klaus Barbie who has jurisdiction over the area."

The mention of Barbie, the Butcher of Lyon, was like an ice cube slipping down Sabine's spine. "Did the Gestapo seize the records?" she asked.

"I know what you're asking—did the Gestapo find the names of the children—but I don't know the answer. The staff has been careful. Coded lists of names were sent to an OSE office in neutral Geneva and many other financial records were hidden off the premises. They couldn't be destroyed outright because when this war finally ends the records will be the only way for parents to trace their way back to their children. But, Sabine, if the staff are questioned—"

There was no need to finish the sentence. The word *questioned* hung in the air, a euphemism for whatever horrors occurred in the sinister cells of Montluc prison in Lyon.

Sabine felt the first stings of panic, as if a frantic bee were trapped in her stomach. "Then we haven't a moment to lose. We must assume the Germans know about the House of Izieu."

"Remember the name will be recorded as The Settlement for Refugee Children from the Hérault. If the Germans even have that name, they will speak first to your friend, Monsieur Wiltzer."

"Pierre-Marcel will tell them the House has a history as a Catholic boarding school and summer camp."

"Yes, of course. But if the Germans become suspicious, they may also want to speak to Monsieur Jean Fridrici, your contact in the Hérault."

"You're right. I'll go to him first, and then to the Paillarès family who will help me find Marius, and then to the Abbey."

"No, my friend. First you'll eat and sleep, because anyone can see the lines of worry on your face. If I poked your shoulder right now with just a single finger you'd surely fall down from exhaustion."

Over the next few days, Sabine met with all her friends and old contacts. They offered her whatever they could, which was always less than what she needed. Since the beginning of the war, OSE and its myriad networks had hidden over four thousand children, spread far and wide among various homes and institutions, and among the families of farmers, craftsmen, labourers, teachers, fishermen, or shop owners, poor or well-to-do, urban or rural. But placements were becoming more difficult to find, and the transporting of children in any number, more dangerous.

A day before her scheduled return to Izieu, Sabine, with the help of Marius and his decrepit truck, had a clandestine meeting with Léon Reifman in the deserted sanctuary of Palavas-les-Flots. They embraced and if they noted any changes in the other's face wrought by desperation, they failed to mention them.

"I've arranged placements for all but eighteen children," Sabine said.

"I can take only six," Léon said. "I can get them into Switzerland."

"Which six? How in god's name do we decide?"

Léon plunged his face into his hands and then looked up. "Let's try to keep siblings together."

Sabine nodded. "Max and Herman," she said, remembering a promise she'd made long ago to a frightened boy waiting in a hotel room with his little brother for a mother that never returned. "Maurice and Liliane, and Paula and Marcel. Some of the older siblings can stay at the Perticoz farm or the boarding school in Belley. How soon can you come?"

"We still have to wait for the snow to melt, for the roads to become passable."

Sabine closed her eyes. For now, the roads were no more than grey pencil lines between mounds of snow, but those lines would soon widen. March, she knew, was unpredictable, either fair or fierce. "I don't know," she confessed. "I'm guessing. Early April?"

"Easter," Léon suggested. "I'll come at Easter when the schools are on holiday and take the children with me when I leave."

Sabine looked away and bit her bottom lip. "I hate this," she murmured. "I hate even thinking about breaking up the House of Izieu. How will I tell the children that once again they'll be uprooted?"

Léon reached for her hand and squeezed it hard. "You have no choice," he said. That was all the comfort he could offer.

When Sabine arrived home to the happy news that all the children were healthy again, she called the adults together and told them everything she'd done and everything she'd learned in Montpellier. "There's nothing I want more than to stay together, but we mustn't underestimate the danger. We have until Easter. Then everyone must go."

Her revelations were met with a long and unhappy silence. The isolation of the House of Izieu was so seductive. Couldn't they stay? Perhaps the Germans would leave them alone. Wasn't it just as perilous to try to leave? But no one spoke these thoughts aloud.

"You still need places for a dozen children. Émile can live with me," Léa offered.

"I'll contact my parents." Suzanne said. "If they're well enough to travel they can come at Easter, and Claude can leave with them."

"There's someone I know who'll take in Gérard," Lucie promised. "I can take him there next week, but I'll come back and help out until Easter."

Mina Friedler said nothing at all. She and her daughter would be together, but she had no idea where they might go.

Finally Miron asked the most difficult question of all. "When do we tell the children?"

Some were in favour of telling them the very next morning so they would have time to adjust, but the others argued that no amount of time could prepare them for leaving the House of Izieu, and they should have one last carefree month together. Miron suggested that if Sabine left the House a day or two before the children, she could greet them when they reached Montpellier and soothe their anxieties. In the end, the adults agreed on this latter course—one more carefree month.

March was like a fresh breeze that swept away worry, or at least made it easier to disguise. The first flowers of the season began to poke out from the ground, and the sun shone almost every day. Spring fever quivered in the air and even the tips of the trees seemed to tremble, anticipating their first burst of green. As a precaution, a bell was hung in the barn and another at the Perticoz farm, and if anyone saw or heard anything suspicious, the bells would ring. The children were told to scatter if they heard those bells, and run into the woods or head for the best places they'd found after months of playing hide-and-seek. If the older children were wary of such instructions, the youngest welcomed the bells as part of a new game.

Though she had much to do in preparation for leaving, Sabine spent as much time as she could with the children as they tumbled in play or chased kites in the gusty March winds, but she could not prevent herself from looking up now and again to study the landscape and the horizon. From village to village, from valley to mountain, the snow was steadily disappearing and the mud drying. Sometimes, she caught Miron or Léa in the midst of the same sort of surveying gaze, and she noticed springtime made the children noisier while the adults communicated in sighs and coded glances.

Finally, when the forest paths were clear and the meadows green, Miron organized a hike into the foothills of the mountains for nine boys and four girls who didn't mind getting dirty or sweaty. Little Sami refused to be left behind, and Miron didn't have the heart to deny him, even though he knew he'd soon be carrying the boy on his shoulders. They sang as they marched along through the forest, stopping now and again to admire a chorus of birds just beginning to make their nests, or a brave squirrel standing erect and sniffing at the new softness in the air. The world seemed to be pulsing with life, sap bursting from the hidden veins of the trees. After a steady climb, they left the forest behind and reached an upper meadow, where they found clumps of cowslips and marguerites.

The heat of midday was evaporating the morning dew, releasing a light mist that lay like a veil over the landscape. So high up, it seemed they were the only people for miles around, and as they climbed higher, the base of the foothill disappeared in a thick fog, and they imagined they were on an island surrounded by a white ocean.

But they were not alone. From across the meadow, a young teenager was waving and running towards them. "Hello," she hollered, finally stopping in front of Sami. She bent over and put her hands on her knees to catch her breath. A camera dangled from a strap around her neck. "Hello," she began again. "You're from the Settlement, aren't you? I'm Marie-Louise Bouvier, Madame Perticoz's niece. I visit their farm often."

There was a buzz of introductions before Sami's high-pitched voice rose above the clamour. His small index finger was pointed directly at Marie-Louise's neck. "Is that a camera? Will you take pictures of us?"

There was a short cough from Miron, and Sami, reminded of manners, began again. "Please, mademoiselle."

"Yes, please," several of the other children chimed in.

"It'll be my pleasure," Marie-Louise replied to a round of applause.

The children laughed and jostled each other with their shoulders, but eventually something like a line emerged, a formation of shorter girls and boys at the front, taller boys at the back. They smiled on cue, easy effortless smiles, and stared into the camera that would hold this day for them forever, while destiny shuffled the cards of their future.

At the exact moment the children were grinning into the camera, Marie-Antoinette arrived at the doorstep of the House of Izieu, calling for Sabine, and looking nothing like her usual self, her hair wild from the spring winds and her green eyes wide with alarm. Quickly, she pulled Sabine into the barn.

"They've sent Pierre away. Transferred him to some other office in France. I don't know why. There was no warning. He's just gone."

Sabine felt something inside herself crack like ice too thin to hold a weight. She did not move her hands or open her arms. She did not try to touch Marie-Antoinette or offer her comfort. She understood there was no possible consolation for such terrible news. Their protector was gone.

For her own part, Marie-Antoinette thought it would have been a healthy sign if she were angry at Pierre-Marcel for not saying goodbye, but she couldn't even manage that. Given the unshakable love she'd felt for him for so many years, all her heart and mind had room for was sorrow, a sense of personal abandonment, and a rising fear for the fate of her friends.

"What will you do?" she whispered.

"The only thing we can do. Empty the house. I only hope we haven't left it too late."

"When?"

"Easter. As soon as the holiday is over."

"I'll come. I'll take as many children as you need. Noelle will leave Belley with her children and join Pierre. I'll keep the house for them. It's big."

"Dear Marie-Antoinette. What of your own safety? What of your job?"

"They didn't send me away," she sniffed. "I'm just a woman, just a secretary. I'm counting on them to underestimate me."

"All right. Come on Easter Sunday. That's the day we'll tell the children and the next day—"

Sabine's tongue tripped on the words. The next day would be the wrench of separation, the plunge back into strangeness and fear, the end of the House of Izieu, as brief as roses or a single line of poetry or the sweet notes of a birdsong, already fading before you can recognize them. She couldn't finish the sentence.

The two women embraced, without speaking another word.

As Easter approached, Gabrielle Perrier made preparations to leave for a short visit to her family, and the children were released from the classroom chores. Amid the bedlam that invariably results when children begin a holiday from school, Marie approached Sabine. "It's Philippe," she began tentatively. "He's not himself, not since that shooting in the mountains. They say men weep only for love."

"What can I do to help?" Sabine offered, appalled that she had not even noticed Philippe was enduring a private sorrow.

"Well, I think, and I'm sorry to ask, but I think we should leave before the children do. He's not a coward, mind, but saying goodbye to all those youngsters ... it's too much."

"I understand. Both of you have been so generous. I can't tell you how grateful Miron and I are."

Marie waved away Sabine's thanks. "It wasn't anything, not for us leastways. You and your man have good hearts. If the house weren't shutting down, you'd have had to drag us away. It's a shame, a great shame, I say."

"Yes," Sabine nodded. Shame was certainly one of many ways to name what was happening in the world.

On April 1, 1944, Sabine packed her suitcase and sat down on the edge of her bed to lean against her husband's shoulder. "I wish you didn't have to go," he murmured into her hair. "When is the car coming?"

"Marie-Antoinette promised to be here by eight in the morning. I expect she'll be here by nine. I'll have time to have breakfast with the children. Now remember, Suzanne's parents are arriving tomorrow, and Léon's arriving on the sixth, and he's picking up Max and Maurice from the boarding school in Belley on the way."

"Where are you going to stay? No, don't tell me. That way, no one can force me to betray you. I'll meet you at the train station in Montpellier in just a few days. Me and Théo, Rénate and Liane—your new and much smaller family."

"Do you think we'll ever come back here?" Sabine wondered.

"I'm sure of it," Miron replied, drawing her close until there was no room for anything else and the imminence of her departure seemed far away.

The next morning, the air was mild and the sky was the colour of pearls. Marie-Antoinette arrived intentionally late, with just enough time to drive Sabine to the train station. She knew her friend would be suffering. Best not to linger. For once, she did not talk in the car or try to lighten the mood. In a series of quick glances, she noted the white knuckles of Sabine's clenched hands and her bowed neck. When finally

Sabine looked up, Marie-Antoinette thought she had the expression of a soldier about to embark on a mission filled with uncertainties and breathtaking risks.

The two women said goodbye, promising to keep in touch, and when Sabine was finally settled on the train, she sighed and closed her eyes. She could summon the House of Izieu from ordinary air the way an alchemist summoned gold from lead, but she could not rewind time or undo its fate.

On Maundy Thursday, April 6, 1944, at around eight-thirty in the morning, the children were having breakfast. Miron was in the kitchen with Léa and Lucie, who had kept her promise by delivering Dr. Bendrihem's son to safety and returning to the House of Izieu to help with chores. They heard nothing but the splashing of water as they did the dishes and the constant chatter of the children coming from the adjoining room.

Léon had been upstairs visiting with his newly arrived parents, Éva and Moise, and his sister, Suzanne, and was just coming down when he saw three men in civilian clothes disappearing along the corridor that led to the breakfast room.

"Run," Suzanne urged. "It's the Gestapo."

Within seconds, two convoy trucks sped into the yard, and fifteen soldiers rounded up the children and loaded them into the trucks like sacks of potatoes. Too late, Farmer Perticoz came running and was warned by a shout from Miron to stay back and hide.

If the people in the town of Izieu had looked up, they would have seen a cloud of dust on the horizon, stirred up by a convoy of trucks, moving like a slow, small whirlwind. And if they had listened closely, they would have heard over the grinding of the truck's gears, the unmistakable sound of children singing. But it was a holiday, and good people were busy with their own affairs, perhaps catching an extra hour of sleep, or preparing for the meal to celebrate the Resurrection of Christ.

At a crossroad, one woman was brazen enough to stand in

the road, refusing to budge, forcing the convoy to stop. She talked at length to a small dark man in a good dark suit, and one small boy—her nephew, she insisted, and she had the papers to prove it—was lifted down from the back of one truck. He was, she protested, not Jewish.

Marie-Antoinette heard about the raid in a frantic phone call from Farmer Perticoz and abandoned her desk immediately, without asking for permission or offering an explanation. She found a German staff car with keys in the ignition and borrowed it. She drove recklessly on the mountain roads, heedless of branches scraping the sides of the car, or potholes that chewed up the tires. In her heart, despite all the stern talk she'd heard from Pierre and her own keen intelligence, she'd believed that nothing terrible could befall a sanctuary where such innocence flowered. She was in a state of shock.

When she reached the top of the hill that overlooked the House of Izieu, she turned off the ignition and let the car coast. When gravity would take it no further, she got out on shaky legs and slowly walked to the front door.

The unearthly silence of the place almost drove her to her knees.

She called out and her voice, in her own ears, sounded like china crashing to the floor.

She forced herself to enter the house, once filled to the brim with forty-four children. She stared at the empty space as if the soldiers had torn through the fabric of the air, leaving it hanging in rags behind them. She looked everywhere, under every bed in the dormitory, up the ladder into the attic, across the yard in the barn. Miron and Léa were gone. The children were gone, and the air in every room echoed their absence.

Finally, Marie-Antoinette stuffed a cardboard box with crayon drawings, school notebooks, letters, and photographs, anything she could find to prove the children existed. She packed up dolls, and small carvings in the shape of animals, and birthday cards. When she carried her burden outside, she heard Tomi whimpering. The poor dog had worn himself out running from place to place in search of the children and consolation, finally collapsing in a dejected heap.

Marie-Antoinette picked him up and said goodbye to the House of Izieu, leaving the door wide-open because everything precious was already gone, and because only the rush of the wind and the battering of the rain—certainly no human hand—would ever be able to scour it clean of the unspeakable evil that had crept up in the dawn and spilled its ugly shadow everywhere only hours before.

The telegram from Marie-Antoinette reached Sabine when she was in the chapel with Abbé Prevost making the final arrangements for the orphanage to take in twelve boys from the House of Izieu.

Family ill, contagious disease.

The House had been raided, the children and adults arrested. The knowledge, coded in simple words, descended with effortless terror like the blade of a guillotine.

Sabine crushed the telegram in her hand and let it drop to the floor.

Abbé Prevost was alarmed at the instant change in Sabine. She was breathing quickly and anguish was rising from her in waves, anguish he could smell, like a sour mix of bitter lemons and creosote. He reached for the telegram and shook his head.

"The children are ill? How unfortunate."

"No Father." She forced out the words. "The House has been cleared out."

The priest still did not understand. Sabine shuddered and tried again. "The Germans have arrested everyone who was there."

"Were they all together?"

"Yes. No. I don't know."

"My God," he uttered, crossing himself.

Sabine was utterly still. She looked strangely emotionless,

though her brain was spinning, as if it had been concussed by a crushing blow. It was the numbness that follows an injury before the pain begins to cut slowly and relentlessly through the dense analgesic fog.

That numbness allowed her to function mechanically for the many hours she worked tirelessly to try to save the children and their supervisors. She rushed from place to place, from person to person. She appealed to the Red Cross in Montpellier, to old friends from OSE, to her old driver, Marius, and the *subpréfet*, Monsieur Fridrici. They could do nothing. She could do nothing.

Finally, she appealed to the Vichy administration for the release of the children, at the very least. She presented her identification papers, in the name of Jeanne Verdavoire, and waited for a long time to be seen by some official who might have the power or the heart to show clemency. Eventually, she was admitted to what seemed to be a huge filing room with industrial lighting, manned by a single official whose name was never offered to her. He had a leonine head and a bony face.

As the man turned away from her toward the open shelving to look for documents of the arrest, an arc of white light from a hanging light fixture swept across his face. For a moment, he looked as if he wasn't in colour, but black and white like a photograph, something flat and two-dimensional with neither thickness nor substance. She wondered for a terrible moment if he was real at all or a spectre.

But the light swung back, and he was standing in front of her, solid and immovable.

"There's no record. There's nothing I can do." His voice was without inflection, a droning sound, emotionless.

Sabine stared at him, incredulous. She brushed the sweaty trails of hair from her forehead with the back of her sleeve, and tried again.

"But there must be something you can do, someone you can call. They're only children."

"Madame. There is nothing I can do. It wasn't a Vichy arrest, but a German one. If you persist, you know what will happen to you?"

Sabine knew this was a question laced with poison.

"You know what will happen to them if no one intercedes, don't you? You know, and still you'll do nothing."

His eyes seemed to darken, to turn the colour of muddy earth.

"Get out," he flared. "Get out or be arrested."

Sabine lifted her chin and held his gaze long enough for him to know exactly what she thought of him, and then she walked away and found the first train she could to Paris.

The city was not as she remembered it. This Paris was scowling and gloomy under leaden skies, which perfectly suited Sabine's mood. She went immediately to the head office of the Red Cross where she met with the director and begged her help.

"Certainly, Madame. We will do whatever we can, but we must be quick. When was the sanctuary raided?"

"The morning of April sixth."

"A moment, please." The director left her office, but returned less than ten minutes later, her face grave.

"I'm so sorry, Madame, but I must tell you that the children arrived in Drancy on the eighth of April."

Drancy. Sabine closed her eyes and wished she didn't know what was whispered about Drancy, but she did. Drancy, filthy, and crowded, existed to feed the trains travelling east to certain sunrise and probable death. She shook her head, as if she could shake off such bad news. She would not think about the children on those trains, or the prayers that fluttered in that cramped space, their wings beating the stale air.

"I must go to them," she murmured, and rose unsteadily from her chair.

"No. You must not. I'm calling Dr. Abrami right now. He's the head of Broca Hospital. Let him try to intercede."

So Sabine waited while Dr. Abrami confirmed that the children, Miron, Léa, Suzanne and her parents were all confined in Drancy. Both the doctor and the director were working furiously to have at least the youngest moved to the hospital.

"We have some time," the doctor assured her. "It's routine for internees to be held for about two weeks before deportation."

But only a few days later, the director informed Sabine that thirty three of the Izieu children and four of the adult supervisors had been sent on rail convoy seventy-one to Auschwitz, and the rest were soon to follow. The haste was never explained.

Dr. Abrami left Drancy empty-handed, but for a single letter written in crayon, addressed to Sabine.

My dearest Sabine,
We are heading for the unknown. Morale is good. The children, parents, Coco and I are all together. Going through Lyon, Drancy, and finally to Metz, I think. See you soon, my dear friend. Hugs and kisses from the little ones and the grown-ups.
Suzanne.

Sadness gathered within her and she could feel it like a cloud in her lungs. The pit of her stomach ached. The hollowness in her chest grew so large it scarcely left room for breath. She hadn't known that emptiness could weigh so much the earth seemed to be pulling at her, dragging her into darkness.

She became terribly ill.

If Sabine had locked herself away from the world for the rest of her life, those who knew her would have understood. But this was not her way. She would not let those innocents vanish, their space in the world simply closing over like water in the fountain at Izieu when she lifted out her hands.

Sabine fought on and fought back, because the story wasn't over yet.

PARIS

MAY 1944

SABINE STAYED ON IN PARIS. There was no place left where she belonged in any case. Her mind was a blank. She had no strategies for surviving the end of the world.

With Berthe's help, she rented a room in a shabby hotel near Place Maubert. The room was spartan—no rugs on the floor or pictures on the wall, just a single bed, a dresser with drawers that stuck, and a scattering of desiccated insects on the windowsill. Down the gloomy hall she found a pungent toilet and a cracked sink for washing up. The hot water boiler in the building wheezed and the pipes knocked and hissed.

During the days, Sabine walked. Though she tried to keep her head down, she kept finding Miron. He was standing in the lobby of a hotel on the Île Saint-Louis reading a newspaper. He was just emerging from a Metro station or walking a dog in Luxembourg Gardens or buying potatoes at the market in Maubert. Her yearning for him was so strong each false sighting rocked her. She often felt dizzy and disoriented. Already she had lost the exact look in his eyes when he said goodbye to her that last morning. Soon there would be nothing left of him but for what she could remember and what she could dream, and she feared the two Mirons would soon be indistinguishable.

Nor did she understand this wounded version of Paris, full of bicycles, queues, sober eyes, and the silence of missing birds.

The language was filled with cautionary euphemisms and codes because the enemy was just around the corner. Even the Parisians' sense of humour had changed, their wittiness weighed down by crude references to various parts of German anatomy. Above all there was a watchful atmosphere, the soldiers' eyes darting everywhere, the citizens' eyes straight ahead, seeing everything and pretending to see nothing. The air smelled of the sweat of both exhaustion and nervous anticipation.

When Sabine could walk no longer, she returned to her hotel. Loneliness leaked through the pores of her skin and curled into the corners of her room and across the ceiling like dark smoke. There was a metallic taste in her mouth and an ache behind her breastbone. The days were losing their shape. Time was fraying, a thread at the cuff. If she pulled it, her memories would unravel.

She looked into the darkness, and saw the House of Izieu, its fragrant spaces and the light it held like wine in a glass. She saw little girls in grass-stained summer dresses, and sisters hand-in-hand, playing tag and climbing trees. She saw little boys and tall boys in wool sweaters coming home from mountain hikes with scraped knees and pine needles in their hair. Perhaps it was summer there already. Perhaps it was always summer there, and gentle, an enchanted place lost in time.

Sabine lay still for a long time, with her eyes closed. She was often awake for thirty hours or more at a stretch before she hit a wall of exhaustion and a sleep so deep it resembled a state of unconsciousness that would descend upon her and protect her from the cruelty of dreams.

Sabine contacted an old friend named Georges Gordon and asked to do something useful. Her instructions were to look for a woman in a yellow dress, sitting on a bench in the Tuileries. On Tuesdays, the woman would be there at noon, carrying a blue umbrella.

The formal French gardens of the Tuileries Palace, which was burnt down during the Commune in 1871, were as carefully laid out as a carpet design with patches of emerald green between straight paths of white gravel, not a pebble out of place. It smelled like grass and freshly spaded earth. Sabine strolled a bit, and then sat down on the bench beside the woman in the yellow dress.

For a few minutes, the two women pretended not to take notice of each other in the manner that was currently fashionable in Paris. Say nothing, see nothing. Eventually, the woman glanced at Sabine. "What's your name?" she asked.

"Jeanne Verdavoire."

"Is that your real name?"

"It's the name on my identification papers."

"I see. You can call me Dorine. That's not my real name either. Who sent you?"

"Georges Gordon. He was a friend of my husband when we lived in Nancy."

"What happened to your husband?"

"What makes you think anything happened to him?"

"You look wrung out."

Sabine sighed. "I've been ill this past month. That's all."

Her lie fell to the ground, heavy as lead, but Dorine didn't dare kick it for fear of what terrible truth might spring out at her. The war spun too many frightening tales. She turned her head and studied Sabine openly. She was unreadable, a cipher. Her hands were folded still in her lap. She hadn't tripped on any of her words, but something dark burned inside her. "You seem unlucky to me," she finally pronounced.

Sabine almost laughed. "There's not a thing left that bad luck can do to me."

"You'd be surprised."

"I doubt it."

"Do you have any particular skills?"

"I'm a nurse, and I—I can draw."

Dorine noticed the hesitation, Sabine's first. She wondered

why. Had she been about to say something else, or was drawing something she had almost forgotten about, or maybe something associated with a painful memory?

"As a nurse, you can get a job anywhere. Why have you come to us?"

How could she explain? Sabine had gone from numerous and enormous responsibilities to none, almost overnight. Where she had once lived in a place so crowded she'd slept in a barn, she was now so alone she was like a moth in a jar. She felt a kinship with all the other lonely people drifting through the streets of Paris. On the nights when she thought maybe it was better not to live in a world without Miron and Léa, her vow to the children saved her. Even though she hadn't been smart or quick enough to protect them from being arrested, a failure she endured with savage self-recrimination, she would pledge her life to them. If she could do one single thing to end the war faster so she might discover their fate or lessen their suffering in the underworld called Auschwitz, she would do it.

She lifted her head and looked at Dorine. "I just need something to do to help end the war," she insisted. "I'm no good at waiting. If you can't use me, say so, and I'll move on."

"Oh, we can use you. You'll be in danger, but you know that already. I hope you're not going to be stupidly brave just because you don't care whether you live or die. Because then I would feel responsible for selecting you, and miserable for not foreseeing any recklessness. More importantly, blind bravery is selfish and puts others at risk. So, please, give a damn."

"You can relax. I'm not brave."

Dorine smiled. Her new recruit was an effortless liar and that would be a boon to her in her work.

Sabine smiled, too. It had been a long time since anyone had worried about her, and Dorine's bluntness was just the tonic she needed to fill her lungs with pure air again. It came as a great surprise to her.

"Are there any people in Paris you need to say goodbye to,

anyone who might need an explanation if you are suddenly gone?"

There was no one. The acknowledgement cut too deeply to speak aloud, so Sabine just shook her head.

"Good. Meet me tomorrow morning at the Gare d'Austerlitz at seven. We're travelling south."

It was May and the French countryside flashed through the windows of the train in a series of white blossoms and bursts of lilac. The changing scenery was the only sign Sabine had that the train was moving, so intent was she on Dorine's words. They were travelling first class, and had a compartment to themselves.

"Who is Jeanne Verdavoire?" she asked.

"What do you mean?"

Dorine sighed, and held out her hand. "Give me your identity card."

Suspicious, Sabine reluctantly gave up her papers.

"When is Jeanne Verdavoire's birthday? Where were you born?

Sabine had to strain to remember the details written on the card. "I think January 27, 1907. Born in Auchy-les-Orchies."

"You hesitated too long. And your birthday is January 28. You'd be arrested for such obvious blunders. What is your back story? You were born in the North, so why are you in the South? Your wedding ring has worn a groove around your finger so obviously you've been married a long time. Details, Sabine, will sell your story. If you can't or won't talk about your real husband, make one up. He should be missing because that's harder to verify in the efficient German records. If he's a prisoner of war, the records could be checked too easily. Stick as close to the truth as you can. Your card says you are without profession. We'll have to get that altered. Are these your real fingerprints?

"Yes."

"And what about the name? Are the Germans going to discover that Jeanne Verdavoire died in her infancy?"

"No. I paid a lot for these papers." Too much, according to Miron, Sabine remembered. "The OSE was careful."

"Ah, so you worked for the OSE. What did you do there? Filing, record keeping?"

"No. No, um, I worked with children."

Dorine, who had a fine, chiselled face, with blue eyes and blonde hair, also had the gift of discerning other people's sorrow, and the kindness to try to soothe it. She'd guessed almost immediately that Sabine was suffering from some unrelenting torment, almost certainly having to do with the children she could not bear to talk about. She decided not to push on the children.

"Your card also says you have blue eyes and blonde hair. We can lighten your hair a bit, and hide it mostly under your uniform. We'll be sending you into a prison as a Red Cross nurse."

"I *am* a Red Cross nurse."

"Yes, but when you're working for us that will only be your cover. You won't be official. I work for the social service section of *Combat*. Have you heard of it?"

"Certainly," Sabine had read issues of the clandestine newspaper that tried to counter German propaganda and delivered real news from the BBC and other, more mysterious sources. "But I've never heard of its having a social service section."

"We try to keep up morale and provide food to the families of resisters, and the men and women already arrested and in French prisons. We're allowed to bring them food parcels, and occasionally we smuggle in news to them. You'll have easier and less suspicious access as a nurse."

"So, I'm just to deliver parcels. What sort of news is in the messages?"

"You don't need to know, but you won't want to be caught with one. Look, Jeanne, you're a smart woman. The Allied invasion is imminent. Combat, along with other networks, is trying to unify the Resistance to assist when the invasion begins. Everyone knows it's coming, especially the Germans. Just keep your head down and don't ask any questions. If you're captured the less you know, the less harm you can do. You will have contact with me and one other agent, that's all. Be careful because my pretty neck is on the line."

"And why is Jeanne Verdavoire travelling south when she was born in the north?"

"You'd better stop thinking of yourself in the third person. And we have one other task for you, one linked to your special talent in drawing.

"When you enter the prison we're sending you to, we want you to notice everything. Find out as much as you can about the layout. Where are the cells? Where are the windows and hallways? How many guards are there and where are they stationed? How many steps are there? Where are the offices? Where is the communications centre—the radios and the telephones? Be as observant as you can without being obvious and then when you return to your room, draw everything as you saw it. Can you do that?"

"I can. I can also speak German. I learned when I was a teenager. It's a bit rusty, but I'll pick it up quickly again."

"Well, aren't you a surprise? Good. Keep your ears open as well as your eyes. This is a French prison, but the Gestapo are everywhere."

"You haven't answered my question. Why am I travelling south?"

"Because this is where your other contact lives. But tell the Germans you came after the demarcation line was lifted for the sea air."

South, much to Sabine's shock, turned out to be Montpellier. It was as if fate kept guiding her back to this hilly city that had altered the course of her life.

"Goodbye and good luck. Your other contact will find you,"

Dorine said, before disappearing among the other passengers on the crowded platform.

Sabine took a tentative step forward, as if she were testing black ice. She stood in line, waiting to have her papers checked, ready to answer questions, but she was waved through quickly. Outside the station, she halted. Where was she supposed to go? She had nowhere to stay, and only a little money left from Berthe. But now that she was part of a network, she couldn't go to her friends for fear of placing them in danger.

At last she spied a friendly face moving towards her. She remembered her old driver very well with his bald head and boxer's build, but she had forgotten the little things, like how he had always ducked his head when he greeted her, and how his smile went all the way to the corners of his eyes.

"Marius," she cried.

"Not anymore," he smiled. "I'm Jean. Such a common name. So hard to check."

"Oh, Marius, it's so good to see you. How are things in Montpellier?"

"The food is terrible. The coffee is nonexistent. Cigarettes are scarce and the Germans plentiful. But the weather is good."

He reached for Sabine's suitcase, which held little more than a change of underwear, a sweater, one summer dress, and a photo of Miron. They walked along leafy streets until they reached the city's central square, Place de la Comédie, and found a table at one of the many sidewalk cafés.

Marius was right. Sabine noted pairs of German soldiers patrolling the square, and a dozen more lounging at the base of the statue of the Three Graces, the city's emblem. Beauty, Charm, and Grace. It seemed that even these goddesses had been conquered, and taken their virtues elsewhere.

"The only thing worth drinking here is *pastis*," Marius warned, ordering two glasses.

The drinks came with a small carafe of water. Marius added a drop of water to the clear *pastis* and watched it turn milky, before downing it in one long swallow. "Any news, Sabine?"

It took some time for her to answer. Gazing at her, Marius could see how loss could suck the air of sound and block the throat. When she finally did speak, he had to lean in to hear her words. "The women and children were sent to Auschwitz. Miron, Théo and Arnold, I'm not sure, maybe Estonia."

"Léon?"

"I don't know."

"Thank God you weren't there."

Sabine looked up sharply. "I'm more sorry about that than I can say."

"That's foolishness. You know it's not your fault. Look around you," he said, nodding in the direction of the soldiers. "Where in this world would those innocents have been completely safe? You did everything you could."

Sabine nodded, and Marius could tell she'd heard all of this before and it was useless to her. He wanted to say that children were resilient, that perhaps they'd survive, that maybe she would find them and her husband again, but it seemed like tempting fate to speak the words, and fate had been so unkind and blind. He remembered how quick-thinking she'd been at the camps, how she had tricked the guards and smuggled out children under their noses. Now he had to call on that spirit again. "Right now we have work to do. Are you ready for this, Sabine?"

She raised her chin. "I am."

"There's a small boarding house just across the square, Rue de la Carbonnerie. It's run by Madame Damas. She's expecting you. She won't ask any questions. In your room, you'll find a Red Cross uniform and a map to the prison. When a food parcel arrives, Madame Damas will let you know. Take it to the prison the same day. When you have something for me, come to this café and I'll find you. Understand?"

"Yes."

"It's good to be working together again. Just one more thing.

Don't be alarmed by Madame Damas. She has the face of a turnip and the temper of a Doberman, but she's on our side." He winked and squeezed her hand, and then he was gone.

A few hours later, Sabine faced another sleepless night in another spartan room, floorboards creaking as she paced. She had everything she needed, and nothing she wanted. When she could stand no longer, she lay down on the bed and studied the face of the young Miron, so confident, so sure of the future, so sure there would be a future. She placed the photo face down on her chest. Maybe his face would melt into her skin and she would breathe in and out with him again in perfect concert.

"Come back," she whispered into the night. "Come back."

The prison was in the southwest section of Montpellier, an old Ursuline convent. According to Madame Damas, the convent was used as a prison as far back as the French Revolution. In the nineteenth century, it housed military barracks and then reverted to a prison for women. It was the presence of the Gestapo now that made the building its most unholy.

Twelve stone steps, Sabine counted, led up to the circular front of the building. Beside the huge wooden front door, there was a bell to pull. Sabine braced herself to face the dreaded black uniform of the Gestapo, but it was a woman in the uniform of the Milice who opened the door.

Minions. Errand boys for the Germans, Sabine thought, but she'd been naïve enough to believe that women had better sense than to join the Milice. Apparently not.

She forced a smile and held out her pass. "I've brought a food parcel for the prisoners."

The woman merely jerked her head as a greeting, and Sabine entered the rotunda. The space was enormous, with high ceilings and a row of windows that looked out into a large courtyard completely enclosed by block buildings, two along the side and one across the back. A series of graceful archways were all that was left of what was once a convent.

Sabine followed her guide to a small office at the shadowy edge of the rotunda, only to face another woman in a Milice uniform, only this one had a tongue. "Open the parcel. Here on the desk," she ordered.

Sabine undid the string holding the parcel together, and waited while the woman pawed through its contents.

"Onions, potatoes, bread, carrots, and an old black overcoat," she intoned. "Hardly seems worth the effort."

"We do what we can," Sabine replied, as pleasantly as she could, all the time wondering if there was a message in this sorry lot. She didn't know where it might be hidden and hoped the woman didn't either. It might be sewn into the lining of the coat, or baked into the centre of the bread, or maybe even part of the onion skin.

The woman waved her hand, apparently uninspired to look further. "You can go."

Sabine was relieved and dismayed at the same time. She'd hardly been inside for more than ten minutes. She'd seen very little.

On the way back through the rotunda, Sabine stopped at one of the square windows overlooking the courtyard.

"Imagine what this must have looked like when the nuns lived here," she said. "Do you think there was once a fountain?"

The guide came to stand by Sabine at the window. "There are no nuns here, more's the pity. The prisoners could use their prayers."

Sabine couldn't hide her surprise. She'd believed that anyone who joined the Milice was incapable of compassion. She looked beyond the uniform for the first time and saw a young woman with red hair and hazel eyes. She had a fierce little face, not pretty, but animated.

"How many prisoners are here?" she risked asking.

"About eighteen in those blocks. But there's a cellar underneath us, and torture chambers. The Gestapo call them interrogation rooms."

"How many?"

"I don't know. I'm not allowed down there."

"Can you get me down there, as a nurse?"

"I'll try. Now you better go."

Sabine made six more visits to the prison, each time adding to her drawings when she returned to her room. Her art training ensured she was precise about dimensions. In fact, her drawings resembled architectural plans. She had the main buildings sketched out, as well as all the windows and visible doorways. She didn't always see the red-haired woman, but when she did she learned where the cellar door was and how many soldiers were usually present during the day. The Gestapo officers, she was told, only came at night.

On the seventh visit, the red-haired woman pressed a key to the cellar door into her hand. "Be quick," she urged. "I couldn't get permission. This is the best I could do."

Sabine acted instinctively. She had no logical reason to trust the red-haired woman, but she did. She entered the cellar, counting steps all the way.

It was not as she imagined it would be. There were no carnivorous rats scuttling across the floor, no flowers of mould blooming across damp walls, no menacing shadows. The space was bright with bare light bulbs hung at intervals overhead. They seemed to be permanently on. Exposed pipes ran along the ceiling, and there was the intermittent sound of water flowing, and the whirring vibration of an engine or a machine, maybe some sort of generator or power source.

There were six cells here, more like cages because their barred tops did not reach the ceiling. Four of them were occupied by shapes slumped on narrow beds. Sabine went from cell to cell, appalled. She saw their swollen faces, black bruises, crooked limbs, bleeding hands. Worse, she saw their eyes, glazed over or desperate, or, once, a flicker of hope. She couldn't help them. She had no keys to the individual doors.

"Who are you?" she whispered to the single man who sat up.

"Doesn't matter," he croaked. "But get her out." He pointed in the direction of the next cell.

Sabine looked in but the figure she saw didn't move. As she was turning away, she suddenly froze, her eyes riveted on a piece of white cotton from a girl's slip caught in the door. It fluttered there for a second like a wounded dove, and then hung limply.

"Who is she?" she asked the other prisoner.

"Monique."

"I'll do my best," Sabine promised, quickly retracing her steps.

The red-haired woman met her at the top of the stairs, grabbing for the key, closing the cellar door and locking it. "Get out of here," she hissed.

Sabine wanted to run, but she forced herself to walk all the way back to Madame Damas' boarding house. She locked herself in her room and worked on her drawings for another hour. Then she changed out of her Red Cross uniform, put on her summer dress, and went to the café to wait for Marius to find her.

She had already ordered a second *pastis*, and was sure one of the patrolling soldiers was regarding her suspiciously, before Marius finally arrived. She had an urge to blurt out everything she'd learned, but a look of caution in her friend's eyes stilled her tongue.

"Come," he said. "Let's take a stroll. We shouldn't linger here."

So they walked calmly and innocently through the square in the opposite direction from Sabine's room and talked of nothing more unsettling than the possibility of rain, or the fine dust blown in from the sea winds that drifted across their skin, while Sabine kept seeing a scrap of cloth trapped in a cage door and the shape of a girl who couldn't move.

They walked all the way to the botanical gardens and found a bench, as if the lush foliage surrounding them would absorb their secrets in the same way it drank in the sunlight and the rain.

"The drawings are done," Sabine began. "I've been down to the cellar, but only once. There are four prisoners there. One of the men, he didn't give his name, says there's a young woman there, Monique. He asked me to get her out."

"Monique is there?"

The name had meant nothing to Sabine, but it seemed to galvanize Marius. "Tell me everything."

In precise detail, she described the steps, the windows, the office, the doorways, the eerily bright cellar, the cages, the handful of soldiers in the courtyard, the Gestapo that only came by night like vampires, and the red-haired woman who'd helped her. She talked until her mouth was dry, as if words were magic spells that could open cage doors.

When she was finished, the two friends sat in silence, listening to the rustling of leaves. Then Marius reached out and took her hand. It seemed almost small in his. They smiled at each other, two souls linked together by conspiracy and danger.

"You've done good work. Don't go back to the prison. You'll be leaving Montpellier tomorrow morning. Dorine will meet you at eight at the train station. Just leave the drawings wrapped up in the Red Cross uniform in your room."

"But Marius—"

"Jean, remember? Goodbye old friend."

He turned away and Sabine watched his large figure gradually grow smaller until it disappeared. So her part was done, that much was clear. She felt frustrated and restless, dismissed and bristling with questions she couldn't ask. Drawings of a prison? She knew what they were for, and now she was to be shut out of the action. But she wanted to act and instead she was being sent away like a schoolgirl who couldn't handle anything more serious than a pencil.

The light was beginning to fade. She had to walk all the way back to her room. Her body began to move, but her mind was stuck on her disappointment. Why didn't they trust her? Why didn't they let her do more?

She wasn't paying attention. She almost collided with a soldier as she re-entered the square. "Watch where you're going," he snarled.

His voice catapulted her back to her senses.

"Papers," he snapped.

While she was fumbling for them, another soldier approached.

"I saw her earlier sitting in one of the cafés. She seemed to be waiting for someone, a man. And then the two of them left the square."

It was the same soldier she'd noticed while waiting for Marius. He spoke in German, but she followed the gist of his words.

"Take her in for questioning," the first soldier ordered.

It happened so swiftly. One moment of carelessness. One moment of thinking only of herself. Perhaps this was exactly what Dorine had tried to warn her about. Maybe she was as naïve as a schoolgirl, after all.

The drawings were the key to everything. She'd been trusted with the most important task of all, and the Germans must never find out.

Now her mind was fully alert, vibrating like a delicate instrument. The soldier was gripping her arm, but she felt nothing. The cafés, the storefronts, the statue of the Three Graces, the people, the square itself—everything seemed to fade away as she tried to keep in step.

The soldier took her to some kind of administrative building, probably attached to the functioning of the now defunct Hôtel de Ville. They entered the nearest office, where Sabine was pushed into a chair.

"Wait here," the soldier ordered.

Sabine leaned her head on the desk a moment, and then sat up straight. This was a proper desk, she thought, with papers strewn across it and a telephone. Someone worked here. Surely the questions wouldn't be too serious. The soldier didn't think she was actually a threat. That notion gave her courage.

Within minutes, the soldier returned with another man in uniform. Again, they talked to each other in German.

"She was in a café, acting suspiciously. Waiting for a man. When he came they left together."

"Who was the man you met?" the second soldier inquired in French.

"It's not against the law to meet a man, is it?"

Wrong answer.

The fist smashing into her mouth stunned her.

Pain lit up the inside of her head. Stars blazed behind her eyelids. She felt a dam burst in her mouth, and she coughed out a spray of blood, blotches of red all over the desk and the papers.

She braced herself for another blow, but what she heard was another voice speaking German, a third man and a very angry one.

"What the fuck? Look at this mess. If you want to question her, take her to the cells. Get this cleaned up. Immediately."

Someone hurriedly thrust a handkerchief at her. She grabbed at it and covered her mouth.

She looked up. The two soldiers were standing with their backs to her, leaning over the desk, intent on wiping up the blood and salvaging the papers.

She had only seconds. She stood up quietly. She backed towards the open door and slipped through into the hallway.

It was only a dozen steps to the entry door.

She covered the lower part of her nose and mouth with the handkerchief and opened the door.

A soldier outside held up his hand for her to stop.

"Please," she said in German. "I came here voluntarily as a witness, but I'm so nervous, my nose began to bleed. If I could just clean myself up." She nodded in the direction of the nearest café.

She waited, her face calm, though her heart was thudding.

The soldier stared at her.

Seconds passed, agonizingly slow.

"All right. Come right back."

Sabine nodded and lowered her head. She marched straight to the café, feeling the soldier's eyes on her back. Once inside, she found the washroom, spit out blood and bits of teeth, and washed her face. She turned her dress inside out to hide the stains and found a kerchief in her purse to cover her hair. Then she walked straight out the back door and disappeared.

Somewhere along the train ride back to Paris, at a lonely country station, Dorine disembarked briefly and talked to a man wearing a fedora. Sabine watched them from the window and thought she caught something wistful in their parting. Perhaps because of Marie-Antoinette, she was attuned to women who fell into hopeless love.

When Dorine returned, she seemed to need several minutes to find the right words to tell Sabine what she'd learned.

"The St. Ursula prison was raided this morning at ten o'clock. A man wearing a Red Cross uniform rushed the door when it was opened to him, followed by half a dozen others. Three of the prisoners in the cellar, including Monique, were rescued. A fourth died. Both the Milice women were killed."

Sabine had nothing to say. She turned her head away and gazed at the landscape. War was never straightforward. She'd helped one woman, only to betray another.

June 6, 1944. Dorine burst through the door of the apartment, her face lit up with excitement. "The invasion, Jeanne. It's finally begun."

Sabine was in the tiny kitchen making ersatz coffee to go with a breakfast of black bread. The cup she was holding crashed to the floor. As she knelt to pick up the pieces, her tears began to flow.

The two women were now living in Dorine's fourth floor

apartment overlooking the main street of the Île St. Louis. Sabine was grateful, both for a room of her own and for Dorine's company, which smoothed out the sharp edges of her loneliness. She still did not sleep for more than a few hours, but when she did her nights were dreamless because her days were crowded with the effort required to navigate a city under occupation.

Paris was practically without gas or electricity. Fuel was mostly newspapers screwed into tight balls and sprinkled with a little water to make them burn longer. The joke was to use pages from the collaborationist *Paris-Soir*, which was already filled with hot air. The *métro* closed from eleven to three on workdays and shut down all weekend. Curfew was at midnight. Skirts that June were short—to save material. Food was scarce and rationing was stringent. Women stood in long, dreary queues for two eggs and two ounces of margarine. The hungrier people became the more willing they were to pedal their bicycles for miles into the countryside to find a farmer equally willing to sell a chicken or a handful of vegetables for an exorbitant price.

Dorine knelt down beside Sabine. "Why are you crying? I'm sensing these aren't tears of joy."

Sabine shook her head. Whenever she tried to talk about her past her throat closed up. For months and months, when she was at the House of Izieu, the invasion was a fairy tale they told the children at night, the magical turn in the tale that would lead to the happy ending of the war. Now it was real, and two months too late.

"You know," Dorine continued. "The best way to deal with misfortune is to talk. I'm here. I'm pretty low risk."

"Misfortune? That sounds like a temporary setback or at worst a broken leg. There's no vocabulary for what happened to us."

"Well then, give me whatever words you have left. And can we please get up from the floor?"

They made their way to the living room, and Dorine opened

the windows wide and let the summer light shine in.

She sat in a chair across from Sabine. "To begin, I think you should know that my name is Denise Mantoux. I come from Aix-en-Provence. My husband is a prisoner of war and I haven't heard from him in months. I don't know if he's alive or dead, and in the meantime, I've fallen in love with someone else."

"The man in the fedora at the train station." It wasn't a question.

"Yes. But I'm a good Catholic and I'll keep my vows until I know if my husband still exists. Now you."

"My name is Sabine Zlatin."

She couldn't go on. She heard a crack like thunder, but that couldn't be right because the sun was so bright. The sound was coming from inside her body. She remained silent. She stared at Dorine, now Denise. The light streaming into the room from the windows behind Denise's chair turned her hair into a wispy halo and dimmed her face.

"Start with the words you remember," Denise urged. She braced herself for she knew the words would be awful.

Finally, Sabine spoke. Her voice had a wavering underwater quality and it was difficult to decipher the sounds she was making as words.

"Sorrow, husband, children, Auschwitz."

Time ceased. A bicycle bell rang from the street far below them. A conversation drifted in through the window. Leaves rustled. The world outside had not vanished.

"Are they dead?" Denise managed to ask.

When Sabine opened her eyes, she saw that the slant of the light had shifted and faded. She didn't know how long she'd been sitting or how long Denise had been waiting for her answer.

"I don't know," she finally said.

"What do you know, for certain?"

"I know numbers. Forty-four children, convoy numbers seventy-one, seventy-three, and seventy-four."

She heard Denise gasp and felt Denise's arms wrap around

her, and then the names came tumbling out: Miron and Léa, Théo, Coco, Nina, Sami, Hans and Max, and on and on into the night she emptied out the House of Izieu until all the people who had helped her there stood beside her in the room and all the tears she had were set loose to glisten in the moonlight.

Denise put her to bed and kissed her on the forehead.

That night she dreamed she was there again helping Philippe and Marie make sandwiches in the kitchen, watching Rénate and Liane pick apples, fluffing a child's pillow, and waving at Miron as he stood at the river's edge—all the small, banal, and utterly beautiful moments that had once made up her daily and blessed life.

When she opened her eyes sometime the next day, sorrow still clung to her, but she had slept for fourteen hours and the dream had soaked into her blood, giving her strength.

As the summer stretched into July and then August, the initial euphoria of the invasion faded. Smug smiles appeared when the Germans erected a signpost pointing to the Normandy front, but sour doubts also arose. The Allied army was a silently approaching thing, like a hurricane spiralling toward the city. It might hit with full fury, or track a different course and miss Paris altogether.

The days of queuing and the nights of darkness went on and on with metronomic regularity. But beneath this placid façade, the men who controlled the Resistance networks in Paris were quietly seething, locked in a political battle of their own.

Sabine was puzzled. "Aren't we all on the same side?" she asked Denise.

"Yes and no. Everyone wants the Germans out, but who steps into their absence is the point of disagreement. The Gaullists or the Communists?"

"Really? Four years of occupation and men are still obsessed with power? Haven't they learned anything?"

"Apparently not."

"How do you know this, anyway? Surely most people believe the Resistance is a united front."

"Yes, unless you work with one group or another."

"Which group did I work for? No," Sabine raised her hand. "Don't tell me. I don't even want to know. And the man in the fedora?"

"He's with the FFI, the French Fighters of the Interior, the Gaullists."

"I see," Sabine said, but she didn't really see. It all seemed crazy to her, this unending struggle for control and domination. It always ended with someone's dreams in shreds, or a fist in the face of the powerless.

She grabbed her shopping bag and set off for another day of lining up for food, but her steps slowed as she reached Notre-Dame. There were many beautiful churches in Paris, but none like this, an eight-hundred-year-old monument to a time when people believed the world was held in something grander than mere human hands. Sabine thought about the centuries of asking in all the churches of Paris for some meaning to reveal itself, and all the centuries that had passed in utter silence, and she was convinced that people were no further advanced than tiny birds flinging themselves from their nests into the air in the naïve expectation of flight.

Two weeks later, early on a Saturday morning still rosy from dawn, Sabine was once again in the square in front of Notre-Dame with Denise, when she saw something astonishing that filled her simultaneously with hope and dread.

Hundreds of men were moving across the square toward the gates of the walled Préfecture of Police only two hundred metres from the church. Bearded and clean-shaven, in shirtsleeves or suits, in berets or fedoras or bareheaded, carrying pistols or rifles or hand grenades or nothing at all, they advanced as one. A priest, his bible in hand, emerged from the Sainte Anne gate of the cathedral and joined the flow of men.

Sabine and Denise couldn't move or speak.

Several minutes later, above the grim and grey roof of the main block of the Préfecture, they saw the French tricolour flapping in the breeze, a singular flag of defiance against a sky of Nazi swastikas.

With or without the Allies, the liberation of Paris had begun.

The next five days were disjointed and chaotic. Nothing was clear. Reports contradicted each other. Spurts of gunfire split the air in isolated pockets all across the city. The cafés were filled with cigarette smoke, tipped over chairs, and shouting. Maybe someone, somewhere was watching a desperate plan unfold, but Sabine lived those days caught up in a bewildering series of events.

No one trusted anything in the newspapers. Instead they read the messages scrawled on walls: *Aux Barricades!* People used whatever was at hand to build barricades on the streets. They pried up paving stones and piled up bedsteads, sandbags, chairs, and subway grills. An antique dealer raided his stock and heaped Louis XVI dining tables and chairs onto the barricade in front of his store, topping it off with a chandelier. On another corner, four men hauled a *pissotière* onto their pile of rubble. Paris had gone back two centuries in a matter of days.

Sabine was unprepared for the noise. After four years of tongue-biting and mute submission, the city was a cacophony of sirens and gunshots, guttural cries and the grinding advance of German tanks. Her ears rang with the whirring of bicycle wheels, running footsteps, and the whooshing sound of Molotov cocktails looping through the air and exploding into yellow flames as they hit their targets.

Her eyes swam with a series of bizarre and surreal images. A bride and groom stood in front of a barricaded *mairie* in the fourth arrondissement, waiting for an official who never came to marry them. Shards of glass glinted in the sun. Char marks stained the pale stone of shops, their awnings blackened and ripped. A woman in an elegant dress wore a Croix de Lorraine armband and the helmet of a fallen German soldier as she stationed herself at the top of a barricade. The Grand Palais, housing a visiting circus, exploded into a mass of flames. The circus horses stampeded. A tiger raced through the streets of Paris, a brief flash of striped beauty, before bullets felled it and a band of hungry Parisians, plates and knives in hand, descended upon the still body. Three SS tanks, like three turkey vultures, positioned themselves in the square in front of Notre-Dame, guns aimed at the Police Préfecture and the glittering glass windows of Sainte Chapelle.

Sometimes, Denise was at Sabine's side. Sometimes Sabine was marooned amid a crowd. In one moment, she was elated and in the next terrified. After the destruction of the Grand Palais, left to burn and pour black smoke into the sky, it was clear the Germans could turn Paris into an inferno. She was incredulous that they hadn't. Every glorious building, monument, and bridge was mined. It would take a single order, a second of time, to turn the world's most beautiful city into a pile of astonished dust.

On the evening of the fifth day of sporadic street fighting, with both hope and light fading, Sabine heard the first sounds of Liberation, the deep rolling waves of the church bells of Notre-Dame. From high in Montmartre, Sacré-Coeur answered, and soon from churches all over the city, the joyous pealing of bells heralded the arrival of the Allies and the imminent end of the Occupation. Windows were flung open, radios blared the *Marseillaise* and American jazz. People sang along, their voices breaking, or sat in their rooms and wept.

Denise pulled Sabine away from the window.

"It's not safe yet."

Not ten minutes after she gave her warning, a volley of gunfire from the German garrison mixed with the sound of the bells.

"We'll wait until morning to go out. Let's get drunk, Sabine, and smoke Gitanes."

Sabine was exhausted, but exhilarated. Her thoughts were like a flock of startled birds, soaring and dipping in circles.

"We don't smoke."

"It's easy. I've seen it in the pictures. You just squint your eyes and look into the distance through the smoke. You look exquisitely bored, as if you can't even remember how the cigarette got into your hand."

"And how did it? Where did you get Gitanes?"

Denise smiled sweetly.

"Ah. The man in the fedora," Sabine laughed. "Are you finally going to tell me his name?"

"Perhaps. If I drink enough wine."

The next day was one of wild contrasts. On one corner, people rushed to greet the French and American soldiers. They cheered and hollered and pressed gifts into their hands—dusty bottles of champagne from closet corners, good luck charms, flowers, fruit, kisses, and even rabbits given reprieve from balcony cages. But on other corners, infantry dug in to face the last menace of German resistance. Sabine and Denise wandered from place to place, staying on the periphery. Sometimes they waved and hugged the people next to them in the crowd. Sometimes they took cover and wished they hadn't seen the grandmother leaping with joy, caught in mid-air by a sniper's bullet, or the German soldier, his uniform in tatters, frantically pedalling a bicycle before a column of fast-moving tanks that passed over him as if he were nothing more than a bump in the road.

"I've seen enough," Sabine said to her friend. "I'll meet you back at the apartment."

As she walked slowly back to Notre-Dame she witnessed a group of Parisians tearing down the hated German signposts, setting their own language free again, she supposed. She passed a young girl, thin as a willow switch, eating a bar of American chocolate with a look of reverence on her face as if she were discovering the sensuality of taste for the first time. She said hello to a man sitting alone at a sidewalk café. He was handing out old postcards of Paris as it had been before the war, inviting the world back to the city of his memory.

Sabine felt a kind of numbness as dusk fell softly over a free Paris, a natural hangover of the day's emotional extremes. Gradually, the horizon became a blue-black line against an even darker sky. Everything that held light, street lamps, lit up windows, the moon, glowed full and bright. The night was too tender to abandon, so she began to wander the narrow streets east of the great cathedral, vacant now with the echoing quality of an empty stage after the players had shrugged off their roles and gone home.

She heard him, before she saw him, an indistinct shape at first, huddled in a doorway.

She took a step closer.

It was a soldier, and with a sharp intake of breath she saw it was a German soldier.

The Germans had ruined her life. They had laid waste to the House of Izieu. Their cruelty had pushed beyond any possible line of forgiveness. Pure hate blazed within her.

The German opened his eyes and looked at her.

She knew he was dying. She could step on his throat right now and he would be defenceless.

Still, he stared at her face and she saw his lips move.

She moved closer until he was less than an arm's length away. She saw he was just a boy, probably no older than Théo or Arnold or Paul Niedermann. Perhaps he had crawled into the alley to hide or simply been abandoned here by those soldiers who could still run.

She knelt down and held his hand until he died. The moment was so brief, like a sigh.

She brushed her hand gently over his face, closing his eyes, and felt something dark lift away from her.

Afterwards, she remembered the weight and heat of his hand in hers, and how quickly his skin had cooled.

She left him where he had fallen and made her way back to the square in front of Notre-Dame. There she saw Denise running towards her. She moved with a lambent glow, partly because of the shining street lamps so long forbidden, and partly because she was in love. She reached for the arm of the man with her and smiled radiantly at Sabine. "This is Jake Shaw. He's from England, and I'm going to marry him."

Without the shadow cast by a fedora, Sabine saw a handsome and intelligent face under a tumble of blonde curls.

It was the night the war should have ended, but it didn't.

Back in Belley where the streets were shrouded in darkness and the blackout curtains were drawn tight, Marie-Antoinette held still, barely breathing and listening intently.

She heard the knocks again. Three furtive knocks at her back door.

Marie-Antoinette lived in a two-bedroom apartment above a lingerie shop with a back door that could only be reached by a rarely used staircase. A person didn't come upon it or climb it without intention.

She opened the door and couldn't believe her eyes. At first she thought she must be looking at a ghost, but when she reached out her hands, the man she touched was solid and real. She pushed his sandy hair back from his face, and shook her head. "Léon." She quickly pulled him inside and locked the door behind him. "My God, Léon. I thought—"

"I know. My sister warned me and I jumped out a window."

He braced himself waiting for her reaction, some sign that she considered him a coward, but all he saw was a flash of joy before the sadness settled back into her green eyes. Still pretty, but she didn't look the same. Something was gone, some spirit perhaps, some lightness. She had always been so extravagant, but now she seemed softer, maybe even vulnerable.

"You don't look the same either," she said. "Maybe it's the beard." She kept her voice light, but she was shocked at how gaunt he looked, how hollowed under the eyes. He may not be a ghost, but he was certainly haunted.

She led him to the sofa and leaned over to kiss his forehead. "Do you need anything? Are you hungry?" she asked.

"No. I just wanted to see you."

She sat down beside him. "What happened? Where have you been?"

He was grateful he could stare straight ahead into the dim room and not have to see her face. He felt the images of that terrible day start to surface. "I'd only arrived maybe half an hour before the raid. I was upstairs with my sister. I swear I didn't hear a thing. I've thought about it again and again and the Germans must've let the trucks glide down the hill, because I didn't hear them. Only the sound of the children in the dining room.

"I was heading downstairs and I saw three men in plain clothes disappearing down the hall. One of them spoke to me, in French, without any accent. I can't remember what he said. Then Suzanne, who'd gone down before me, turned back and told me to get out. *It's the Germans. Get out,* she said. I jumped from the window and laid flat on the ground. If the Germans had bothered to look, they would've found me easily. I often wish they had. They took my parents, my sister, and my nephew. I delivered Max and Maurice from the boarding school in Belley right into their hands. If only I hadn't picked them up on my way, they would've been safe."

"If only. If only. That will only end in madness, Léon."

"Have you heard anything? Have you heard from Sabine?"

"I sent the telegram. I found out the children were sent to Lyon and then immediately to Paris. To Drancy. They were all deported. That's all I know."

Léon shuddered. There was no place for his thoughts to settle that wasn't a quagmire of guilt and anger and regret. Every day he had to struggle not to sink into the earth.

"Sabine?" he managed to ask.

"I'm sure she followed them to Paris and tried to intervene, but I can't be certain where she is now. You haven't told me where you've been."

"Monsieur Perticoz has been hiding me in his barn. But his wife is worried that the farm is being watched. So I slipped away a couple of nights ago. I don't want to put them in any more danger."

"Fine. You can stay here. You just have to be careful not to move around during the day when the shop downstairs is open. You might find it a bit crowded, but it won't be for long. Paris has been liberated and the Germans are getting ready to run. They won't try to defend a backwater like Belley. Philippe says the Resistance is ready to fight."

"Philippe is here?"

"Nearby. He and Marie weren't taken in the raid. They'd gone on holiday. Like all of us, they were devastated."

"But you said it might be crowded. I thought that meant someone was already here."

For the first time, Marie-Antoinette smiled. "Someone is. Gérard Bendrihem, the doctor's son. Lucie had always intended to hide him with me. He's sound asleep right now. You'll have to share the bed or sleep on the floor."

"Tell me, how do you know the order for the raid came from Lyon? Perhaps it came locally, from someone in Belley."

"I made it my business to find out. I still work in the *sub-préfecture*, for the Germans now. They're careless around me. Reassuringly unimaginative. How threatening could a dim little secretary be? I only wish I could speak German because then I would know even more. Whatever information I can get I pass on to Philippe."

It was a glimpse of the old Marie-Antoinette. Still irreverent. Still smart. He watched her cross the room and rummage in a drawer. When she came back she held out a gun.

"Here. Take this, in case you need to protect the boy."

The gun looked German, but he couldn't be sure. He didn't

know much about guns. He took it from her and hefted its weight. "I used to not believe in these," he said wearily.

"I'm told they still work, whether you believe in them or not."

"But what about you? Are you safe working in the same office?"

Marie-Antoinette shrugged. "I treat them with the same hypocritical politeness as they treat me. I'm fine," she lied.

She decided not to tell him she woke up every morning disbelieving and found it impossible to reconcile the happiness of her time spent at the House of Izieu with her despair at its fate. He didn't need to know that nothing was clear to her any longer, that everything was cloudy now like the water in a vase of dying flowers, that the only time she smiled was when she was with little Gérard. Instead, she coaxed him into eating some bread and the last of her cheese. She gave him a blanket and urged him to sleep.

"Goodnight, Léon," she whispered, being careful not to wake the child, his limbs sprawled, his face relaxed, his breathing sweet and deep and strong.

Unbelievably, miraculously, agonizingly, the war finally ended.

Paris saw its share of revelry and revenge. Some collaborators met the rough justice of the street—a short noose and a long struggle on a lamppost. Others slithered away, and still others faced formal charges in the courts.

Denise and Sabine sat in the kitchen, reading about the plans for the Nuremberg trials. Klaus Barbie had been charged, but not arrested. He seemed to have disappeared from the face of the earth. The prospect of his being found guilty *in absentia* left a sour taste in Sabine's mouth.

"The war is over, but nothing seems to have changed. Even justice is hit or miss," she sighed, pushing the newspaper away.

"Oh, just watch," Denise insisted. "One thing will change for sure. There'll be a national amnesia. Everyone will have been in the Resistance and no one will admit they collaborated. Vichy itself will be buried. And as for women? We'll be expected to return to our household duties and not make a fuss."

"Well at least the government is talking about giving women the vote for the contributions thousands of women made to the Resistance."

"Maybe, or maybe just because our story fits so neatly with the De Gaulle myth of a unified and reborn France. I doubt we'll see many women, even the heroines of the Resistance, given positions of power."

"So what will you do?"

"My husband is dead. That's been confirmed. So I'll marry again. But I won't give up what I've learned about my abilities and myself. Maybe I'll start a business or go back to school. What will you do?"

"I still don't know where my husband is, or what happened to him. I don't know what happened to any of the people I loved."

"Well, I have an idea. Until Jake comes back from England, I'm going to work with Henri Frenay in the Ministry set up to help returning prisoners of war and deportees. You might be able to find out what happened if you come and work with me. That is, if you think you can bear it."

"I can bear anything to find out. I'm just not sure what I'll do when I know."

Frenay, who had helped found Combat, negotiated with De Gaulle to procure a building large enough to provide medical assistance and temporary shelter to the thousands of prisoners of war and concentration camp survivors making their way back to Paris. The Hotel Lutétia, a beautiful Art Nouveau building in the Saint-German-des-Prés area of the sixth arrondissement, became Sabine's second home. She and Denise were quick to appreciate the irony of the site, for the Lutétia had once been the centre of German counter-espionage, its gracious ballroom the venue for glittering parties to entertain the commanders of the occupation. In their haste to flee Paris, the Germans left behind a dozen refrigerators filled with meat, cheese and butter, and a cellar full of the finest wines.

Sabine soon discovered that her secretarial skills were negligible. She couldn't type a word, but her organizational skills were brilliant. Within a few weeks, she was able to procure vital medical supplies and piles of clean clothing and linens. With her Red Cross connections, she set up a radiology centre and a staff of workers to help deportees find their families. Denise was thrilled when Sabine was asked to become the director of the repatriation centre. "After all you've been through, and all you've done, you're the perfect choice, Sabine."

But though she was happy to serve, Sabine found the work emotionally gruelling. Pictures of the still missing lined every wall of the Lutétia's huge lobby, and every day letters arrived from every corner of Europe from people still searching. If every name weighed an ounce, and all the names were piled on top of each other, the desk where she was sitting would buckle and the floor underneath her would crack open. The building itself would shudder and sink into the ground. Sabine felt the crush of those names like an iron bar pressing down on her shoulders.

Many of the people pouring into the hotel every day had touched the very border of death. They were fragile and exhausted. Some of them had lost their limbs, and some had lost their minds. These poor senseless wretches would wander this way and that, with only the air to talk to because people avoided them and averted their eyes. Sabine thought of them as holy fools for they lived in the purity of the moment. They had lost their reason and thus, also, their grief, their fears, and their memory. She treated them with special gentleness, helping them remove their rags and put on clean clothes, and feeding them tiny bits of food so that their shrunken intestines would not burst.

Most of the time, the repatriation centre was surprisingly quiet. There was the low humming of voices and the occasional ringing of a telephone, but the deportees were unsettled. They looked down at the shining floor and up at the chandeliers as if they couldn't quite believe in them. They seemed eager to ask questions, but feared to disturb anyone and so held their tongues until spoken to by one of the workers. They were grateful for the slightest touch or acknowledgement.

But every few days, a shouted name or a cry of joy, a miracle of recognition or reunion, would shatter the quiet. Heads would be buried in embraces and tears would flow and a life would be reclaimed.

Sabine longed for the day when this might happen to her. She studied every face. Her heart jumped each time she saw a child. She pasted photos of Miron and Théo and Arnold on the lobby walls. And then one day, her eyes met those of another woman. A tremor of recognition. Léa?

Sabine stood up, but her legs were shaking so badly, she sat down again. She tried to follow the woman with her eyes but she was quickly gone. There was an ache so hollow and lonely in her stomach that she felt faint. Perhaps she was only seeing another memory or an apparition.

"Sabine." The voice floated around her, light as a feather, brushing her skin as if it were a caress.

"Is it really you, Léa?"

"It is. I'm here."

Slowly, Sabine rose to her feet. The two women stood face-to-face, their hands tracing each other's bodies as if they were blind. Sabine could feel the bones under Léa's skin. Her fingers brushed the numbers tattooed on her arm. But Léa's gaze was steady, her eyes bright, her soul untouched and unsullied. She smiled and suddenly Sabine's grey world was shot through with colour again, like fireworks bursting across a night sky.

"The children?" Sabine whispered.

"It is thanks to the children that I'm here to tell what happened that day. My love for the children saved me, but I was unable to do the same for them."

"All of them?"

"Remember them the way you loved them."

Sabine pressed one hand over her mouth and the other one over her stomach, as if to keep her screams locked inside and her body in one piece. The anguish she felt could rock the room, but nobody except Léa seemed to notice the trees crashing to the earth and the sun exploding. They thought the world was just as it had been a moment ago.

Léa stayed for four months with Sabine and Denise, growing physically stronger every day. The House of Izieu was like a bruise, painful to touch, but with gentle coaxing from Denise the other two women began to set free the splendid lightness of those days: Coco dressed as a tomato, Barouk's glorious voice, Suzanne's magical dance.

Sometimes they talked all night and sometimes they laughed.

Léa did not speak of Auschwitz. Whenever Sabine had the courage to ask, which wasn't often, she would tell Sabine not to think about the children's last week, but to hold dear instead the year of joy she had given them. She would not say little Émile was torn from her arms by a guard, the same guard who had kicked her aside with a boot to her abdomen when she tried to follow. She would not describe the column of children marching hand-in-hand to the gas chambers. Instead she swore she felt the children's presence in the world, in the beauty of twilight and the smell of lavender, in roses that bloomed despite the wreckage of war, and in the innocence of birds. As she always had, she taught Sabine how to bear the unbearable.

When she felt they were strong enough to part, Léa told Sabine of her plan. "I'm leaving at the end of the week. I'm going to Palestine. Will you come with me?" Léa already knew the answer to her question, but she asked it anyway, for friendship's sake.

Sabine shook her head. "There's still Miron, and the two

older boys. It's probably pointless to hope, but I need to stay where he might find me."

When the day came, Denise and Sabine accompanied Léa to the ship, *Exodus*. Her whole life was in one suitcase. They embraced and Léa placed her hands on either side of Sabine's face. "My dear friend," she whispered, as tenderly as she could. "Don't wear your pain like a medal. Please do something with it."

Sabine heard those words for days afterwards. She pondered what she might do. She had no desire to parade her sorrow, but neither could she allow the crimes of the past to slip unnoticed into the darkness of the occupation. Denise had been right. Already, France spoke of *les noir ans*, the black years. People were eager to forget, to blot out bad memories like a spill of ink on a pristine page.

Her decision to travel to a conference in Geneva was a declaration of her devotion to the children of Izieu. She would tell their story, no matter how much it hurt to revisit those days, as testimony to crimes against humanity.

But even as she set out on her journey—her suitcase was under her desk and she had a ticket for an afternoon train—her past lashed out at her again.

She happened to glance down the hallway where pictures of the missing still hung, waiting for someone to claim them. She saw a small man with red hair studying the photos. Something about him called to her and she went to stand beside him.

"I'm Madame Zlatin, the director here. Do you recognize someone?"

They shook hands and the red-haired man pointed to the photos of Miron, Théo, and Arnold. "These three men, I know them. We were in the same prison."

Sabine reached up and took down the picture of Miron. Though her hands were shaking, her body was rigid, as if a steel bar were running down her spine. "This is my husband. And these boys are my children."

The man stared at her. She saw his face was pale and as wrinkled as a winter apple, his eyes cloudy. Perhaps he was mistaken.

"Are you sure?" she moaned.

"We worked in the mines. But one day, when the Russians were approaching, the Germans told us to chop wood in the forest. As soon as we were hidden in the trees, the Germans opened fire. These men and a dozen others were killed. This was July 31, 1944, in Tallinn in Estonia. I am sorry, Madame."

He reached out and placed a hand on her shoulder. She could not bear even an ounce more of weight. The steel bar in her spine snapped and she collapsed to the floor.

To assuage Sabine's suffering, Denise postponed her wedding and hid her one photo of Jake in a drawer in her room. It seemed almost grotesque to her that she could be happy about her future when Sabine was facing a void. She marvelled that her friend could still walk and talk, that she hadn't been driven witless by the enormity of her losses.

"You don't have to do that," Sabine insisted. "I've been mourning my husband since the day I last saw him. And now, kindness itself to the end, he's taken my nightmares away with him. It's the two boys, those brave, handsome teenagers that my heart aches for, the last of the children."

"Surely not the last."

Sabine raised her head.

"You're not discounting those who are living, I hope," Denise continued. "The babies you rescued, Dianne and Yvette, will be toddlers by now. What about Paul Niedermann and Henri Alexander, safe in Switzerland, or the children who stayed at Izieu for only a few months before being reunited with their families or smuggled across the border? It might do you some good to see them, or see your friend with the name that always reminds me of a queen."

"You mean go back to Izieu?"

"I don't know, Sabine. I can't pretend to advise you. But listening to you and Léa, I could see it was a place of great love. Perhaps it still is."

Sabine didn't respond, but several days later, she smiled at Denise. "Her name is Marie-Antoinette, and she is rather like a queen. I'm going to visit her. What do you think?"

"Well, your suitcase is still packed."

Sabine had forgotten how rejuvenating the countryside could be. A scattering of tiny villages huddled around church spires. Through the window of the train, she gazed out at long stretches of green and golden fields. When she left the train, she saw the leaves of a thousand trees resplendent in the sun, and heard the birdsong and bees and the rustling of tall grasses like faint music from a thousand violins.

Marie-Antoinette was waiting for her just outside the offices of the *subpréfecture.*

Everything that could or should be said happened in the moment their eyes met and each saw the subtle changes pain had wrought in the other. A stranger might have seen no visible alteration at all. A clairvoyant might have seen a deep purple aura, the colour of a thundercloud. But these two women read the silent etchings of bereavement as clearly as if they were branded on their foreheads.

Between them muteness was eloquence. Words were superfluous because what use would a sentence be when any sentence uttered about Izieu would be filled with stutters, pauses, and gasps for breath? Once that moment of meeting each other again was over, they felt freed of a burden and were pleased to be with each other.

"Tell me," Sabine pressed, as they walked the streets of Belley on their way to Marie-Antoinette's apartment. "Have you heard from Pierre-Marcel?"

"Oh, yes. He was sent to Chantellerault near Poitiers for the remainder of the war. He's something of a local hero now. When the Germans were leaving, he negotiated their safe retreat in exchange for their not destroying the Henry IV Bridge. Noelle and the children are with him, and they're happy to stay there. Belley has too many ghosts."

"Was he sent away by the Germans because of the House of Izieu?"

"I think so, but I can't be sure. It might have been because they suspected he was supplying identity papers to the Free French."

"He was?"

Marie-Antoinette grinned. "My own father recruited him."

"But he wasn't arrested?"

"Pierre was too clever for that. I think the Germans actually admired him for never bending his head to Vichy, and he was so loved here, arresting him would have stirred the people against them."

"And you still miss him?"

"Sometimes. He sends me postcards signed, *with affection, Pierre*." Marie-Antoinette rolled her eyes and laughed. "Come on. I have a surprise for you."

She unlocked her apartment door and led Sabine into a pretty room, flooded with light. A boy of about twelve looked up from the book he was reading and smiled. He had a delicate nose, large brown eyes under straight brown hair, and a shy glance. He was a beautiful boy. When he stood to greet her, she could see he was tall for his age.

"Gérard?" Sabine cried. "Is it you?"

Woman and child embraced as Marie-Antoinette looked on proudly. "Gérard is going to be a doctor like his father."

Gérard nodded. "I'm grateful every day that you found me, Madame Sabine. Marie is my new mother now."

Sabine raised an eyebrow. "You're allowed to call her Marie, and not Marie-Antoinette?"

"The longer name seemed too formal to us. I'd prefer to call her Maman, but I'm to honour the memory of my parents, so we settled on Marie. I'm the only one allowed to call her that. It's special."

They ate dinner in a festive mood and talked about Izieu, which Gérard recalled from his brief time there, as a raucous summer camp. When the boy had retired to bed, Sabine asked about the fate of his father.

"It's difficult to piece together. I understand he was forced on the death march to Gross Rosen when the SS evacuated Auschwitz in 1945. He died of exhaustion in March of 1945 at Buchenwald."

Sabine was silent for some time. "I often wonder if my visit to him alerted the Gestapo to the presence of the House of Izieu."

"We'll never know. Certainly he was questioned at Montluc prison, and no one kept secrets there. But the Germans seized records from the raid on Chambéry, too, and might have easily found reference to the House of Izieu there. Or there may have been an informer. There was an investigation here that threw suspicion on Lucien Bourdon, a farmer in Brens near Izieu. Apparently, he accompanied the Gestapo on the raid, but he swore he was commandeered to give directions only. There was no proof of a denunciation.

"A second man, André Wucher, was also accused because his son, Réné, was with the children and released. Réné's aunt stopped the convoy to rescue her nephew. That's how we learned that the Germans took the pig Farmer Perticoz had given Herman for Christmas. But we'll get no answers from Wucher. He was executed in August, 1944, by an anonymous group of resisters with their own scores to settle. But I swear, Sabine, that no one in Izieu ever betrayed the children. The villagers continued to hide the children they had until the end of the war, and they mourned those lost deeply."

"I wonder if there'll ever be an end to mourning."

"Mourning, yes. Remembering, no. I used to believe that constant sorrow would make me grow wise and strong, but I overestimated myself. Eventually, I decided to be happy again, for me and for Gérard. It's what the children would want for you."

"You make it sound simple."

"I didn't say it was simple, but it's possible. It's like those stories about a rabbit kept in a cage for so long that when the door is opened, the rabbit is afraid to move. You have to take the first hop. You're the only one who can open the cage door."

With that, she kissed Sabine on the forehead, and said goodnight.

Their excursion to Izieu the next day in Marie-Antoinette's new car was a hymn to their common past, the summary of a story disappearing in the distance, with no possibility of redress. They stood together at the top of the hill overlooking the House of Izieu, bright in the sunlight. The Rhône still flowed as it had for centuries, and the sight and sound of that flow was soothing.

"I gathered up everything," Marie-Antoinette said. "All their pictures and drawings, letters, and toys. I kept them for you."

"Thank you."

"You'll think me ridiculous, but this place still seems inviolable to me. I still see the children by the fountain, on the terrace, through the windows. I hear their voices in the trees. Léon calls it a hallucination, not of the mind, but of the soul."

But Sabine didn't think her friend was seeing things. The children had purposely left traces of themselves, messages that could be read by anyone who had loved them. She could sense their presence. She felt like an actress after a performance returning to an empty stage, contemplative, still hearing the echoes of the brief world she'd created with her words and actions, still aware of the magic.

"Where is Léon?" she asked. "Why hasn't he tried to find me?"

"He feels ashamed to be alive. He thinks he should have saved them, or at the very least, been arrested with them."

"But that's so wrong."

"Yes, it is, Sabine. He's built a cage for himself, too."

Sabine stood for so long without uttering a single word that the light began to shift and the breeze grew cooler.

Marie-Antoinette waited patiently.

Finally, Sabine turned to her. "I'd like to design a simple stone monument, maybe the head of a boy and a girl against a Star of David. I'd like it to be placed at the crossroads between here and the village of Izieu. Do you think that's possible?"

"I think the villagers will be very pleased to help you."

Later that day, Sabine sent a telegram to Denise: *Coming home. Plan your wedding.*

She thought about how Denise had constantly had to hide her own happiness and curb her own joy for fear of seeming insensitive. She thought about how many hours she'd listened, how weighed down by compassion she must have been, for there was nothing heavier than carrying another's pain and being powerless to lift it.

Sabine braced herself to open the door of her cage.

THE TRIAL

THE YEARS DRIFTED BY like leaves falling from autumn trees, barely noticeable in the moment and yet slowly accumulating. Sabine lived in a large apartment over an atelier in Paris where she sold paintings of figures drawn from theatre, dance, and the circus. She became well known as a designer, and often thought of her father as she sat at her drafting table. In the evenings, if the weather was mild, she liked to linger on her tiny balcony and admire the greenery that flowed over the railings like Rapunzel's hair in the fairy stories Marie-Antoinette used to dramatize for the children on the terrace of the House of Izieu.

There was a school near her apartment and she often watched the children walking in crocodiles in the street. The children of Izieu were never so orderly, and the thought made her smile. They were more like wild ponies full of skittish energy, roaming free in a sea of grass under an innocent blue sky.

It took many years but eventually she learned to accept even her most painful memories, for without them it would have seemed as if she had never been young, or in love, or as tender as a mother. She had friends who were dear to her. Berthe still visited from Montpellier. Denise had married her Jake, but could not bear the drizzle of England and so returned to France with her husband and daughter, a sweet, rosy girl. Sabine had entered a bistro one day in 1968 and had found Philippe either by accident or fate. His mother, Marie, had retired to the Jura, but Philippe missed the sensual freedom and relative anonymity of Paris. He showered her with kisses when they met and insisted on cooking for her. She ate at his bistro twice a week and he never allowed her to pay and never served her anything made with apples.

"There are no apples allowed in my restaurant," he teased, "not after living on them for three months."

Among her friends, there was no need to speak of the past, and Sabine did not tell her story to strangers or passing acquaintances. If they were invited to her apartment, they might notice framed photographs of a man with hair brushed straight back from a broad forehead, or two handsome teenagers, or a group shot of smiling children in costumes, but she didn't offer to explain who they were and there was something about her demeanour which forbid her guests from asking.

Twice a year, Sabine travelled to Izieu: on April 6, the day of the raid, and on July 31, the day of her marriage to Miron and the day of his death. She placed flowers at the foot of the memorial and visited with Marie-Antoinette and Gérard, all grown up now and a doctor just as he'd promised. The villagers always welcomed her and she was grateful that they shared her need to commemorate the past in this tiny corner of France, even though the rest of the country and most of the world did not seem to notice.

In what had become a relatively peaceful and useful life, not without some comfort and pleasure, there was one friend Sabine could not reach. Léon Reifman finally came to visit her, sometime in the late 1950s. His appearance shocked her, for his face was so gaunt he reminded her of the wrung out deportees who had once wandered the lobby of the Hotel Lutétia. All the fight inside him was gone, and his eyes emanated darkness.

She made him coffee and listened while he told her of the mood swings that plagued him and the migraines that blinded him. Nights were worse than days, and most days he felt he was pushing against gale force winds. Each face from his memory was a portal to misery. He'd sunk to a place she'd already climbed out of and she didn't want to go back there, even if it might help him to have company.

Sabine shook her head. She tried patience, kindness, consolation, and reason, but nothing she tried could penetrate the stone wall of his perfect sadness because Léon, she suspected, did not want to live a life that had been spared for no reason that he could fathom. She knew it could be seductive, that perfect sadness.

Eventually, she resorted to a direct attack. "I never thought you a coward for jumping out a window, but perhaps you're one now." She did not mean to be cruel. She only wanted him to focus his eyes on his own life, but she might just as well have slapped his face.

He flinched from her words and hung his head.

"You might try to visit Léa in Israel," she urged, more gently.

"To be among other Jews mourning their lost families, you mean?"

"No. To be among people rebuilding their lives."

Léon left her home soon after and she let out a breath she didn't realize she'd been holding.

Many years passed before she saw him again. The second time, he brought Paul Niedermann, as tall as ever and twice as handsome as Sabine remembered. He was drawn immediately to her photo of Théo.

"We promised each other we'd meet up again after the war. He taught me how to swim, and I pretended to teach him how to court Paulette. We were best friends."

Sabine noticed the way Paul's smile began at his mouth and then crept up into his eyes.

"I'm a photographer now, and a translator of technical documents. I wouldn't be anything if you hadn't taken me in, Madame Sabine, and if Léon hadn't helped me cross the Swiss border." He shook his head. "My life was saved simply because I was too tall for my age. Imagine that."

"Yes, imagine." Léon repeated.

Sabine thought she saw a spark in Léon's eyes when he spoke. Perhaps, after all, he'd found some consolation in the utter arbitrariness of the universe. She wished him well.

Sabine did not pay much attention to the aftermath of the war, except to notice that Paris had become lovely again. Hatred of the Germans was like an addiction she wanted no part of, for it corroded the insides of the hater more than the hated. She knew that Barbie had put himself beyond the reach of justice. There were escape routes, ratlines they were called, for those Nazis with foresight, looted money, and secrets to sell. The Americans whistled in the wind, folded their arms, and were up to their necks in collusion.

All of that changed in the early 1970s when she was visited by a young lawyer, Serge Klarsfeld. He had a round face, kind eyes behind black-framed glasses, a determined chin, and a mission.

Barbie, he told her, was in Peru, living under the name of Klaus Altmann. "We, my wife, Beate, and I, want to have him extradited. Will you help?"

"Bring him to France and I'll testify on behalf of the children of Izieu. But I can't help to identify him because I never saw the man."

"I swear to you, Madame, he will return to France. He will stand trial."

"I already know what he'll say. *I was a soldier. I followed orders.*" Sabine had heard this kind of rationalization before and still found it breathtaking in its cowardice. There was always some excuse, a finger to be pointed at someone else, an anonymous order to be obeyed.

"Madame, he signed the order that sent the children to Drancy. And we have a witness, Raymond Geissmann, director of the Union Générale des Israélites de France in 1943-44. He tried to stop the executions of Jews at Montluc prison, Jews whom Barbie had arrested. Monsieur Geissmann asked that they be deported instead, for no one knew for certain then what deportation meant. In his answer, Barbie revealed that he certainly knew, and so betrayed himself."

"What did he say?"

"Shot or deported, there's no difference."

Sabine sagged in her chair. Was a man who could say that, and still send forty-four children to certain death, capable of remorse, or was he a soulless mechanism? "He will say the war was over long ago."

"Perhaps. But we will try him for crimes against humanity, for which there are no statutes of limitation."

"I'll testify."

"One last thing, Madame. People are often disappointed at these trials."

"Meaning?"

"They expect Nazis to radiate menace. They will especially expect that of this one, given his crimes as the Butcher of Lyon. But all you'll see is an old man, stooped and balding."

"I hope not. I might be tempted to pity him then, and he doesn't deserve it."

After Serge had left, Sabine followed every bit of news she could find on Barbie for almost a decade. He had aligned himself with the Bolivian army and instructed them in his special skills of interrogation and torture. He was rumoured to have been instrumental in the capture and execution of Ché Guevara. He ate at the finest clubs, and rubbed shoulders with drug lords and dictators. The first attempt to kidnap him failed. He skipped back and forth over the borders of Peru and Bolivia as free as a bird.

She stopped reading. To even think about him was to teeter on the edge of an abyss, a yawning void that promised to plunge her into whirlpool of howling demons and madness. She backed away from that threat, backed away from hate and revenge, and thought that justice wasn't meant for this world.

But Serge Klarsfeld never gave up, and in the early morning of February 5, 1983, a small miracle occurred. An airplane landed in France carrying Klaus Barbie, who was immediately taken to Fort Montluc in Lyon, the very place where he had once interrogated the forty-four children of Izieu.

It took four years to bring Barbie to trial, four years of searching for witnesses to testify, four years of gathering strength and sifting through documents to find the telegram signed by Barbie and sent to Paris, addressed to the head of the German security police and to the attention of the Gestapo department for Jewish affairs. That telegram gave details of the roundup at Izieu and included the deportation order to Drancy.

On May 27, 1987, the sun was shining when Sabine, white-haired and eighty years old, arrived at the Lyon courthouse. She hoped the trial would be dignified, and not a carnival of hate. She shied away from the flashing cameras and looked into the faces of those who stood with her: Léa and Léon, the schoolteacher Gabrielle, Paul Niedermann, and the still lovely Paulette Paillarés. She embraced Madame Halaunbrenner, the mother of Mina and Claudine, and Madame Benguigui, the mother of Jacques, Richard, and Jean-Claude. Only her youngest child, Yvette, had survived, because she was too little to reside at the House of Izieu.

The courtroom was huge and solemn. When Sabine entered, it fell silent as a church, as a stone, as a grave. She had to lean her head back slightly to see the judges, so high did they sit presiding over the lawyers and the reporters and the people who were here to tell what they had seen with their own eyes.

She stood up straight. There was something compelling in her gaze. When she spoke, her words were as sharp and clear as glass. She spoke without hesitation or sentiment or tears, nothing to blur or soften the edges of her words.

She had papers—letters the children had written, pictures they had drawn and signed to each other, birthday cards and photographs. She had facts, dates, numbers, and names. Forty-four names. Her husband's name. She had evidence.

She did not look at the murderous man with the black eyebrows.

"Above all," she said, "I want to say to Barbie's defence that Barbie always said that he only dealt with members of the Resistance and *maquisards*; in other words, enemies of the German Army. I ask you, the children, these forty-four children, what were they? Were they members of the Resistance? Were they *maquisards*? What were they? They were innocent."

Barbie pled not guilty as she'd always known he would. She wondered if he truly believed that. She wondered how he hadn't noticed when his crimes became so heinous.

When Sabine left the courthouse, dazed and as wrung out as a dishrag, one voice she hadn't heard in a very long time penetrated the babble of reporters and their thrusting microphones. She felt a strong arm reach across her shoulders and carve a path for her through the throng. The man led her to a waiting car, and a few minutes later she was driving through the city with Marie-Antoinette and Pierre-Marcel. She was overjoyed to see them.

"How did you know I was here?" she asked.

"My dear, all of France knows," Pierre-Marcel shrugged. "The media have stripped away the illusion of a nation of resistors and exposed the depth and breadth of collusion. It's time for France to look in the mirror without flinching."

"Are you here to testify?"

"No. I'm here for you, and because Marie-Antoinette said so. You'll remember how persuasive she can be."

"Just drive, Pierre," Marie-Antoinette smiled. "We thought lunch in the countryside would be restorative."

But the meeting among three friends was so much more than lunch in a pleasant garden. As she always had, Marie-Antoinette lifted Sabine's spirits, boasting without apology of the achievements of the remarkable young Gérard, the best and most handsome doctor in all the country if you believed everything she said. Pierre-Marcel spoke more modestly of his family and his career in the civil service.

"We have a surprise for you," Marie-Antoinette interrupted, "and we thought today was the best time to tell you because testifying must've been an ordeal. You tell her, Pierre."

"I was coming to it, before you interrupted."

"Well then, what are you waiting for?"

"Sabine, I'm thinking of filing papers with the Ain *préfecture* for the founding and management of a Memorial Museum for the Children of Izieu. We'd have to raise funds to buy the house, but after the trial, because of the trial, I think the government will help. What do you think? Will you be president of the *Maison d'Izieu?*"

"You mean the House will always belong to the children?"

"Yes. And I think people will come and learn about them and the guardians who loved and cared for them."

"Then I say yes, a thousand times, yes."

The trial of Klaus Barbie came to an end on the third of July after twenty-three sessions. Sabine and all of her friends attended to hear the closing arguments of the defence. The courtroom was crowded, the atmosphere as heavy as the stifling heat.

The defence, in the person of Jacques Vergès, rose to begin his summation, his final plea to the jury. His voice was deep and sonorous, his stature impressive.

What happened next has never been explained and never forgotten.

Before Vergès had spoken even a dozen words, a violent storm erupted, with thunderclaps so booming he could not be heard and he was forced to sit down until the storm passed.

He stood again, a bitter smile on his lips, and resumed his speech. At that instant, the bells of St. John's Cathedral in Lyon started to ring as if nothing could hold them back, wave after wave of deafening sound. Vergès was forced to sit again, as if overpowered by some greater force.

Those who believed were certain God had made an appearance in the courtroom. Others, for whom there could be no miracles, were grateful for the fortuitousness of coincidence.

Vergès finally said what he'd been prepared to say and the jury filed out.

Most of the crowd spilled out into the courtyard to wait. The air was still thick with humidity and anxiety. Sabine could feel it clogging her lungs. Her cheeks were hot. She watched people milling about as if knee-deep in mud, their limbs clumsy and heavy.

Time passed. An hour felt like a month. Two hours was a year.

Six hours later, at forty minutes past midnight, the court was called back into session. The crowd surged forward and held its breath.

The verdict was announced: Guilty of Crimes Against Humanity. Klaus Barbie was sentenced to life imprisonment.

There followed an astounded silence, one so profound Sabine swore the world must have stopped spinning, everything and everyone frozen in place.

She closed her eyes, the unbearable sorrow of a lifetime written across her face. Her testimony had finally been heard.

Three friends met in a small café in a side street in Paris to say goodbye, each of them alone, but together. They talked and laughed and remembered, and the taste of the wine was like honey in Sabine's throat.

She looked from face to face. Perhaps Léon was seeing little Claude tossing him a ball, or his sister, Suzanne, twirling a strand of black hair around her finger. Maybe Léa was seeing the desert blooming in Israel, or the shadows of children moving across the sand. Sabine was seeing Miron, his head thrown back, watching the stars brighten over the flow of the river.

She placed her hand in the middle of the table. Léa put her hand on top of it, and then Léon did the same. Each of them alone, but held together by the House of Izieu, a light that would shine forever through the thunder and darkness of the world.

EPILOGUE

REMEMBER US, THE CHILDREN OF IZIEU.

We were loved. Some of us were too young to know fear. Some of us were relieved to reach fear's end.

Remember that we sang in the trucks and held hands on the train. We moved forward as one and dried each other's tears and kissed each other's cheeks.

Now we are running free, running barefoot in the woods and among the wild flowers and long grasses of a summer of endless numbered days. Our souls have settled in the trees like birds at dusk. Our laughter is in the leaves.

We are there in the corner of your eye, just over the rise of the hills, in the quick current of the river.

Honour us. Be amazed for us. Remember us.

HISTORICAL NOTES

I wish the essential facts of this story were not true, but they are. By the time I visited the House of Izieu, its history had already been written with an ending that couldn't be changed. Sabine and Miron Zlatin existed. The children of Izieu, whose names are listed at the beginning of this book, existed. I have given them words and personalities, and I have filled in their days since history cannot record everything.

In fact, the only characters that come completely from my imagination are the driver, Marius, the red-haired Milice woman in Montpellier, the young girl who keeps goats outside of Chambéry, Jake Shaw, various German soldiers and officials, and the nameless man who throws himself into the face of an oncoming train.

In my research, I relied on Sabine Zlatin's memoir, *Mémoires de la Dame d'Izieu* and Serge Klarsfeld's books, *Remembering Georgy: Letters from the House of Izieu* and *The Children of Izieu: A Human Tragedy*. Sabine's exact words, spoken at Barbie's trial, are taken from *The Children of Izieu, 6 April 1944: A Crime Against Humanity*, a booklet published by The Musée dauphinois. Suzanne Reifman's letter, written to Sabine in Drancy before leaving for Auschwitz, is also taken from this source. The incident that occurs when Sabine is being interrogated in Montpellier and yet manages to escape custody is taken from Margaret Collins Weitz's *Sisters in the Resistance*.

Perhaps this book would never have been written had my husband and I not stumbled across the House of Izieu almost as if fate were leading us there. We were profoundly moved by what we found, and though the story is tragic, we remain grateful that so many lives and so much love can never be erased.

ACKNOWLEDGEMENTS

Thank you to my friends and family who offer me so much support and tolerate my long silences. Thank you especially to those faithful first readers, Arthur Haberman and Fran Cohen. I feel privileged to know and work with Luciana Ricciutelli, the heart and soul of Inanna Publications, who treats all of her authors with respect and generosity. Thank you to everyone at Inanna for your professionalism and friendliness.

Finally, and always, thank you Arthur, for being beside me on the day we discovered the House of Izieu, when we saw the children eating lunch under the apple trees, and where we both left a piece of our souls.

Jan Rehner is the author of four previous novels. *Just Murder* won the 2004 Arthur Ellis Award for Best First Crime Novel in Canada. *On Pain of Death*, a historical narrative set in World War II France, won a bronze medallion from the IPPY group of independent publishers in 2008. *Missing Matisse*, her third novel, was longlisted for the ReLit Awards in 2012. Jan retired as University Professor from the Writing Department at York University in 2015. She has visited France many times and continues to live in Toronto.